PROOFREAD OR DIE!

PROOFREAD

OR

DIE!

Writings by Former Students & Colleagues of

David Foster Wallace

Introduction by Charles B. Harris, Ed.

ISBN: 9781943170159

Cover Image: Leslie Raine Carman
Cover and Interior Design: Jane L. Carman

Fonts: Garamond, Courier Prime, Proof 3, and Proof 7

Published by: Lit Fest Press, Carman, 688 Knox Road 900 North, Gilson,
Illinois 61436

Moving
Literature
Forward

for David

Contents

Contributors

Introduction

Fiction

Nonfiction

Drama

Contributors

Contributors

Becky Bradway is currently revising *Into the Beautiful New*, a long biographical novel about the poets Vachel Lindsay and Sara Teasdale (and the early modernist era). She has published a craft book/anthology on creative nonfiction (*Creating Nonfiction*, Bedford/St. Martin's), a collection of essays (*Pink Houses and Family Taverns*, Indiana University Press), and about fifty stories and essays at various magazines. She lives in Denver and teaches in the MFA program at Wilkes University. She completed her PhD from Illinois State University in 1998.

Jane L. Carman is a former Sutherland Fellow and founder of the David Foster Wallace Conference at Illinois State University where she received her PhD. She is founder of the reading series Festival of Language and a reading eXperiment, as well as Lit Fest Press, all of which allow her to promote fellow writers and scholars while she works to move literature in a forward direction. Her book, *Tangled in Motion*, was published by Journal of Experimental Fiction Books in 2015. Other creative and critical work can be found in *elimae*, *580-Split*, *American Book Review*, *Devil's Lake*, *Pequin*, *Blue Collar Review*, *JAC*, *Santa Clara Review*, and others.

Ricardo Cortez Cruz is the author of *Straight Outta Compton* (FC2, 1992) and *Five Days of Bleeding* (Black Ice, 1995), novels short and funky. His f(r)-ictions (over 50 peaces [sic] of him) have appeared in numerous journals and anthologies, including *Litscapes: Collected Writings 2015* by Steerage Press, *Fjords Black American Edition*, *Mandorla: Nueva escritura de las Américas*, *Packingtown Review's* 2009 inaugural issue, *Fiction International's* abject/outcast issue, *African-American Review*, *Crab Orchard Review*, *The Kenyon Review*, *The Iowa Review*, *Obsidian II: Black Literature in Review*, *Postmodern Culture*, *In The Middle Of The Middle West* edited by Becky Bradway and featuring a collaboration with his cousin Rodney B. Cruz, *Not Guilty* edited by Jabari Asim, and Kevin Powell's anthology *Step Into A World*. Back in the laboratory like Dr. Funkenstein and dropping some serious science, Cruz has created a third body of (s)language—*Premature Autopsies: Tales of Darkest America*. Laying the tracks down for a new black avant-garde aesthetic and remix [counter]culture, Cruz is Professor of English at Illinois State University.

Trevor Dodge is the author of a novella and three collections of short fiction, the most recent of which will appear from Subito Press in 2017. His most recent work appears in *The Butter, Green Mountains Review, Little Fiction, CHEAP POP, Hobart, Monkeybicycle, Gargoyle, Metazen, Juked,* and *Nailed.* He lives in Portland, OR and can be found online at www.trevordodge.com. He earned his MA in Creative Writing from Illinois State University in 1998.

Andrew Ervin's first book, a collection of novellas titled *Extraordinary Renditions* (Coffee House), was published in 2010. In 2015, he published his debut novel, *Burning Down George Orwell's House* (Soho). As a master's student at Illinois State University, he studied fiction writing with Curtis White and Ricardo Cortez Cruz. He lives in Philadelphia.

T. Louise Freeman-Toole's first book, *Standing Up to the Rock* (University of Nebraska Press, 2001), which was based on her Illinois State University master's thesis, won the Pacific Northwest Booksellers Award and the Idaho Book Award in 2002. David Foster Wallace wrote a blurb for the book jacket, calling it "A moving and very very fine book." Freeman-Toole has received fellowships from the MacDowell Colony, the Steinbeck Fellowship Program, the Howard Foundation, and the Bridge Foundation. She was writer-in-residence at the Klondike Gold Rush National Historical Park and The Island Institute. "Heading North" is an excerpt from Freeman-Toole's unpublished memoir, *Asylum in the Woods: A Memoir of Secret Love in the Far North.* She lives in Anchorage, Alaska.

William Gillespie has published 10 and 5/6ths books of fiction and poetry under six different names—most recently *Keyhole Factory* (keyholefactory. com) by William Gillespie, published by Soft Skull Press—and hosts the radio show *Rock Geek F.M.* (rockgeekchic.com). His press Spineless Books published, among others, Karen Green's first book *here/gone.* He received his MS from Illinois State University in 1997.

C.S. Giscombe's poetry books are *Prairie Style* (2008), *Giscome Road* (1998), *Here* (1994), all from Dalkey Archive Press; his book of linked essays (concerning Canada, race, and family) is *Into and Out of Dislocation* (North Point, 2000). His recognitions include the 2010 Stephen Henderson Award, an American Book Award (for *Prairie Style*), and the Carl Sandburg Prize (for *Giscome Road*). *Ohio Railroads* (a poem in essay form) was published in 2014, and *Border Towns* (essays on poetry, color, nature, television, etc.) will appear in 2015. A former member of the Illinois State University English faculty, he currently teaches at the University of California, Berkeley. He is a long-distance cyclist.

Stacey Gottlieb holds a BA in English from Cornell University and an MA in Creative Writing from Illinois State, which she attended as a Sutherland Fellow. Her short fiction, essays, and reviews have appeared in numerous publications including *Sycamore Review*, *Quarterly West*, *Spork*, *Pindeldyboz*, and *Current*, the journal for the New York Foundation for the Arts. She has been awarded residencies at the Edward F. Albee Foundation in Montauk, New York, and Vermont Studio Center in Johnson. She works as a freelance writer and editor in New York City, and is completing a first novel.

Charles B. Harris is Emeritus Professor of English at Illinois State University, where he chaired the English Department for fifteen years (1979-1994). His books include *Contemporary American Novelists of the Absurd* (1971), *Passionate Virtuosity: The Fiction of John Barth* (1983), *The Holodeck in the Garden: Science and Technology in Contemporary American Fiction* (2004), and *John Barth: A Body of Words* (2016); his articles on American fiction and the profession of English studies have appeared in numerous scholarly journals and essay collections; and he is publisher emeritus of *American Book Review*. He is past president of the Association of Departments of English (ADE). In 1997, the Modern Language Association honored him with the Francis Andrew March Award for Exceptional Service to the Profession of English.

Kymberly Harris. A member of Rogue Machine Theatre, Skylight Theatre, AEA, AFTRA, SAG, and the Dramatists Guild, Kymberly is an actor/writer/director who has appeared on stage at Labyrinth Theatre, the Public Theatre, Circle in the Square, Next Theatre, where she originated the role of Holly in Eric Simonson's *Bang the Drum Slowly* opposite Tracy Letts, *It's Only a Play*, opposite Thomas Sadoski, Josh Radnor, and Lisa Kudrow (2014), and several award winning independent films. She created (writer/actor) a pilot that is in post-production with Paul Kampf Studios for 2016, and is directing her first short film adapted from her award winning play *Rose's Turn* in May 2016. As a playright, several of her plays have been produced in NYC, Los Angeles, and Chicago. Harris founded TheatresCool to teach method acting to kids, teens, and adults in Bloomington-Normal, Illinois, and currently teaches acting at The Lee Strasberg Film and Theatre Institute in West Hollywood, at AMDA, and to private clients. She holds an MA from Illinois State University in Theatre, and a double MFA in Acting and Playwriting from The Actors Studio Drama School, NYC.

Amy Havel lives in Maine, and teaches at Southern Maine Community College. She studied with David Foster Wallace at Illinois State University, and received a Rona Jaffe Foundation Writers' Award for her fiction. Her writing has appeared in *Conjunctions, Avery Anthology, Failbetter, Adirondack Review, Tarpaulin Sky, Small Spiral Notebook, Portland Press Herald, Portland Magazine,* and *Pindeldyboz,* and her stories are anthologized in *The Way Life Should Be: Stories by Contemporary Maine Writers* and *Consumed: Women on Excess.*

Doug Hesse is Professor and Executive Director of Writing at The University of Denver. He's currently President of the National Council of Teachers of English and previously was President of the Council of Writing Program Administrators and Chair of the Conference on College Composition and Communication. He publishes mainly about creative nonfiction and about teaching writing, one of his essays winning the Donald Murray Prize. Among his books is *Creating Nonfiction* (St. Martin's), co-authored with Becky Bradway, who did the real work. From 1986-2006, he taught at Illinois State University, where he was variously Director of Writing, Director of Graduate Studies, Director of the Center for the Advancement of Teaching, and Director of the University Honors Program.

Gregory Howard teaches creative writing, contemporary literature, and film studies at the University of Maine. His first novel *Hospice* was published by FC2 in April 2015. His fiction and essays have appeared in *Web Conjunctions, Harp & Altar,* and *Tarpaulin Sky,* among other journals. He lives in Bangor, Maine with his wife and cats. He graduated from Illinois State University in 2001 with an MA in English.

A D Jameson is the author of *Amazing Adult Fantasy, Giant Slugs,* and *99 Things to Do When You Have the Time.* He studied creative writing at Illinois State University and is currently a PhD candidate at the University of Illinois at Chicago. He is writing a book on geek cinema.

Brian Monday received his master's degree from Illinois State University, where he was awarded a Sutherland Fellowship, served as Production Director for the Unit of Contemporary Literature, and studied under Curtis White and David Foster Wallace. He has since taught English at Westosha Central High School, in Salem, Wisconsin, and has written a book of poems, *A Little Breath,* and a collection of short stories, *The Klein-Bottle Boy and His Ontological Dilemma.* Brian is currently studying the workshop critiques that Wallace offered him and hopes to collect other such critiques in a book that explores the nature of Wallace's teaching. He lives in Trevor, Wisconsin, with his wife and two sons.

Scott Rettberg is professor of digital culture in the department of linguistic, literary, and aesthetic studies at the University of Bergen, Norway. Rettberg is the author or coauthor of novel-length works of electronic literature including *The Unknown, Kind of Blue, Implementation,* and others, and he is the author and co-producer, with Roderick Coover, of films including *The Catastrophe Trilogy, Three Rails Live,* and *Toxi*City* and the CAVE immersive VR narrative *Hearts and Minds: The Interrogations Project.* His work has been exhibited online and at art venues including the Chemical Heritage Foundation Museum in Philadelphia, Rom 8 Gallery in Bergen, Beall Center in Irvine, California, the Slought Foundation in Philadelphia, The Krannert Art Museum in Illinois, the Inova Gallery in Milwaukee, and elsewhere. Rettberg also frequently publishes critical and theoretical work related to electronic literature, digital culture, and digital art. Rettberg is the cofounder and served as the first executive director of the nonprofit Electronic Literature Organization, where he directed major projects funded by the Ford Foundation and the Rockefeller Foundation, and from 2010-2013 led the HERA-funded collaborative European research project ELMCIP: Electronic Literature as a Model of Creativity and Innovation in Practice. He received his MA from Illinois State University in 1995.

Suzanne Scanlon is the author of *Promising Young Women* (Dorothy, 2012) and *Her 37th Year, An Index* (Noemi, 2015). Her fiction has won *The Iowa Review* Fiction Award, and appeared in publications including *Hobart, DIAGRAM, Electric Literature*'s Recommended Reading, and *BOMBMagazine.* Her fiction has been anthologized in *A Kind of Compass, Stories on Distance, Tramp Press,* and in *The &NOW Awards 3, The Best Innovative Writing.* Her nonfiction has appeared in *Essay Daily, The American Scholar,* and *The Millions.* She teaches creative writing at Columbia College Chicago, Roosevelt University, and in the University of Iowa's Summer Writing Festival. She is currently working on a novel-from-life, titled "Scenes of Interrogation," inspired in part from her brief time spent in Bloomington-Normal.

Ben Slotky is the author of *Red Hot Dogs, White Gravy* (Chiasmus, 2011). His stories have been published in *Golden Handcuffs Review, Juked, Requited, McSweeney's, Cheap Pop, Santa Monica Review, Clackamas Literary Review,* and other places. "Dear Retarded Black Kid" is from *An Evening of Romantic Lovemaking,* his recently completed novel. He was a Sutherland Fellow at Illinois State University, where he received his MA in Creative Writing in 1997.

Curtis White is a novelist and social critic. He is the author of seven works of fiction, including *Memories of My Father Watching TV* (Dalkey Archive Press, 1998) and five works of non-fiction, including the international best seller *The Middle Mind: Why Americans Don't Think for Themselves* (HarperSanFrancisco, 2003) and *We, Robots: Staying Human in the Cyborg Era* (Melville House, 2015). He is Emeritus Distinguished Professor of English at Illinois State University, where he directed the creative writing program for many years.

Introduction

Charles B. Harris

Introduction

I first laid eyes on David Foster Wallace in a New York City hotel room in December 1992. We were interviewing candidates for a fiction writing position at that year's Modern Language Association convention. As chair of the Illinois State University English Department, I presided over the interviews, about a dozen of them, as I recall, several involving writers with more imposing writing credentials than David had at the time. He quickly charmed us with his wit, intelligence, and what we suspected—and he knew we suspected—was a feigned insouciance. The faux indifference was protective, of course: David never really believed he'd get the job. In his letter of application, he had written, "I alert you in advance that I am both caucasian and male." Because most of us interviewing him were scholars, not writers, he felt compelled to inform us that he was "really really smart." During his on-campus visit, when a faculty member asked why the department should hire him, David responded, "Who else?" Then, during the post-interview dinner with the hiring committee at a local Chinese restaurant, David went out of his way to assure me that, as a literary model, John Barth was dead, even though he knew I had spent my career reading, teaching, and writing about Barth's fiction.

We interviewed and eventually hired the pre-*Infinite Jest* David Foster Wallace. But we were struck by the early genius evident in his first novel, *The Broom of the System* (1987), written as an Amherst undergraduate thesis, and his follow up short story collection, *Girl with Curious Hair* (1989). He had also contributed three fine essays to Dalkey Archive Press's *Review of Contemporary Fiction* (RCF), whose forthcoming Younger Writers Issue featured David (along with William T. Vollmann and Susan Daitch). Published in summer '93, just before he joined our faculty, that issue included David's landmark essay "E Unibus Pluram: Television and U.S. Fiction," his now famous interview with Larry McCaffery, and a brief selection from his novel-in-progress *Infinite Jest*. The issue quickly became a collector's item.

We had just attracted Dalkey and *RCF* to our department the year before, where it joined *American Book Review*, the innovative fiction press FC2, and a few other presses and journals as part of a center we were developing that combined the creation, reception, and publishing of innovative literature (the center became the Unit for Contemporary Literature, 1994–2004, described by D.T. Max in his biography of Wallace as "the oasis for experimental writing in the prairie"). David shared our excitement about the project. "I'm keen to have a chance to be part of it," he wrote in a note to me, and he eagerly accepted a part-time assignment with Dalkey. To be sure, that assignment was designed in part to reduce his teaching load, but David took it seriously, editing a special "Quo Vadis" issue of *RCF* ("The Future of Fiction," Spring 1996) and vetting several Dalkey fiction translations.

David's decade at Illinois State University was his most productive period. Not only did he finish *Infinite Jest*, the work that will ensure his permanence, but he assembled his first essay collection, *A Supposedly Fun Thing I'll Never Do Again* (1997), and his second collection of short fiction, *Brief Interviews with Hideous Men* (1999), as well as completing his nonfiction book on mathematical infinity, *Everything and More* (2003). During this prolific period, Wallace also wrote most of the stories and essays later collected in *Oblivion* (2004) and *Consider the Lobster* (2006), respectively, and he began his final novel, *The Pale King*, auditing advanced tax courses from ISU's Accounting Department as part of his research (the novel, published posthumously by Little, Brown in 2010, is set in a branch of the Internal Revenue Department). He bought a modest home on the edge of town, adopted two dogs—Jeeves, from a local pound, and Drone, a stray, from the street—and threw himself enthusiastically into his new role as a college professor.

Despite the success of Wallace's fiction and nonfiction workshops, he preferred other assignments, even volunteering to teach composition courses, a rare choice among senior professors. Not surprisingly, neither his classroom methods nor his course syllabi resembled anyone else's. He began his graduate seminar in contemporary American fiction by admitting to the students that he had either not finished or, in some cases, even *begun* reading the assigned novels. "English 487... is basically a contrived excuse/incentive to read several interesting, difficult U.S. novels," he explains on his syllabus. "Class meetings are intended to function basically as the proceedings of a large, sophisticated, energetic reading group." After warning that the course would require reading "an average of 250–300 pages of very dense, high-level fiction every week,"[1] he entreats: "For heaven's sake do not remain enrolled in this class if you're *not* going to be in a position and/or mood to do this much close reading." Determination of final grades—described in the syllabus as the only respect in which Wallace would be "the actual 'instructor' here"—includes the following criterion: "fidelity of attendance, alacrity of carriage, doing every m.f.ing *shred* of the reading...." And in a final vintage touch, Wallace complains about the chronic inefficiency of local bookstores. The odd order of the reading assignments, he explains, "is due to the monumental shitheadedness of the ISU Bookstore System's mechanism for ordering and delivery....Feel free to join me in being pissed, and to complain both to the English Department and to the management of our two bookstores." During my fifteen years as Department Chair, I evaluated hundreds of faculty members and, in the process, read hundreds of course syllabi. David's were the only ones I know that were R-rated.

Although former students praise his teaching, what they remember most fondly are interactions that accentuate David's signal personality.[2] All remember that omnipresent bandana and the fact that David chewed tobacco while teaching, expectorating it discretely, even delicately, into a cup he held in his hand. One student, Scott Rettberg, recalls the time that Wallace, who hated the fluorescent lighting in ISU classrooms, instructed his class to bring their own lamps to the next meeting. Most complied, only to find that the room lacked a sufficient number of plugs for the lamps, which, in any event, kept sliding off the slanted classroom desks. For the rest of the term, the class met at David's home. Another student, Rebecca Kaiser, remembers that Wallace loaned her his pickup truck when he learned that she was having car trouble, then promptly forgot that he had done so. In a subsequent class meeting, David offhandedly mentioned that he had somehow misplaced the truck he

1 Wallace assigned two books each by Don DeLillo (*The Names* and *Ratner's Star*), William Gaddis (*A Frolic of His Own* and *JR*), and Cormac McCarthy (*Blood Meridian* and *Suttree*), in addition to *Omensetter's Luck* by William H. Gass.
2 The following reminiscences have been gleaned from tributes read by David's former students at a memorial service sponsored by the Illinois State University English Department on November 1, 2008.

had purchased with MacArthur "genius" grant money. At the end of the period, Kaiser quietly returned David's keys. A third student, Marty Riker, recollects a visit from Wallace, accompanied by his two dogs, while the student was dogsitting in the country for another professor. Driving home on unlit rural roads, David accidentally hit a deer. After depositing his dogs at home, Wallace called Riker and asked if he would meet him to help find the deer, which had disappeared in the high grass along the roadside. After a long search, they located the dying animal, its hind leg irreparably broken. Trying to hide his tears, Wallace said to Marty, "Tonight I have been a bad human being."

As the last two anecdotes suggest, David was unusually available to and generous with his students, whom he invited to call him Dave. Although David was a private, even shy, person, whose phone was unlisted, who avoided email, and who remained largely incommunicado to his adoring public, he made an exception for his students. As one of them, Tim Feeney, wrote:

> Here was a guy who waited no more than a week or two before giving an entire undergraduate prose class his home telephone number and who encouraged us to call him pretty much whenever we waned to, insisting that if he were asleep or busy, his phone was in another room in another part of the house and he wouldn't hear it, so go ahead and call and he'd return the call as soon as he could. And, if we didn't call, many of us probably baffled, here was a guy who would proceed to call *us* to talk about class and what we were working on and whether we needed help with any of it.

This concern was reflected in the time he spent grading student work. "Every story or essay I ever turned in," wrote Lynn Bulgrin, "was returned to me with six to eight paragraphs of constructive criticism from one of the most insightful and active minds I've had the opportunity to encounter....It wasn't uncommon for Dave to have written in two or three different colors of ink on your paper as he sat with your work, read it multiple times, and commented on at each sitting in his inimitable style."

Feeney amplifies:

> He was a guy whose typewritten response to a workshopped creative writing piece was occasionally longer than the piece itself, and his response would come with handwritten notations and further thoughts, and he'd return his copy of your workshop

piece and it would look like he'd taken on the challenge of covering every bit of white space with his reactions, and then he'd go ahead and include his home phone number again in case you wanted to talk or if there were anything unclear about what he'd written.

As David told Jason Hammel, he was there to provide his students with the help they "needed and deserved."

But if he was generous with his students, he was also, as D.T. Max points out in his biography of Wallace, "a pedagogic hardass," who "penalized for lateness and for absence and grammar and spelling errors, trying to wean a lazy generation from dangling participles and subject/verb disagreements." At least one graduate student "fired" him as a thesis advisor because of what she perceived to be his unreasonable resistance to the standard argot of the field of English studies. The title I've chosen for this anthology is an actual directive Wallace scrawled on a student paper. About that directive, Trevor Dodge, whose work is represented in his collection, writes: "I'm… attaching a scan/screengrab from what's probably my favorite of the comments Dave made on my work. One of these days, I'm going to have that phrase 'PROOFREAD OR DIE!' tattooed onto me." Anecdotes such as this one, which illuminate aspects of David's classroom influence, have been included as introductory headnotes for many of the contributions.

Wallace's signature style is of course the style of *Infinite Jest*, whose encyclopedic form, long, syntactically dense sentences, footnotes and other extra-textual paraphernalia (these also turn up in some of his essays), and comically exaggerated situations (The Year of the Depend Adult Undergarment) are immediately recognizable. But Wallace mastered many styles, vexing the definitional boundaries of whatever genre he tried his hand at, and he tried his hand at many. He also read widely, not only the writers he loved, like DeLillo and Gaddis and Cormac McCarthy, but also popular genre writers, like Thomas Harris and Stephen King and Tom Clancy. And he encouraged his students to do the same. As David's colleague Robert McLaughlin recalls, "When a student asked him what…authors they should be reading, I expected him to name people like DeLillo, Pynchon, and Auster—authors I knew he admired—but instead he named a number of authors of popular fiction, like Thomas Harris, from whom, he said, would-be authors could learn a great deal about structure, plotting, and character." The last thing David wanted—or would tolerate—would be for his students to imitate him.

Not interested in acolytes, he encouraged them to develop and pursue their own artistic inclinations.[3]

This anthology also includes works by faculty who taught side by side with David in the Illinois State Creative Writing Program during his years here. More than just academic colleagues, they numbered among his closest friends. David found the program's commitment to innovative literature congenial to his own taste and literary temperament. At Arizona, where he had earned his MFA, David often felt constricted by the writing faculty's bias toward conventional realism. At ISU, by contrast, he considered himself "the least weird writer" in the program.[4] As their contributions to this volume demonstrate, Curtis White, noted social critic and author of such experimental fictions as *Memories of My Father Watching TV* (1998), C.S. Giscombe, whose innovative poetic meditations on race and place have won numerous literary awards, and Ricardo Cortez Cruz, whose *Straight Outta Compton* (1992) is often regarded as our first "rap" novel and who is himself a graduate of ISU's Creative Writing Program, all trouble the conventional boundaries of literary form. In addition, David interacted with John O'Brien, founding publisher of Dalkey Archive Press, and Dalkey editors Steve Moore, who read early drafts of *Infinite Jest*, and Bob McLaughlin, the well-known literary scholar, all of whom were members of ISU's English Department at the time. The result was a rare catalytic convergence of talents mutually beneficial to students in the program and to the faculty who presided over it. As White, who directed ISU's Fiction Program, remembers:

> When David came to ISU, he always called me, much to my surprise, his "mentor." But the real debt was just the reverse, as I tried to tell him many times (not with much success). David was

---

3 As Max observes, Wallace "battled any young man who reminded him of his younger self." When his student Ben Slotky "wowed his classmates with a voicy, ironic short story," Wallace took him outside the classroom and told him he had 'never witnessed a collective dick-sucking like that before.' Wallace promised to prevent the 'erection of an ego-machine' and strafed the student with criticism for the rest of the semester." As Slotky's story in this collection as well as his subsequent publications attest, Ben went on to develop a distinctive style, as inimitable as his early mentor's.

4 The description occurs in a letter from Wallace to Corey Washington. I suspect David was joking, but he always considered himself to be a much more conventional writer than he actually was or ever could be.

Charles B. Harris

what I needed in my immediate environment as a constant challenge to me as an artist....In short, David made my own best work possible....I missed him from the day he left town.

As do we all.

The contributions in this anthology reflect the aesthetic breadth that David fostered in his classrooms. They represent multiple genres—fiction, nonfiction, even a play—and a range of voices, styles, and forms. A handful of the contributions in the anthology have been published elsewhere, in little magazines or online, but the majority of them appear here for the first time. Not all of the former students represented in this volume worked extensively with David, though most took at least one course from him. A few of the stories and essays were initially written for one of his classes or as part of a thesis he directed or co-directed, but most were written later, as former students progressed into their careers as professional writers. In one way or another, all of the works collected here reflect David's influence, either on individual writers, as mentor, or on the writing program they studied or taught in. Except for Doug Hesse's essay about team-teaching a graduate seminar with David, none of the contributions is *about* David in a strict biographical or autobiographical sense, although characters who resemble him do turn up in a couple of the works that, though wholly imagined, may play off of actual events involving him.

I know that David was proud of the students who came to study with him and his colleagues at Illinois State University during his eventful decade here. I'd like to think he'd also be proud of this volume, which records the ongoing accomplishments of a group of writers he nurtured in the earliest stages of their development. I dedicate this book to ISU's writing and publishing program during the exciting years that David taught here, to the students and colleagues who studied and worked with him and whose growing body of work continues to bear witness to his influence, and to David himself—colleague, teacher, writer, and friend.

February 21, 2016

PROOFREAD OR DIE!

Fiction

Becky Bradway

The Hell Hole

Oh, it would be nice if I could throw some little anecdote out here, something very cute. But I can't imitate it. I would never try to nail down Dave's wit. He could barb others, barb himself, and really, it was just a blast to spar with him in that way. He was kind of a teaser; that is, he was the kind of guy (it's always a guy) who teases the people who he really likes, and is rather deferential to those he re- spects, and is just flat-out mean to those who he doesn't. He'd tease me, I'd jab back, and it was good times all around. And I'm not exaggerating a bit. We got along famously for quite awhile. And it wasn't flirty, exactly, or at least not the kind that felt risky. It was more the way that brothers and sisters treat each other. And he was just the same with my daughter. I never had a friend like that before, and I will never have one again. So you'll get no cute anecdotes from me. It's too big a loss.

So one night they walked and ate and drank, and took a cab to a black and tan where they heard a real jazz singer (the West wasn't exactly overflowing with black people). Then, although it was already past her bedtime, they did what Mae had been insisting on since they got to New York: they went to the Hell Hole.

Mae had heard about The Golden Swan, a.k.a. the Hell Hole, from her sister Marguerite, a drug-consuming actress who was happy to let Mae pony up the family income. Marguerite had moved to New York six months before and had already hunted out a slew of arty-but-hardcore dives.

"The Hell Hole is where the real Villagers go," said Mae.

"And the Irish gang from the Bowery," said Vachel, sounding nervous.

"That's exactly what I mean! I love the flannel!"

"I don't know."

"You don't like it?"

"I've never been there."

"But how bad can it be? It's full of artists."

"And thugs. Addicts. Prostitutes. It's not a place to take women."

"There are women there."

Anita patted his arm. "Don't worry about our respectability. Mae and I have been everywhere. We grew up near the Barbary Coast. We can take care of ourselves."

Vachel considered. "Some of the Art School gang goes there."

"So, see."

"They go to get sloshed—but if you want to go, we'll go."

"Hooray!" said Mae. "I love dives."

"A dive is a dive world round," said Anita, who had seen a lot of shit-holes in her life and wouldn't mind moving uptown where she could listen to this young songwriter people were talking about, Cole Porter, and drink champagne while leaning against a Steinway piano. But her curiosity had led her to many strange places that could later be turned into prose. She imagined the scene in the smoky Village club: slobbering drunks, satire and stabs, dramatic tears as a heroine leans over the prone body of her deliriously handsome and brilliant sculptor lover, sepia background and piercing light from a single overhead bulb. Moral. The end.

The Hell Hole was a dark weatherbeaten building in the shadow of the El. From its front door hung a once promising sign of a life-sized gilt swan, because this was in actuality The Golden Swan, a name of beauty for a bar favored by a pack of aging Irish gangsters, the Hudson Dusters. Vachel had walked past it many times, never going in, sensing that his type was likely to get pounded; the Hudson Dusters were a crew of hijackers at the least and murderers at worst. Yet the Hell Hole was the favorite of hard drinking artists, a place of vague threat that remained open when all else closed. And women were allowed to smoke right at the tables.

Ladies and couples had to enter through the back into a separate room; the loud and conspiratorial front bar wasn't to be disturbed by females, who could, it was said, destroy the lifelong camaraderie of a gang. So into the back they went, through a dirty glass door into a room thick with tobacco smoke and the soot from a potbellied stove. Round beaten tables packed with drinkers were crammed together and when they came in, everyone took note. The room was dim, lit by gas lamps on the wall; the place felt oily. In a corner were several tables filled with artists and writers—they stood out among the other drinkers and flirters, who were an interracial mix of high and low, of deposed heirs, anarchists, and prostitutes, late night journalists, the chronically unemployed and some neighborhood shopowners, and the drunken wives of the men in the front room. They wound through them all to get to the oasis of artists who, wherever they went, set up an encampment. He caught the eye of Max Eastman, who sat against the wall with his newest actress. At another table he recognized the artist John Sloan; at an adjoining table were Eugene O'Neill and a young woman and, at another table, could it be?—John Reed with someone new. "Hellooo hello," introductions all around, and everyone looked surprised and impressed that he was with two movie ladies and they were warmly welcomed while from the other room came the noise of a drunken fight. But no one paid attention to that.

As soon as they sat at Max's table, Anita was set upon by his flame, a wishing-to-be actress named Florence Deshon. She was at least ten years younger than Max, and her eagerness was oppressive. Anita, Vachel could see, was trapped. Max looked annoyed and pretended to be deep in conversation with Floyd Dell about the war, and Vachel joined in.

"Wilson will keep us out!"

"He's got the election in the bag."

"I'm backing him all the way; what else can we do?"

They told Vachel that the old crew of socialists and anarchists were upset with them because they were promoting Wilson rather than the sure-to-lose socialist party candidate. They thought *The Masses* had sold out.

"Christ, we get hate mail," said Floyd.

"Too radical; not radical enough," sighed Max. "Where's the reason? Everyone runs on emotion."

"We'll avoid this war if Wilson wins," said Vachel. "If he loses, we're doomed."

And so that talk went. Why did none of them look optimistic? Maybe it was the general gloominess of the bar. Probably not, though. Everyone ordered more liquor. Vachel ordered ginger ale. Gossip came, getting up to speed.

"Who's your little girl and the mick?" said Max.

"The mick?"

"Your Irish maid actress, who is she? God, I don't watch movies, though that's all Florence goes on about."

"That's Mae Marsh, the goddess," said Vachel. "And Anita is the best writer in the movies."

"As if movies involved writing," laughed Floyd. "She's cute, though. So tiny! What is she, four-ten? A bug! What eyes! But her teeth are a little horsey."

"How can an actress look so lovely on screen and in real life be just like any Irish slut on the east side? I guess it's the silence."

"She's not a slut," said Vachel, so taken aback he could hardly speak. "She's beautiful."

"See that girl by O'Neill. She works for *The Call*—that's a socialist rag," said Floyd. "Good little journalist. Strange serious thing. Name is Dorothy Day. She's O'Neill's sidekick—here night after night, and they talk and drink and sing songs together. O'Neill calls her his pal; I don't think they're fucking. She might be renting my back room soon. She's a sincere little sprite, don't you think?"

Dorothy was a slight, boyish, long-legged slip with her foot up on the chair, her hair messy, long bangs flopping into her face. There was something about the way she leaned forward, with an intense stare that seemed familiar, what was it? In front of her, three shots were set in alignment. She listened intently to O'Neill, who, in turn, seemed to be addressing no one in particular, but was half-distracted by the murmurs being exchanged by John Reed and the new girl.

"That Dorothy might be a good tap for *The Masses*," said Max.

"But who is that with John Reed? Where's Mabel Dodge?"

"Mabel is gone for good. She followed him somewhere for awhile. Mexico? It didn't work out."

"I think she's in Santa Fe."

"Reed's new girl is Louise Bryant, some pretend bohemian from Seattle, a deposed wife. He brought her back after he visited home. It's love or something."

"She's got him by the balls," said Floyd.

"You don't like her."

They shrugged.

"She's been hanging around with us in Provincetown. We all were writing plays this summer. She's pretty when she's naked. She likes to show off her body. I can't knock that," laughed Floyd.

"She has a little talent," said Max. "Not a bad writer. Not great, either."

"Reed is mad for her," said Floyd.

"What is it about Reed, the way he'll observe some war and then come home and let a woman tell him what to do." Max was still looking with annoyance at Florence Deshon, who was doing a lot of hair tossing for poor restless Anita.

"Ah, the fate of men," sighed Floyd, "weak at the quintessential beauty of the pussy."

"Reed's been sick," said Max, as a way of excuse. "Not insane sick," he explained to Vachel, "but physically. He's has this kidney ailment and he's going to have to get it removed."

"He could die," Floyd added. "And in the meantime that nutty bitch Louise is fucking O'Neill."

"Wait, what? So how does Jack go following wars in Europe with kidney disease? And—so his girl is with O'Neill?" Louise Bryant wasn't paying a bit of attention to the playwright. She was looking up into Reed's eyes, laughing. Vachel found the machinations of love in the Village both predictable and dramatic—there was always something sordid going on, but it was fascinating nonetheless, a melodrama of artists who could do nothing but stir up passion as they tried to stave off boredom. Though Vachel never partook, he never judged it (the way Sara did); he found it entertaining and read it as cautionary. "Poor Jack."

"She's a mad bird let out of the cage."

"I think she's in love with O'Neill," said Floyd, leaning back, his cigarette balanced between two long fingers. "Or maybe O'Neill is in love with Reed. I can't quite tell."

Max said, "Reed will kill himself with his fanaticism. He's a believer and adventurer and sets death aside. Until now, anyway. Now he's just laid up. So he writes plays and looks like he wants to jump out a window."

"His plays aren't good," said Floyd. "Too many lectures. He's losing his soul."

John Reed did look wan, even a little grey, a hulking man leaning into the small darkhaired woman with the big eyes and free laugh. There was something of Christ in his troubles, some desire to suffer in his pursuit of truth. The violence and injustice had permeated his body and wounded his soul. Vachel had never seen war and prayed he never would; the race riot taught him how far men could go. How often could a poet go into that hell and come out undamaged?

In the Hell Hole his old friends seemed suspended. The decline of the moldy swan in the glass case along one wall of the bar seemed an omen of their own decline. Though all of them spoke of hope, there was little hope in this place. The grandfather clock beside the case displayed the wrong time.

Everyone laughed and drank, but it felt that a knife blade might flash; a woman slipped money into her garter.

"Lindsay, man!" John Sloan motioned him over to his table, to where Mae had now situated herself and had let her red hair out of its pins, letting it flow in waves over her shoulders. Mae was roughly beautiful, like a servant in a Vermeer, and she laughed a little too loudly for these artists who Vachel was fairly sure wouldn't give her the time of day. Sloan was very much married to Dolly, and he was pretty sure that the other artist, the painter Charles Demuth, was homosexual. But poor Mae clearly had her eye on all of them, blinded by visions of berets and absinthe, which was really not the way of the serious ones.

Introductions for Vachel, with the main one being to an abstract artist from France, Marcel Duchamp, who Vachel had read about and puzzled him no end. He had seen Duchamp's *Nude Descending a Staircase* a few years before at the Armory Show and respected its sense of movement. It reminded him of chrono photographs of motion, and of Muybridge's early film experiments, and a part of Vachel wished that he had done this himself. His friends had fought angrily about it at the time, which to Vachel meant that the painting probably did as it was intended. But Duchamp had since left his paintings for *things*: A ball of twine between glass plates. A steel comb with the inscription that translated: 3 OR 4 DROPS OF HEIGHT HAVE NOTHING TO DO WITH SAVAGERY. What did this mean? Why? He was a Frenchman in the midst of the most horrific war in history, gas mud entrapment with no end in sight, his country destroyed, flight into exile. Why a comb? What did the epigram mean, if anything? Art was tilting in directions that Vachel didn't comprehend. He was afraid of what it meant for him. Though he had no objections to what others did, he didn't grasp what they wanted. It seemed to discount the pressing situations around them, breaking ground simply to do it. Maybe there was a need to dismiss the horror through the absurdly ordinary. He appreciated Duchamp's lack of pretension, his willingness to take art to the level of the mundane found thing. But they spoke a different language. And in Duchamp's case, it was literally different, as the fellow spoke very little English. He was a thin, sweet faced young man in a brown raincoat, bright blue eyes, very polite, quiet, watchful. But cold, too; if he knew who Vachel was, he didn't acknowledge it. Mae oohed over his accent. And Sloan, older, the chronicler of the ugly beauty of the city, the subtle painterly satirist, was his friend. It was a strange world.

Since there was no place to sit with the artists (who always made him feel inadequate, as he thought of his old failures), he moved on to an empty chair by the girl, Dorothy Day, who was gazing out at the room. Reed's girl had gone to a table far across the bar, and now he and O'Neill were drunkenly singing some sad Irish song.

"Usually they don't start that til two." She turned to him.

"The Irish songs bring all the lonely rebels home," said Vachel.

This girl with messy hair didn't wear an iota of makeup. She wore a longish skirt the way you might wear pants, with one leg up and the fabric draped over; she was skinny, like she didn't eat much. Though she seemed to be taking down the shots, judging by the glasses in front of her, she didn't have the bleary look of drunks. She looked, if anything, like a smart and observant college girl. Or boy. Did it matter?

"You wrote General Booth." He nodded. "I like that poem. It had a certain…messianic call. A call to good works as redemption. That's interesting to me.—I heard you at the U of I last year."

"You did?" He thought back. "Oh—you sat in the front?"

"You remember! I was a student."

"By Lord," Vachel boomed, embracing her. She was very thin but steely, steady with little give. "You had a watchful face. You yelled louder than everyone!"

"Did I?" she laughed.

"Your hair was different."

"Oh, I was just a kid. Though I was working for the socialist papers then, too."

"You should have come to talk to me."

"I'm talking to you now."

"So you are."

"I admire what you did on the road, reciting in the fields, working with the hands, generating a song of the people. I've read your road book, too, the gospel of beauty book, the essays? I love those. They show that your poems really are of the people, though I don't know if you learned from the workers, or if they learned from you and you all created a new kind of song."

"Well, I don't know," Vachel laughed. "I heard music everywhere I went, chants on the streets and songs from the windows. I don't know where mine came from; they just appeared. Maybe the heavens."

"I wonder if your performances are a waste of time."

"What?" He was completely taken aback. "But that's how you got to hear the poems."

"But trying to sing to two thousand dimwits who aren't paying a bit of attention, who are laughing at you—why would you do that?"

He often wondered. He told her about reaching all the people, including the young, adding sheepishly, "And they pay me."

"Your poems sing on their own, on the page; if they are looking at you and critiquing your performance, they lose all that. They don't take your message seriously. Also, my friends didn't know why you wore such a fine suit for your performances if you're singing songs of the people."

"It seems polite. And colleges scare me."

"Not me." She finished off a shot and set the glass down with a definite thunk. "They're fools. They know little of life and what's more don't care to know. They close their eyes to the truth of the world and let words wrap around them for protection. It's rules, all rules. I rarely read the assignments. Just books of my own choosing."

"Me, too," said Vachel. "I didn't finish."

"My work on *The Call* and with the people of the street is so much more important than some paper degree. I don't need a professor to tell me what to think. They want to steal my soul."

"I couldn't agree more."

"They have no appreciation of the spiritual side of being. They are giant heads, all head and no heart and no hands for work. They are the most useless humans in the world, aside from the rich."

"Well, there are a few good ones, like Robert Henri—"

"I grant you, but the essential people work in the soup kitchens and the churches; they do their work and don't presume the knowledge to teach. The truly essential people, the ones who change things, are humble, not arrogant. I think you're at heart a humble man, but all of this applause might damage you."

"Oh, they're only clapping over that odd fellow on the stage. That's not me.—I want them to hear the gospel, isn't that important? So many people don't read."

"Then preach to *them*, the people of the street. Not to college children."

"You certainly are blunt."

"I don't like to waste time."

He put his chin in his hand and contemplated her. It wasn't any kind of romantic contemplation, because her intensity scared him. He was just trying to understand.

"Where did you come from? And why are you here?" He gestured at the people beyond their circle of tables.

"Here in New York? Why, to know the good neighbors of the Lower East Side."

Becky Bradway

"No, I mean *here*. In the Hell Hole."

"Do I not look the type?" She pulled her other leg up to the chair and settled back and looked around. "I like these people."

"These artists, you mean?"

"Of course not. The people. Look at them. All struggling in their sad depravities. All in need. Their emotions and impulses pulling at them. Desperate for friendship or love or liquor. Look at their faces; they've fought through life. They understand things a professor can't, that you and I can't."

Vachel looked. He had seen many such faces on the road. He came to see them not as a mass, but as individuals—to learn not to expect too much or too little from any one of them until he got to know them, to read their eyes and hear their stories. "But they're no better or worse than us. Some of them are quite happy and will hear any story you want to tell and will give you their last slice of bread. Others will smile and knife you in heart because they're like wounded dogs."

She gave him a disbelieving smile. "Your books all trumpet the great democracy, the voice of the poor. Yet here are the poor."

"I've known the poor in their homes and their labor marches, too, and at the settlement houses, and in the mines and farmhouses. I hear their stories when they walk with me and when they throw me out. I agree that we have to know them to fight for their rights. But I don't need to drink with them to know."

"Liquor can give us a shared bond, help us understand one another. People loosen their tongues and their true selves come out and I want to see that and understand, I want to hear the saddest confessions. Life is here, Mr. Lindsay.—You shouldn't be patronizing about my choice to witness, just because I'm a woman."

"But to gamble with your health. Aren't you afraid?"

"I'm rarely afraid. I've never been threatened or harmed. And if I stay too late, there's always Gene or Hippolyte or someone. I'm safer here than walking down Fifth Avenue."

"I wonder." He often wondered what drew certain women into the bar life. He had known many of them when he did his temperance visits, and sometimes he would ask and they would tell him. Usually it was an abusive parent, or a need to sell themselves, or some destructive romance that left them searching for companionship. But maybe this girl just wanted the company of the artists and anarchists of the Village, the dangerous ones. She didn't seem driven by the self-destructive self-pity that brought many to drink; she wasn't crying in her whiskey.

"I devote my life to justice for the poor," she said. "I can do this at the IWW, I can talk with the girls on the Lower East Side—I live there now. In a tenement of Jews. And I work at night and come home at five in the morning and see thugs lurking in the alleys or bums sleeping, and smell the bread baking as the world begins to wake. And I know the kids playing on the street, their friends and quirks and sweetness and meanness, and I share my books. I know of the parents who help their families and the ones who disappear into subterranean dives leaving the babies alone. To help, I have to know. Don't you agree?"

She was a Joan of Arc. But was she really this, or was it just some fancy of hers, the way young people got ideas, a fleeting idealistic passion let go of in a year for something easier? And if she truly was following the gleam, would God protect her?

"Can't you find these people just as well at the Salvation Army?"

"Ah, I can't stand their moralizing. Sometimes I go to the homeless shelter at the parish and prefer that."

"You go to church?"

"I go to Mass. I'm not a Catholic, but I go to Mass. I like the ritual of it, and I like the worship of Mary, the mother. I have no interest in a rageful, paternalistic God."

"Same with me!" And Vachel began telling her of his gospel, of his own church of disciples, and she didn't look away or interrupt him. She listened, closely, her knees to her chin. An evening's acolyte.

Fuck this, thought Anita. Why couldn't she escape the actresses? No matter where she went, Hollywood followed with its pathetic ambitions, its parade of weak accomplishments and need for slavish attention. Florence Deshon, Max Eastman's flame, was pretty and young like all the rest; she had been in a few good New York plays. Who knew if she could act, but that didn't really matter; she'd get her moment in a scene, slinking around in a skimpy costume—an extra for a party or a harem—and then get cut, back to the ugly apartment to dream of being the Biograph Girl. Anita agreed to give Florence's name to a producer, but cautioned her that this meant little. Even the popular, well employed actresses had troubles; it was never enough, would never be enough. They were great gaping holes of ego.

She wished she could escape it. Max Eastman, who she tried to talk to because she admired his magazine, kept glaring as he nursed his liquor,

Becky Bradway

blowing off her name-drops of great books. He was furious that she (or what she represented) was luring Florence away from New York.

"Movies are cheap," he said, more to Florence than to her. "Simple stupid stories."

"He's just drunk," the girl said, going back to talking about her good reviews.

And what about Vachel, the poet who was supposed to rescue her from Hollywood? He was talking to a girl. A girl who looked like a boy, at that. From the sound of it (his voice carried, even over the player piano playing Irish tunes), they were talking religion. Well, that didn't interest her at all. She had only been in a church twice in her life, both times to retrieve her father who, after a drunken bender, thought he needed deliverance. Lindsay's religious streak made her uncomfortable; she could never live with a Bible thumper. As for Mae, she was all wrapped up at the artists' table, leaning into this Charles Demuth who was dressed very dapperly and seemed both embarrassed and amused. Mae was so bad at these things. Really, she'd be better off a dull housewife in Santa Monica.

Anita had to extricate herself.

From the front room came loud arguments of old boozy friends, a sound familiar to her from the many seaside establishments of the Barbary Coast. She was used to rough old men and couldn't care less. She went to the swinging doors that separated the front and back bars and leaned in.

The room was the usual—tables crammed with men, men lined up along a battered bar. Above the bar was a huge mirror with a picture of a man (some politician, no doubt) set off by a giant X of shillelaghs with shamrocks along the frame edges. Tucked around the bar mirror and stuck to the wall were hazy photographs of horses and jockeys and naked girls. The room stank of stale beer and piss, just like home. At the bar was a pack of thugs. Must be some of the Hudson Dusters gang, who looked if anything like Hollywood clichés, which was how the world generally appeared to her. They were burly, dirty, wearing caps, some with scars and broken noses, long beyond their fighting prime. Some had probably been handsome in their day. She had nothing against them, though she knew they weren't really characters and probably had killed people and maybe still made a practice of it. Being tiny, she knew her vulnerability; she also knew that people left her alone and that most older men felt some need to protect her, as if she were a child and not a woman. She used this to her advantage. Some of the Hudson Dusters stared at her; a couple of them smiled; a bouncer moved in her direction. And so she took in the tin ceiling, the filthy window, the bent bulk of the fellow behind the bar who leaned in the way of a sickly man trying to look strong. Life beat down men like this; if they weren't murdered when they were young, they declined into a frail age of rotting kidneys and crippled joints. She didn't fear them. Besides, they nearly always adored her because she'd listen to their endless blowhard stories.

What must they think of the artists in the back? No doubt they found them annoying and just took what they could of their money. She wondered how many times the Hudson Dusters had mugged some pretentious writer in the alley. But that seemed to be the Village—the tough immigrants butting up against the mannered artists who had descended in a wave in search of cheap housing on charming streets, all of them pushing back the old rich, and now the entire pack shoved aside by tourists and developers buying up the old lodging houses and hotels and tearing them down for spiffy apartments for which they could charge premium rent. The poor Hudson Dusters and their anachronisms; the artists should be glad the gang didn't shoot them all dead.

As they eyed her, she wished she were a man so she could stay in this noisy room with its nostalgic Irish music and just talk and listen, hear the stories as sordid as they were, and maybe beat someone up herself, why not?

"Back with you," said a squint eyed cliché, a hatched-faced man who looked as if he'd never smiled in his life. He took her by the shoulder, turned her around, and gave her a surprisingly gentle push back into the "family room."

Damn it.

Eastman's friend Floyd Dell came up and took her elbow. "I see you've met Lucky Louie." Dell stood close and looked down into her face, his flop of sandy hair drooping over an eye. He was pale and ingratiating, well dressed, hovering—a ladies man, easy to spot; Hollywood dripped with them. This was not her type, and though he talked to her charmingly about New York welcoming a Western flower blah blah, and he seemed likable and smart, she was put off. She hated insincerity for the purpose of the almighty lay. She preferred the harmless Vachel, though she wasn't sure what she wanted to do with him. In truth, though, she already kind of liked someone, her director for the Fairbanks films, John Emerson, though she wouldn't say this attachment was quite love. Mr. E.—what she always called him—was much older, needy and possessive, and took credit for her work, and she didn't want to think of him now that she was away. They had never slept together, because he was busy sleeping with so many other women, and because she was too busy and didn't care. Still, she found herself comparing everyone to him. Their work enmeshment—what she liked to think of as a partnership of great minds—bled into all else. He had taught her much about movie-making; he was funny, though morose and moody and alcoholic. The trip to New York was in part an experiment in perspective, to put Emerson at a distance and see if she could get by completely on her own. So far, she didn't miss him.

For a further sampling of men, she sat beside John Reed. He said hello, said "call me Jack," and asked her about herself and was kind, though very distracted by the girl Louise, who had crossed the room and was laughing raucously with some theater types; maybe he was also distracted by some-thing in his past, or something he wanted to do. Restless, legs moving, hands shifting, and when he heard she was with the movies he lost interest. So she asked him about his war reporting and politics, and he began to tell her about Europe when he saw something; he abruptly stopped, pardoned himself, and walked to the bathroom. Poor guy. The Hell Hole, it seemed, had faded into the background for Reed, and he saw little of it and all of Louise. Not like his friend O'Neill, who noticed everything while downing shot after shot. Oh, she knew this brooding Irish type, all right. So darkly appealing on the sur-face. So much trouble underneath. He was listening intently to the religious discussion between the girl and Vachel.

Then Mae stood and pointed. "Fuck, Anita, isn't that Barrymore?"

"Of course not—wait, crap."

And in stumbled John Barrymore, maybe the best living actor, greet-ing the room. And he headed right to their tables where he seemed to know them all, and he suddenly recognized Anita and Mae and said, "By the Great Gawds!"

"And thus is Hamlet," murmured O'Neill.

Barrymore hugged her, reeking as usual of whiskey and sweat from hours of being on stage under lights and possibly days of forgetting to bathe, except for his hair—his hair was beautiful, golden, waving to his shoulders; he was slight, graceful, almost ethereal, and he bleated out "God damn!"

Barrymore as Hamlet, performing in the theater he loved, in the city he was bred to; night after night of brilliant declamation to a skull led him to get stinking drunk. Pain, death, sad suicide, and she believed he felt every bit of it.

People in Hollywood laughed at him, calling him a great ham, but Anita found him sweet and gracious. He was no good with women, though he had plenty; he was frail and passive, and a part of her was enraged at his actor brother Lionel for bringing him to Hollywood, where there was far too much money and far too many women. For some reason he liked her, though every time he saw her he patted her on the head and called her some variation of "delicate flower of the bold word." Which made her laugh.

Everyone at the table moved to make room for him, despite how bad he smelled, and he chose a spot between O'Neill and Dorothy. Vachel then leaned across Dorothy, who didn't seem to mind, introducing himself loudly and declaiming lines from *General William Booth*, which Anita found embarrassing. Yet in a grand compliment, Barrymore responded by finishing the poem for him, performing it much more subtly and less bombastically than Vachel, making it sound British.

Vachel complimented Barrymore on his movies and Barrymore said, "That crud. Lindsay, movies are games, as easy as a stroll, a slum if you will—a means of cash—and I never watch them, most especially not my own."

"But movies can be the greatest art," Vachel began, and before he could get on the soapbox, Barrymore laughed. "In film there's no way to see and hear who's before you—it's trivial, run by money men. Might it be art in some abstract way? Not now. The time for artistic freedom is past; it's all a business now. Best instead to look out upon the eyes and the breathing mass, the life that is real theater."

Vachel looked completely deflated.

"Ah, perhaps someday, Lindsay, long after we're dead."

"He's right," said O'Neill. "Theater allows risk. Every time a gamble."

"Not that Mae hasn't given some lovely performances. Not that our little daisy Anita hasn't given us hilarious words," said Barrymore, ever the gracious flirt. "But they are lone voices transcending the mess, and Mae, you may never find a director the likes of Griffith again."

Mae shrugged. "Yeah, you're probably right."

"But enough! Who cares!"

"Yes, who does care?" murmured Dorothy. "It's all a panacea."

Barrymore talked awhile to O'Neill, and then someone across the room began yelling for him, and he bowed to the table and went off into the crowd. Nearly everyone in the place stared at him; he seemed a Renaissance throwback, with his long coat and tight pants and wavy long hair; it was as if time stood still, or there was no time.

Then a pause. Everyone forgot to talk. It was that late hour. Women were falling into men; men were sliding hands up their legs. Some were very well dressed, the slumming alcoholics. The sawdust floor smelled more strongly of spilled liquor, and the smoke from the cigarettes held by nearly every man and woman was stifling. At a table she saw a foppish blonde man, handsome, snorting cocaine or heroin through a rolled up bill, then passing it to a much older man with a beard, the bohemian sage type. If there were syringes in the bathroom, she wouldn't be surprised. Morphine, heroin everywhere she went. In L.A., so many bright talents shooting up, arriving late to the studio in the morning after long nights, then eventually fired, left to die or sleep on the street or stumble back to Bumfuck Ohio. In the Hell Hole the feeling was edgier, the drugs more of a statement, some proof of radicalism—what crap. She was surprised when in a few minutes the same blonde man rushed to the table to embrace Eugene O'Neill from behind in a big hug, hanging about his neck like a jeweled chain.

"Goddamn, Louis," laughed O'Neill, peeling away the fellow's arms.

O'Neill introduced them. "Anita of Hollywood, Vachel of Poetry, this is Louis Holladay. His sister is Polly, owns a restaurant."

"Ah, you're Polly's brother." Vachel jumped up and pumped the wan fellow's hand.

"That's right," said Louis. "Gene's my oldest pal."

"College roommates," O'Neill explained. "Louis, take this shot and order more."

Louis was as good looking as a department store manikin. A lot of cokeheads were good looking in a sensitive sort of way. Why was that? Why were they so light and thin (well, she knew girls who used it for weight loss; what was she thinking?).

"Where did you go to college?"

"Harvard, of course," said Louis. "Every Villager has been to Harvard. Haven't you noticed?"

"Just the men," Anita clarified. "And then there are the Hudson Dusters."

"I mean the artists, the ones who count." And Louis laughed. Although he could have pulled a chair over to her, he instead pulled up between O'Neill and Reed and hung on pathetically to both of them.

"Anita and the redhead over there are from Hollywood."

"Oh Christ," said Louis. "The wasted desert."

"I take issue with that," said Jack Reed.

"Then why don't you move back to Portland and take the dentist's wife with you?" He poked Jack in the ribs, like he was teasing.

"I can't do any good there. I'll agree that the West can be empty, but it does have beauty, a freedom and spirit, tranquility."

"It's so," said Anita, though she took issue with the tranquility part. Boring, more like it. "But I'd like to come East."

"The West might as well be the moon. I don't even know why it's in America."

And Vachel launched into his theory of the United States being five distinct countries, which sounded both crackpot and correct.

"Too bad Europe's not one country," said Louis. "Then it could have little civil wars instead of one big bloody one."

"Goddamn, Louis, what will you do when you're drafted?" said O'Neill. "They'll shoot you dead on the spot, you're such a wastrel."

"Aw fuck that. There'll be no draft. Americans don't give a shit about Europe."

And so came that argument. No, no draft, they said, but behind it was fear and worry, scheming to figure out what to do, drinking to forget they had to figure out what to do, and more drinking, and more bashing of Germans, then of the British, and of the "pansy" French, applause for the Russians who would just revolt and say no because "they're the strongest of the lot," said Reed, and more debate, and more liquor, and she noticed Vachel nervously looking around as the talk grew heated, but she'd heard it all before, and the girl Dorothy Day didn't seem to care (she seemed to be taking revolutionary notes), and in fact it was all very entertaining and funny. Ah, the ways to subvert the war effort, with bombs, the stealing of papers, the bashing of recruitment office windows, barnstorming every event attended by the president so he wouldn't forget which of the electorate was really boss, fuck John D. Rockefeller and the warlords, rise labor, defeat bankers, et cetera. And they said Tom Wallace, the owner of the Golden Swan Hell Hole, and his cronies were shipping arms to the IRA who when they weren't trying to blow up the British were shipping the guns to the Germans to do it….Ah, the talk of drunken revolutionaries who couldn't get up.

"And what do you think, Hollywood?" O'Neill asked her out of the blue.

"Me? We won't go to war."

"You sound pretty fucking sure," said Max Eastman, who now somehow ended up beside her. Who knew where his wife had gone.

"Everyone I know is against it. Hollywood is full of Europeans fleeing the war. The Jews are all sending money to help their families escape. The German directors and actors are all laying low here—they think Germany's gone mad. How can we go to war when people oppose it?"

"Some want it, just to fight," said O'Neill. "Patriotism fever. Makes men feel valuable. Fuels governments. Takes down movements."

"Christ, such a pessimist, buddy," said Louis.

"Not everyone is a radical or an intellectual—remember that. That way you won't be surprised."

"Sixty percent of Americans oppose the war," said Max.

Dorothy leaned toward Lindsay and said, "This kind of talk makes me seek out the cathedral. Because it's quiet and beautiful. If there are prayers for peace, and a great hope…."

O'Neill looked at her appreciatively, but shrugged.

"Aw, fuck it," said Louis. "I don't want to think about this shit. We are in the ultimate center of ultimate thought of ultimate idea, we are our own republic, we cannot be touched."

And the Frenchman Duchamp smiled in the corner.

"What do you think, Marcel?" Eastman said.

He gave a little shrug. "People are attracted to chaos. You will go."

And on it went and the night went on, and eventually talk of the war turned to gossip. Mae gave up on Charles Demuth (who left with a very handsome man) and tried Duchamp who seemed to be his own entity, then moved on to Floyd Dell, who naturally seemed receptive if a bit snobby about it, smiling smarmily as Mae stroked his hair. Mae was an idiot. Max left, arguing with Florence, and Reed left with his wandering lady Louise while O'Neill watched them go, and then he and Dorothy matched shot for shot, talking God and Heaven with Vachel in a way that seemed very strange to Anita in the Hell Hole which spun like something out of Dante at the end of the night, the smoky gas lamps giving off a furtive haze as yelling came from the front room with the potential of real violence (Anita had learned to recognize what was camaraderie and what might become attempted murder), and the waiter angrily put empty glasses into a bucket waiting for them all to leave, and somehow it all felt warm and boozy and solid, more real than Fifth Avenue with its wealth, infused with nostalgia for other battles in other lands, so strange, strange to long for lands where none had been.

And O'Neill began reciting a poem from memory, a long ballad, a poem her pop and his pals used to recite around this time of night, *The Hound of Heaven*. He recited sonorously, but plainly, as if the story had really happened or was happening now.

I fled Him, down the nights and down the days;
I fled Him, down the arches of the years;
I fled Him, down the labyrinthine ways
Of my own mind; and in the mist of tears

I hid from Him, and under running laughter.
Up vistaed hopes, I sped;
And shot, precipitated
Adown Titanic glooms of chasmed fears,
From those strong Feet that followed, followed after.
But with unhurrying chase,
And unperturbed pace,
Deliberate speed, majestic instancy,
They beat—and a Voice beat
More instant than the Feet—
"All things betray thee, who betrayest Me."

And so on, this long song, O'Neill reciting in a kind of brogue. It was eerie, and the artists sat transfixed, bleary, staring from O'Neill to the door as if they expected Jesus or a demon to come in.

Then from across the room came another voice. Barrymore began singing with O'Neill the last verses of *The Hound of Heaven* loud enough to be heard even by the Hudson Dusters, who came into the room at first annoyed but then enrapt—that Irish thing again.

I stand amid the dust o' the mounded years—
My mangled youth lies dead beneath the heap.
My days have crackled and gone up in smoke,
Have puffed and burst as sun-starts on a stream.
Yea, faileth now even dream. . . .
And now my heart is as a broken fount,
Wherein tear-drippings stagnate . . .

It was only a moment, never to be forgotten by some. Children of the theater, both with famous fathers, one for the first time having a play produced in Manhattan, the other giving away his soul in what would probably be his greatest performance, for who could top being the best Hamlet anyone living had ever seen? Both young, they both carried all possibility, yet seemed profoundly sad and ill-fated, as if they were already in the throes of defeat. *The Hound of Heaven* was the regretful cry of a man assessing his life—Anita knew it well—fearing beyond, pursued by the hound to redeem himself before it was too late, to face the anguish of the self and transcend it to commitment, to stop finding comfort where? in this very bar. The poem seemed to accuse them, and why were these two divine drunks singing it to them? This sense of impending trouble and judgment pervaded their lives— everyone drowning, haunted by guilt—yet it felt unreasonable, even melodramatic. Europe might be destroying itself, but they were safe across the waters;

their lives were mostly fun, bubbling with ideas; they were free to choose who they wanted, where they wanted—they weren't bound to horrible jobs, and realms of justice were just within their reach. So why did they feel pursued?

Or maybe it was just two more drunken Irishmen, singing songs of loss and fear, accusing themselves of flight, running from tradition and belief as they washed away in booze and pining.

When they finished they tossed back their whiskey in perfect synchronization—the show was done, there were no hounds. Barrymore tossed his wavy hair, O'Neill blinked as if emerging from a dream, and there they were, still in the Hell Hole.

Jane L. Carman

Baby Stories

infinitely inspired

Story 1: A baby is born. It is born inside out, the heart flutters beyond its cage, intestines slither past their walls spiraling around the body, circling legs, suffocating stories. The little heart beats. The parents see the heart beat, cannot look at the face until the heart stops. The face is pink, then gray and blue. They bury the baby in a cedar box beneath an oak tree. Every day for 31 years, the mother swears she sees the baby's eye or toe or face in the sweet angles and curves of the tree's bark. Every day for 31 years, the father works. For a few years, he pretends not to think about the baby. After that, he believes he does not think about the baby. Every day for 31 years, the parents do not speak of the baby. Friends who ask are told it was a false pregnancy. There are no more babies, because there is no more sex.

Story 2: There is a baby born and nobody wants her. She is, after all, a girl. She is carried to the side of the river and tossed away. She cries when her skin smacks against the cold, gray water, but the cries do not last. As she floats away, there are little fish searching for soft eyes and flesh. There are large fish tasting for baby. Once she hits the water, she feels nothing. They say, Babies aren't human until they are dressed. This baby never wore a dress.

Story 3: There is a baby born. In the beginning she belongs to one father or another and one mother. The first father tells the second father that he can keep the baby because the first father doesn't have enough time or money or breast milk to support the baby. Since the second father possesses the mother (and therefore the breast milk) and because he owns 400 acres of cropland, he should have the baby. So the second father takes the baby, not knowing who she truly belongs to. He calls her his.

Story 3: There is a baby born to a mother who doesn't really need a baby to keep her man. She places the baby in a plastic basket (because she cannot find her nicer wicker basket) and sets that basket on a fencepost on a dirt road. The mother selects that particular fence post because there are two good geese at the bottom to guard the baby, and because the road is isolated enough that nobody will see her dump the baby but not too remote, so somebody might find the baby with the intention of keeping it. There is also a creek, tall grass, and a lot of wild berries in the area, so the baby, when it learns to pick berries and eat grass, will have plenty to eat. A lot of individuals claim this baby.

Story 4: A babyless mother on a Harley sees an infant checkered with sunburn, covered in dust, sitting on a roadside in a patch of lilies and cattails. The babyless mother scoops up the baby and puts it on the Harley's gas tank. Together, the two ride until the babyless mother and the motherless baby are lulled into a state of near sleep by the good vibrations of the Harley. Eventually, the baby rolls off of the gas tank into a new patch of lilies. Oblivious to what is happening, the babyless mother remains babyless when she cannot remember whether or not she really had a baby for a few hundred miles or if it was the lack of sleep and her tendency to eat horseweeds that had her only thinking she had a real baby and was no longer babyless. For the rest of her life, the babyless mother sends silent prayers and incantations to the once-hers baby. The sounds of the babyless mother morph and grow as they reach the baby who is, eventually, no longer a baby.

Story 5: There really is no such thing as a baby.

Story 6: A father who loves his baby for reasons he cannot understand (because he has never met the baby but can only imagine what it is like to have a baby) can only imagine that the baby must love him back, because that is what babies do. This father thinks about his baby, the same baby that he gave to another man. As he thinks about this baby, new stories begin to form in his mind. He pictures himself washing the baby, feeding and watering it. He imagines dressing it for school, watching it ride away on the school bus wearing clothes he made from sheep and goat skins. He imagines the baby wearing a feed cap he found at the grain elevator. He imagines making fishing poles out of branches from an old oak tree and fishing for crappies and bluegills, filleting the fish, and having cookouts behind the house where he imagines the baby will grow strong from eating mutton and potatoes and fish and dirt. He imagines how tough the baby will be from wrestling hogs to the ground and chasing geese. He imagines the baby living with him forever, forever letting him hold and feed it.

Story 7: Ladies who find themselves pregnant out of wedlock should make sure the baby is either not born (by eating controlled amounts of rat poison or by drinking castor oil or by having somebody jump on the prospective mother's stomach or by use of a stick aimed at the problem) or go into hiding for a long enough period to have the baby to be discarded (in a river, feed to livestock, or abandoned in a wooded area) or left on the doorstep of a church very early on a Sunday morning.

Story 8: Possible fathers of babies produced out of wedlock should pay off the mother or enter into an undetermined period of emphatic denial. Of course, there is nothing to be ashamed of. As a man, one has certain needs that have to be fulfilled.

Story 9: A baby is born to a married mother and father. This, in itself, is nothing extraordinary. In fact, this is how babies are supposed to be born. This baby lives with the mother and father for nearly 9 long years doing baby things and getting the sort of attention babies crave, things like: food and water, clothing, a temperature controlled climate of approximately 60 degrees in the winter and 85 in the summer. The baby is held an average of 7.3 times a day through the age of 9 months, 6.77 times a day from 9 months to 17 months at which time the holding is decreased to 4.85 times a day for the baby's own good. By the time of the baby's third birthday, when there is a cake and a father wearing a clown wig, the frequency of being held graduates to 0.4 times per day. Being mature, the baby learns to do simple chores and is ready to be on its own for hours at a time by the age of 5.129, and, by the age of 8.56, the house smells too much of mature baby and the mother has to leave in search of herself, a self that is lost almost immediately after the birth of the baby, a self that is particularly slippery and illusive, for the mother has been searching for this self for most of her life (or at least since the age of 8.56). Shortly after, the father understands the depth of the baby's self-sufficiency and spends weeks at a time at meetings and conventions or working the fields or at the homes of special friends. The baby learns to make both toast and omelets, how to collect eggs and milk from the farm animals and berries and vegetables from the garden. Eventually, the baby, understanding how mature it really is, leaves the home in search of a job and a dog with which it can share leftovers.

Story 10: An abandoned baby is found in a trash barrel. The baby is abandoned by a 24-year-old mother who is later charged with attempted murder. Had she left the infant at a fire station, police department, or doctor's office (it is not clear whether this office has to be that of a medical doctor) there would have been no charges filed. Five years prior to this incident, a baby is found under a stairwell and later adopted. The same year a 15-year-old can't tolerate the shame or grief or depression that sometimes accompanies the birth of a baby out of wedlock or the birth of a baby to a teenager, a teenager who might be called a whore or a slut or a bitch or a worthless piece of shit that should have been aborted herself or murdered or taught a lesson through rape or another form of physical pedagogy. A year later (and having learned a lesson about how abandoned babies might be discovered), a 16-year-old places her newborn in a garbage bag before dropping it in a shed behind her house. This baby is not adopted. Two years before a baby is abandoned in a trash barrel by a 24-year-old mother somewhere in the south, a baby is found alive under a tree at a hospital. Since there must be a doctor's office in the vicinity, it is likely that the mother, if found, will be able to declare amnesty.

Story 11: An 18-year-old man is charged with raping a 5-month-old baby girl while her mother is in class at the local high school. The baby (who requires surgery and cries hard enough to either vomit or overfill her lungs with melancholy) might have been crying too loud for the man to tolerate or the man might have been on drugs or drunk or the baby might have been asking for it or the man might have just needed to satisfy a primal urge to dominate or to get off. Fifty years earlier, a mother castrates her newborn son. The infant's screaming or the shame of having a disfigured child or the understanding of the possible spiritual or legal consequences is too much, it works its way into the mother, slips through her cells as she lines up a revolver to the temple of the infant's head, then to her own. She pulls the trigger once. A century earlier a father rapes a 10-month-old daughter who bleeds to death and is placed (along with several rocks and flowers) in a burlap sack and sent to the bottom of a river that flows into the Mississippi and then into the Gulf of Mexico. It is unclear how far the body, bricks, burlap, or flowers travel before being consumed by fish or mud.

Story 12: A baby is born dead, the cord wrapped around the neck. Two days earlier, the mother complains of a series of violent movements in her womb and calls her doctor who says that there is absolutely nothing to worry about and to stop overreacting and that he will see her at her next appointment and that the baby will be still for a few hours to a day before it is born, which it is. The baby is still, and it is born.

"Baby Stories" was published in *Devil's Lake* and *Tangled in Motion* (Journal of Experimental Books, 2015).

Ricardo Cortez Cruz

Longing for Home

…The first joint of David Foster Wallace's that I ever explored was Signifying Rappers, *a cut 'n' mix project breaking down the meaning of rap. That book was a great gift [read: a loaner/ loner], a sort of white boy shuffle generously given to me by a dear and former Illinois State University colleague, Ron Strickland. I always wanted to sample it. The DFW story that most stays with me is the one told to me back in the day by Curtis White, my mentor. In truncated fashion, White got me thinking about David for good, who apparently had been thinking a lot at that time about brown recluses.*

"America is our motherland now—there's no changing that fact," I say to Girl in unrealtime, taking a good look at her. We're in a time warp. She's a woman with a black black face, hanging around in cellars and in every crowded place, but she laughs. Our Main Street features an automatic teller. We are surrounded by cock-blockers and hoes and groupies and tricks. *Just remember to say your prayers*, I hear my momma warning us. Girl maintains herself and holds her position. But because I am carrying Girl's retro ghetto-box with a slow jam tape I made for her, I withdraw, afraid that niggas might rob us.

"Please take your money," the white teller says quickly, straight outta the box.

"Today's mind is a machine," I say to Girl. But when I turn to look, she runs to the john. Calling for help, I hack into a stolen smartphone that asks if I'm a robot before letting me download anything on it. I reflect on how us black men's grandmothers are constantly calling us "thugs" and how that hasn't helped matters any but rather instead turned a nigga into a cyberpunk.

(A Mr. America wearing mirrorshades hurriedly loads a clip and heads toward us in seeming slow-motion, slinging a 12-gauge and a Tec 9 like The Terminator, and, for a moment, we believe and we shut up and focus on him to see if he's coming for us, a single drop of sweat falling from my brow and spattering against the sidewalk like water/melon tossed from a rooftop where the city is so seedy.)

The world's so ratty and dark outside that Girl and I decide to drop inside a shady/shabby place called Chelsea Hotel, policemen already profiling us, following our black behinds like we kids in a candy store.

Mark/America, according to the name/tag on his chest, ducks behind the counter as if remixing a book there. Who shot ya, I want to ask Mark, 'cause there's something about him that speaks to me. However, I get quickly distracted by the velvet paintings of African tribal leaders off the wall.

Girl gives a bill to a huge, muscular German woman in charge of the desk.

"Card or roll," says the humming German woman thinking she's Joy Denalane, shooting us a look, and Girl smiles and shows her some plastic, a Chase Bank Card.

Picking up the pace in this place where roach performs birth and re-birth, we climb the winding stair of this chocolate building on 125th Street. The clerk checking out Girl's ass and shaking her big head, eclipsed by a graphic poster saying "Funf Tage des Blutens" behind her. Caught up in wars of Armageddon, we walk around the funkadelic maggot brains playing board/bored games on the stairway and dart into the hallway of the third floor.

A stray Negrophile hanging around in chinos holds his head and slides over on the steps, then watches us through a brown bottle of warm Canadian mist, our bodies swirling for him, I assume, making him feel even more trippy. Listening to drill music, he offers us a rag for five bucks, a dirty hand towel or something supposedly from "the half-white and half-black prophet Muhammad who had walked this earth as a peddler of silks and snow," he says. As we pass on by, I accidentally catch the man's leg and see the melted nougat stuck to the sole of his feet. Negro catches a glimpse of Girl's monster tight-ass jeans which say "Guess." Ready to make a move, he puts out a cigar, ashes trying to bury themselves. A dark cloud covers/clothes his face as if he's the executioner, Death spying on us again. We cannot see his expression, cannot know if he is smiling. Blackout.

We proceed through a corridor feeling a little nauseous. Lying niggas all masked up. Brown recluses retreating. Legs pulling back to prevent themselves from being stepped on. Signifying rappers in glitz and gangster-dom re/presenting lounge music and trying to play us for attention. Then suddenly Girl stops walking again.

Secondhand smoke's the worse kind. After getting higher by the second, Girl opens her alligator purse and, with a quickness, whips out her key and uses some speed to unlock the door to our room. Before we go in, we notice how depressed the door is. Our gaze turns to the hallway colored with graffiti and tattooed with labels from Campbell's soup—perhaps remnants from Basquiat, the first black NYC street artist to break into that chic, avant-garde art scene with Andy Warhol etc. He fucked a woman here before, too, the desk clerk had told me in front of other tenants, spitting in my face. But then, he died at the age of 27 from a heroin(e) overdose. "Maybe one sweet day they'll do a movie on him and *The New York Times* will say it's 'Powerful! It will change your life forever!' and movie critics like Siskel and Ebert in the old days will give it two thumbs up," Girl says. She's still mad, trippin', that we couldn't catch a taxi, that we had to hitchhike just to get here. Just to put our face up in the place. "Let's keep on walking," she says.

"Which way is up?" I ask, and Girl grabs my hand so we can travel the stairway to heaven.

Now we're standing in the hallway, Girl noticing that the walls have ears. Shaking a bit, Girl turns the key and we step in. I'm ready to get my money's worth, but the first thing that hits us is the blackness of this cramp space, accompanied only by the red and blue neon lights spotlighting us. The room's window appears to be made of low-e glass [with a thin coat] and broken and wide open, the ledge doused with sexual blood. Rotten wood saying "just be good to me." O', the moon enters the room, then has the nerve to hide from us. I start "PLAY," pressing all of the buttons, and set the ghetto-box down on the floor, Billie Holiday singing "Fine and Mellow."

Just as I'm considering hitting on Girl, I feel her tapping my ass.

"Goddamn!" Girl shrieks. Goddamn: All I can see is Girl's skinny, scrawny, anemic-looking figure; she's blue. "All I can see is you," Girl says, taking off her clothes. Her body is porno/graphic. Vanessa Blue. But the source of brilliance. A genuine diamond for a blood like me. A Blue Nile princess cut.

Everything is touching.

"You're completely red," she says to me. We are silhouettes. We fall onto the bed by accident, rubbing against each other softly. "Baby, come and taste my soul," I think. "Show me all the places you want me to touch and want me to go."

There's a street fight going on, but we don't care. Nobody cares. Tonight's the night for love. Chances are we'll have some romance tonight, O. I put Girl's hand over my heart. "Yo', feel the thunder roaring," I say. Lightly, winds are blowing. Outside our door, the wino listens to us as we explore the uncharted depths of our space, our intimate zone, like two ships in the ocean. Déjà vu. I have the feeling that he has been here before, a voyageur/ voyeur, the ancient mariner or some shit like dat.

We hear him gently kissing those dark lips. We feel sorry for him. He plays for pennies, blowing into the hole of his woman while she moans and groans as if begging him to quit. "If love could talk, I think it would sound like this," I say to Girl who places her hand over my heart.

"This is our time," she says. She calls me "Savior." Lighting up a ciga- rette, she searches for incense, wine, and candles, a tiny, little fireplace in the room. She is red-bone now. The atmosphere is calm, peaceful, tranquil tonight. "These are the halcyon days of our youth," Girl proclaims in the mood, happy, standing in front of the little window breeze, watching people on the street smoke dozers, her shit tight.

I know everybody, I mean, everybody is my nigga. "There go Mr. Wright," I say, pointing at him, giving him the finger. He looks at Girl as if she's snatched.

"Uh-uh." Girl stands with her arms reaching out and legs far apart. I can tell that she is feeling totally liberated, completely hellacool. This is her moment of epiphany.

Rocking Monet costume jewelry, she reminds me of Lisa Bonet in *A Different World*. For the first time, I noticed running water in the sink.

"For as long as we are together, we can be carefree," she whispers. "We can be …"

"Now or never," Billie Holiday vocalizes.

"Must be the music," Girl says, "turning me on. Let's get intoxicated. Fall in love again."

Our world is always so full of bass/base.

"The Life You Save is Always More Than Your Own," a billboard says.

Our world is full of base/bass.

Thunder in the ghettoes. After vaping and lighting up with each puff, beautiful, big booty women with blu Cherry Crush, vacuum lungs, and breasts transforming into walloping raindrops make their butts clap. They prove niggas are actors. They play the role of Foxy Brown or Cleopatra Jones in a blaxploitation film, a B movie.

Ricardo Cortez Cruz

"Wake up," they say to me like Coffee.

Half-dossing in a blue funk, Slim, after dozing off, sits in a small living area, reclining, resting, facing his front door and watching a black-and-white TV set up on top of some stackable milk crate. The picture's cloudy, but Slim sees himself changing in it; that's all that counts. From a broken bottle, traces of a perfume, Pure or Amazing Grace, still emanate. A monster fluorescent bulb dangles directly above Slim's big head, the spotlight on him, a 380 Special by his side, a revolver suitable for outlaws Jesse James, John Wesley Hardin, "Wild Bill" Longley, or Dick Glass. Sucka's hot. And fragile. He never thought he'd be so fragile.

Outside, mis-streeted, the boys dabble in vitamin C, powder, sucking on sugar tits, whatever white lady they could get. So-called policing the "gayborhood," they hang out with their dogs and drool over their makeshift raps. They kick rock, girlfriend, to the curb, enjoying themselves. Jiving about running a train on one of the jezebels, sexy mamas, chicken heads, Aunt Jemimas, or crack/crank whores. Jibing on that. Keeping a battering ram handy, they rail on and on 'bout how they like "Summertime, Summertime," which contains a sample of "Summer Madness" by Kool and the Gang.

Even when Slim masturbates, the beat is hot. Hot tracks flowing down his arm while he cries himself a river.

"We are not going to have any 1932 Gestapo-type raids on anyone," promises the mayor of New York City on TV in response to his receiving an off-the-pig Christmas card and his children getting a coloring book depicting black children challenging white law and order in the 'hood. "If someone who has been drinking in the middle of the night decides to be a spook, that's catharsis," the mayor adds. "However, we are not equipped to deal with black comedy or hyperbole, so if somebody says they are going to kill a person, we take that quite literally. After all, white citizens are primarily decent but frightened for their lives." Our mayor is privately gay and, like J. Edgar Hoover, a contributor to the FBI files later obtained under the Freedom of Information Act. Let's get one thing straight: There's nothing wrong with being or feeling gay. But, definitely, there's something seriously wrong with you if you don't want to help your own brother or sister or support black people.

The mayor confirms that, indeed, there have been threats by the radical chic to burn down The White House. "Cipher this, I'll burn the mother/fucker down and beat the President (the punk) to death with a marshmallow," says King Lord God Allah Patrice Lumumba, taking over the mike at a recent jam in the park, according to reports. He's a five-percenter, a civil servant I would later write about, another minister who the CIA instructed an agent to poison, and the member of this growing militant gang who claims to have taken over the reigns/rains. As if the result of some Vodun Order, he's been resurrected, says the news. A slight, goat of man destined to be punished for the errors of others. He must have seen it coming, but his glasses only framed half of the story.

GANG LIFE CONTAINS SHORT LIFE SPAN.

My flesh and blood(s) even scare the hell outta me. Crabs—crips with the blues—creep around like it's nothing. The spirit of storms and war and creation and the see and the forests and the trees. Niggas with locks on top of their heads and bucking the system smoke the trees, a whole set of them in bondage as either guardian of the grave or evil spirits taking the form of an animal.

"Later tonight, around midnight, after a test of the Emergency Broadcast System, we plan to send a messenger into our ghettoes," the mayor says, "to let families know that we mean serious business."

With the scene/seen creating part of the backdrop—the eerie ambience of the whole day, Slim sprawls out in a LA-Z-BOY reclining chair in the place where he handles his business. He looks for the papers under his feet, but can't find jack. Thinks *maybe that's how it's 'sposed to be.*

THE TIMES WELCOMES EXPRESSIONS OF ALL VIEWS.

The TV announced that OJ Simpson had been found "not guilty" and public reaction has escalated into black and white rioting. This was Baltimore, Ferguson, MI, Little Rock, South Carolina, you name it. For the last hour, Slim had squirmed, eating up all the stuff delivered by the orient express, all types of people dying outside, crying like babies in their sleep. Sick and tired, Slim finally became lifeless. His clock had ticked and ticked, then suddenly come to a screeching halt when he started chewing over those two Robocops who had visited him and forced him to sign a statement that he never had a chance read. "Could arrest you for possessing an illegal firearm," one of the cops threatened while Slim lit a cigarette that burned the arm of the chair a

Ricardo Cortez Cruz

bit. Slim's hands had said "no" and refused to budge, but the other of them rash-skinned, steroid-looking Rocky cops ironed them over the table and made the brother talk. "What kind of bitch calls himself 'Slim'?" the cop asked. His partner pissed in Slim's cup of dirt, mud, while he wasn't looking.

"Don't be deceived, there is no justice except strength," Lumumba said, dreaming *of going back to Africa and leaving these boys to their own black-ish narrative theory.*

We now know that all of the black victims are connected to a series of bizarre and grisly murders—they were discovered to have numerous, and quite pronounced, post-mortal injuries which unfortunately I am unable to further elaborate on at this time, the TV announces.

As soon as the heat left, some freak named Babylon came running into the place with a girlfriend whom she introduces as Destiny. Babylon is hold-ing Destiny's hand, leading her on. They say they work for Mary, the mother of all whores.

"The only thing Mary Mack loves is Gs, cold cash, lots of bones," Slim says to both women, but they ignore him because it's no secret to anyone in Harlem that Mary is a black widow, female trap-door, or at least some kind of poison.

"Lucky for you, I ain't going to hurt you," says Slim.

"If it ain't bad luck," Babylon says, "look out your window and check out the rot, I mean, riot happening in the street. I swear, the angel of death is definitely white and out to fuck us all, not that it surprises me or anything. I even felt myself being grabbed everywhere while I was on the street. And, believe me, I'm pretty goddamn blessed to have gotten away."

But I can tell you this, we've found a slew of botched black bodies contaminated with some serious diseases, killers that are germicidal, tuberculocidal, fungicidal, virucidal, and bacterial, such as herpes simplex types 1 and 2, e.coli, primary syphilis, influenza, hepatitus, staph and strep germs, malaria, Human Immunodeficiency Virus Type 1, en-cephalitis, Black Death, necrosis, and even dirt under their nails. At this time, I am not at liberty to discuss the suspected origin of these diseases or why some of them have made such a strong comeback. But their impact upon this society has proven to be overwhelming and perhaps as ubiquitous as necrophobia.

"For the first time in her life, she's a free woman," Destiny whispers sarcastically.

"Ain't this a bitch," Babylon mutters, making room at the table for the brothers who ain't here, turning around to grab for a chair, showing her back, pulling her hot pants out of her ass. Instead of "bitch," she should have said "mug." "This city's going down fast," Babylon insists. "And here we are, Destiny and me – once again, we end up trying to find some protection and security from a man!" She lifts up her leg and puts one foot on Slim's seat, but Slim knows that something ain't right. Babylon's nylons be ruint, and she paints Mac red fingernail polish on her thigh to try to bring her run to a stop while wondering if Destiny plans to disappear on her once again because, as it turns out, Destiny is actually a Cassandra. The world is funny like that, people always already more than what they seem.

"I shall prove to be what I shall prove to be," Lumumba stresses, according to the broadsheet, the extra. "I don't fear anybody."

One thing is certain, people in the black community have gotten frantic, frighteningly desperate, reaching for anything—more than just drawers—to try to find help, a panacea for their various problems. I've seen women squirting breast milk into their babies' eyes. Men rubbing themselves with spider webs to stop themselves from bleeding. Large groups of people wandering about during the daytime while eating garlic to lower their high blood pressure. The shit just got real.

"Did you know that somebody outside has put blood over your door?" Destiny asks, "just below where your business sign says 'Speedy's.' And these violent kids outside . . . see them? They're like little monsters. They still think Tupac Shakur is alive. 'How you know?' I axed them. 'He made two more movies, did a new album, experienced the same gridlock we see,' they say. 'Whoopee, so what?' I said. 'His name spelled backward means that he is caput, finished, ovah,' I said. 'Well, not really,' they said. 'Nobody's perfect, but the man is a Saint. That's what, how, he's representin' when or if you're smart enough to see his initials reversed. We saw it on BET, MTV, BuzzFeed. It's also being broadcasted on WebTV, Netscape, WorldStar HipHop, BlackBottom, Hot Ghetto Mess – streamin' in those fancy white stores we raided on Madison Avenue. You go to prison, and they'll tell you in the projects the same damn thing. The Best of Deathrow.'

"'Yeah, whatever,' I told them."

"'One day this will be his street,' they said. '2 Pac Boulevard or Avenue.'

"Nowadays these boys don't know when to slow up . . . 'You ever heard of David Blaine?' they ask me. He does street magic. 'It's kind of painful, but he can plant his palm on the ground and keep spinning his hand around in circles, twisting his own arm. See?'

"These little bastard kids twist my arm. Their hands are gritty. Bloodstained. They pass around rocks and candy covered with grime. They tell me, 'After doing his dive of death and drowned alive, this illusionist and endurance artist came back with revolution.'

I'm not supposed to say this on air, but what I am suggesting, what's happening here, is, ah, something reminiscent, ah, of germ warfare. You know what I mean?

Ricardo Cortez Cruz

"What's wrong wit Quincy M.D.?" Babylon asks, no longer able to channel her anger. "I mean, look at him! There's a shadow hanging over him, a fuckin' line of sweat above that nigga's top lip. It's so obvious he's selling us out. Nigga's barely able to talk, walk the walk."

"One day we'll learn," says Destiny, going into a rant. "Somehow people started fighting over race and words once spoken became too difficult to recall so we fought some more over who cursed whom first and, wham, bam, thank-you, ma'am, before we even knew it every wigger and nigger in the city with a private Bigger Thomas living in his goddamn skull is toting a hot gun, and, trust me, there's a lot of them out there, and just out there, whacking folks and hollering fire, all in the name of survival."

"Girl, what the fuck is wrong wit you?" Babylon asks, looking at Slim, feeling a sorted attraction between them. "She's babbling and shit 'cause she's been giving up booty for the same roughneck since she can remember. And, I guess, until she met me. She's tore up. In the street, he done beat her ass real good, I guess. Got her looking in the rearview mirror. That's why she so terrible and super stupid now, jaw(n)ing all that bullswanky.

"Come. Sit down in this chair, girlfriend, before you make yourself too sick to do anythang."

"Look here, my mama done died a long time ago. You should be worried about yourself, sista. I ain't the one who thinks I'm the cultural center of the world. I got no shame. So don't be trying to tell me dat I'm too weak to do anythang."

"Yes, you keep saying 'anythang'—any thang, anythang—like you're hot yourself and want something right now," Slim says to Babylon. He squeezes his crotch area, thinking "the best thangs in life are free."

"No, uh-uh, wait a minute now ... I didn't say 'any thang.' Don't try to tell me I said 'any thang.' You said 'any thang,' not me. I know when I say 'any thang,' okay, so back the fuck up."

"Something ain't right," says Slim. He can smell himself. Even his character is flawed.

Hoping to declassify himself or lesson/lessen his burden, Slim, in true Religion fashion, believes he has nothing to lose. Nothing to lose. Nada. Not a thang.

After contemplating it, Slim grabs Babylon by her back pack and kisses her—hard, cruelly, indifferently, in the beginning of what was at best a very complicated love-hate relationship. This time, she remains impenetrable, reaching for his piece, a Colt Python, a Combat Magnum. There's a confusion of tongues.

"To experience the passion of hatred is to know the force of love," Lumumba said. According to the extra, the ass-wipe, his followers demonstrated deadly silence at the rally.

Microsoft word. That is to say, we catch ourselves talking quietly to ourselves, processing our own thoughts, reviewing and editing our language, then making comments, underscoring the importance of this entire moment, auto-summarizing what has really surprised us about life. We finally have a room of our own, a design for life we actually want—a polyhedron with an open window, a 23-inch diagonal viewable that comes with clouding and backlight bleeding. In ec(h)o-saving mode to reduce energy usage, we feel a part of a touchscreen with magic upscale for enhanced picture without degradation. It's got a congruent polygon as its base, parallelograms for sides, power surging through us. Now, we can't help but to look down on people. After I enter Girl, she says she feels the entire space, including us, swiveling around. Girl puts us in game mode, poses "will you be my hero?" In the meantime, we keep hearing squeaks, little funny noises. I look in the dark for a mouse.

Girl pleads with me to let her please me. "This is the nineties or the beginning of crack in 1985, black to the future," she says, "tell me what you like." She speaks in micro, soft word but asks for word perfect.

"Get with the program," she says. "Take advantage of your control. Don't try to escape, to get out of this one. You wanted me, and now you got me. Remember, Daddy: I'm nothing but a black hole/ho, but I'm your black hole."

We roll around on a generic brass bed that leans to the side, two vertical supports forming right angles with the low-profile box spring. A pair of restraints, Hiatt hinge style handcuffs, becoming part of just another notch in the bedpost.

"Now that you've turned me on, do something," she says.

"What would you do if I was Josephine Baker begging you for a banana?"

I'm silent. I'm thinking enough with the dirty talk. I pump my brakes, then I get in that ass, looking up to her, saving my energy, star compliant, hoping and praying that she doesn't have any type of bug.

"You a bit rough," she says, undergoing a sort of metamorphosis. "Don't even try me." Still a little in the dark, she screams, then calls out for God. "God …help my ass!" she hollers.

Ricardo Cortez Cruz

You said you wouldn't hurt anyone, you dick, perv," exclaims Babylon in holier-than-thou fashion. "Not even yourself." She grabs Slim's mojo and refuses to let go.

"If I could bang, pound, or get nasty with any famous body or diva, Phyllis Hyman be who I'd want for the booty," I hear my stepdaddy stress. "I ride dat for all it's worth." He was a big dreamer that would say anything while listening to drug ballads.

"What if I told you that you are supposed to care *for me*, feel *for me*?" Slim asks his audience.

"Could the problem be that nobody wants to try hard enough to read me, to know what *I* be feeling deep inside?" he asks. "Is it my fault that I'm not believable enough? Shoot. If I tell stories, it's because in the end hue-man lives need and deserve narration.

"I'm the motherfucking hero," Slim says, his voice becoming, pretty, androgynous. See every life brings a moment of intense hatred, body insemi-nated with foul/fowl thoughts. "Pay attention."

"Code red!" yells Slim. Since/sense his period of violence had just begun.

We hear the sounds of human suffering like that of a Nazi concen-tration camp. Naked, we look out the window and see Batty Boy beating Richard Wright's black boy with a nightstick and Billy. Throwing coke all over him. Caning him, forcing him to roll around on the ground until his zipper busts open.

Now Batty Boy is Hitler, A-gay. He dictates the action while some oth-er boys in blue just stand around and obey.

"Strip search the little niglet, take his bling and draws and swag!" Batty Boy shouts in front of a large gathering of folks from the neighborhood. One thing to clarify: It's not Batty Boy's sexual preferences that make him whack to us. It's his use/misuse of power. The wailing on one another.

Blanketed by all of the blackness, Girl gives me a rod, some pump-action stuff. "Smoke him," she whispers. "This is for the community, for all of us. 'Cause this superfreak took advantage of me. The rape is over. He's not like you. He's super kinky. When he inserted his object inside, he tried to hurt me. Called me weak. Swore he was aiming to take this 'pussy' out. Unless you kill him, he'll do it again.

"I'd hit him with a little fire and desire," she urges. She baits me. "Go Rick James on his crazy ass for the sake of you and I. Give it to him, baby! This might be your last chance to enjoy some of that loose juice. Be cold-blooded. Then let him smell himself once and for all!"

"There's no dictionary to describe the way you look, in my book, Dirty Harry," Girl spits. "Peckerwood."

"Did I ever tell you what happened that day I showed you the honey-comb hairbrush by Cold Steel in the furniture store?" Girl asks. "The brush that pulls off to reveal a 3 ½-inch dagger that you gotta thrust into an attacker? The snub nose .38 I easily concealed in a belly holster? The bear mace used to make a blind motherfucker walk around like Frankenstein?"

"I have a vision," Lumumba said. "I ask all of you not to shrink before any sacrifice."

"Can you do it," Girl asks, placing her hand on my shoulder, "from up here, while we're so high?"

"I can see over mountains," Lumumba said, "reach out and touch the sky."

I pulled the trigger and closed my eyes. Pop! Pop! Pop!

"Take care of yo' momma for me," I remembered my stepdaddy saying, taking a shot of Jim Beam and gurgling like a stabbing victim, but still unwilling to give up the Devil's Cut.

I had been wandering for the longest, wondering if I could ever do anything right.

Then I saw the cop Batty Boy go down in the 'hood, reaching for his Glock 22 with more stopping power but no longer able to draw on instincts.

My head still sticking out of the window to catch some fresh air, I waited to see if Batty Boy's demise, downfall, would make me feel better, more whole ...make me feel satisfied. Time regressed for me. I paused, held myself back, while Ice T shouted "cop killer" from outside. Not that Ice T thought he was venting something controversial or anything; he just believed everybody hated the cops. In any case, that was the ice opinion. Anytime you kill a man, folks will obviously freak out or trip, even or especially if it is a cop.

I'd probably get life for this one. I waited.

They say that at night when it's black, you can see the stars if you look hard enough. James Brown. The Queen of Soul. All of them come to Harlem sometime. Fly ladies, wined and dined, leave with apple bottoms, dirty pillows, and torpedoes ready to go.

For me shit happened. Except there came this feeling of deep emptiness, extreme loneliness, perpetual poverty.

"Because there are no stars in the sky is no reason to assume that darkness is eternal," said Lumumba, called by X "the greatest Black man who ever walked the African continent."

I'm messy. Reminiscent of MacBeth.

"Look at me!" Girl shouts, tugging and pulling on me, shaking my big head, trying her best to snap me out of it, reel/real me back in. "You did it, lover! What's done is done!"

Now remember, I told you from the beginning that I was America's new nightmare. I'm young, black, and gifted, but full of grit, shit, and mother wit, no doubt.

People criticized Lumumba in an attempt to decide whether or not he was serious: "A whole new world," Lumumba chanted. "Only when the monsters exit, the angels enter."

With his lyrics of social protest, the Prime Minister Lumumba impatiently picking up the mic reminded me, us, of spoken word edutainer Gil Scott-Heron. The dope way he spat out his sentences, everything feeling chemical and undeterred by going every witch way but loose. This, course, went down before the cocaine cowboys of a coup roped Lumumba and seized his imagination/ass, offered him—drugged from his crib, dosed, shocked—time to kneel and pray, lined him up alongside a couple of black cats by a big/dead tree and some weed after days of blackwater torture. He was trembling by the edge of the grave before bullets around him paralyzed him. Reformed souljas, Pygmies with weapons as tall as them going ballistic and the chicken slaves of Mobutu waited in the shadows or wings. They busted Patrice's balls for big fun in a boxing match, then blasted huge holes in all of his sorry ideologies and philosophies in front of darters also expecting to be blown away. They buried his political views deep. Wetting the bed of dirt to the extreme. "Bitch," they spat at him, rifling through a rainforest of his important papers. His shredded shirt too late in going green like the Hulk, but his eyes still a Banner for freedom. Shady, harboring no sense of mercy and pulling Lumumba's leg about having sympathy, Pygmies with sawed-off shotguns raised by Fear chopped off every limb imaginable, including those in the wind still reaching out to them, pieces of the man all over the place. Then the members of this rogue midnight band employed a pungent dark brown agent – the oil of vitriol – to liquidate all perceived as a threat to their society. Afterwards, they spread his bones and scattered his ashes out so the black diaspora would remain undisputedly invisible. In an image that recalled the holocaust, the burned body's fat from this "Head-Nigger-In-Charge" (HNIC) ended up used as fertilizer for nommo, the gold in his teeth taken as war booty. They shove(l) what was left of him into a box that he couldn't get out of. Badly affected standbys/spectators/specters twitched for him. At dawn, after so artistically dismembering the minister & peeling his cap, the goddamn elder members of the coup went off, looking to plant the seeds of more bitter oppression. Before they left the scene, waving off the human botflies, the firing squad picked up a kilo of cartridges. They took a lot of poetic license. These ignorant/brutal/badly infected child soldiers left behind a child and huge waste, costing them an arm and a leg. Body parts with the needles stuck in them seemingly forever, for the record. Warding off the snake-birds and the boobies, the previously abducted Congolese women with hacked-off breasts, they left an assemblage of tracks laid down that kept talking nothing but smack behind their backs.

"Believe it or not, when it comes down to it, you can find many of your favorite Disney classics right here in the ghetto," my stepdaddy once said. "The beauty in the beast. The lion king. Snow white. Even Cinderella tail."

"It's a small, small world," Girl says, leaning out of the window trying to spit on the cop's body while it rested in a fetal position. Airplane noise almost drowns her out. Nightcrawler from black forest edges along the side-walk in an effort to sneak a peak at her cockpit.
"But we can go anywhere," she adds, covering up her mosquito bites. "Anywhere."

"Rewind that mixtape, start that Memorex full of slow jams," said Girl. "One day soon, I gonna make babies," she repeated from her gut thinking.
"You wish," I said, lacking class, rubbing my anaconda, what I'd also like to believe is a magic lamp.

Ricardo Cortez Cruz

People have asked me why I always sound so angry. I say, "Because I am supposed to be a motherfuckin hero but nobody can understand me."

"All of the Lord's greatest creations must bleed," my buddy Sporting News once said, spray-painting over the fourth wall at the theatre and seeing red.

The curtain drawn, we jump over the dead body and leave the theatre. "Jesus," my boy Herod says to me, galloping like an animal to catch up again, "what a spectacle this thing was."

White people restoring historical features of the theatre stare at us, look down on us, because we're dressed in hip-hop fashion designer clothes but have no jobs. A bunch of fancy, foreign, luxury cars keep blowing like we're outside Studio 54, standing on stardust.

"The streets are alla dat," Sporting News says to one of them honkies. Rebels.

Think about it. If you were us, wouldn't you hate constantly feeling like you've been ripped-off, like you always had to do something to get even?

"You keep stroking that cock!" Obsession shouts from Slim's boob tube. His PornHub portal loaded with X videos, MILFs such as Brandi Love, and mature content. "I need 12 inches or more," the stars say through the screen like Vanity. "Do you think I'm a nasty girl?" she asks.

"Just shoot me!" Slim cries out in ecstasy, agony, squirting in his boxer briefs, wetting himself. Obviously to avoid denouement or anyone feeling sorry for him.

"Shoot, give us our money back now, our ends," I order the German manster—the gold digger, space queen—at the front, from the counter. Despite Girl standing beside me. SPITE/BEING back in our minds.

I figure, in the end, I like being what I am. Even if does sometimes eat at me—fuck up my insides, as far as I am concerned, I ain't about to quit.

"Hey…next place or so-called 'safe' space we trek to, keep it 100 and say my name, badass, say my name!" Girl crows on a warpath, ingesting dark liquor, like she's a freakum genie in the bottle and Destiny's Child.

Contains: *Five Days* [Nights] *of Bleeding*, "Break" by Jean Grae, replayed elements of "Tossin' and Turnin'," and bootlegs from *Straight Outta Compton*.

Ricardo Cortez Cruz

Trevor Dodge

Final Adjustments

I'm…attaching a scan/screengrab from what's probably my favorite of the comments Dave made on my work. One of these days, I'm going to have that phrase 'PROOFREAD OR DIE!' tattooed onto me. ;)

1) From underneath the car, you noticed which three things first?

    A) sagebrush, oil leak, rusty spot

    B) rusty spot, animal fur, flat tire

    C) flat tire, other flat tire, other flat tire

    D) daylight, shadows, starfield

2) The 45 minutes it took to drive here. Tell us what you discussed.

    A) How Apple Maps got us lost that one time we tried to find a sex shop

    B) Nothing. We listened to Harry Potter and the Goblet of Fire for the 30th time and shushed one another when either of us tried to comment or initiate any sort of conversation

    C) Everything. And still had half an hour to spare, so we turned on Harry Potter and the Goblet of Fire to burn out the rest of the drive

    D) When to stop and how to angle the tires so we could sure the car wouldn't get stuck when it was time to leave

    E) Which body part of the other we would eat first if the snowstorm got real bad and we were stranded there like that married couple in California that one Thanksgiving who took a wrong turn and ended up burning everything in the car with them to stay warm, even the rubber parts, and weren't found until the following summer, with each other's bones mixed together and indistinguish able at first and second glance, like pieces of a jigsaw puzzle with all the notches rounded off

3) Which of the following best describes your sense of self when it's clear the other person isn't into it and wanted you to stop?

A) panic

B) loathing/groveling

C) equivocation

D) suffocation

E) indifference

F) chivalry

4) Towels?

A) yes

B) no

C) forgot em

D) wet wipes

5) Who did you call first?

A) dad

B) mom

C) no cell service

D) battery died

E) left phone on dresser charging

F) phone stolen with wallet and purse at 7-11 on way back

G) tow truck

H) 911

I) you

J) pharmacy

K) self

6) Use the spectrum below to rate your ability in recalling events in their full accuracy. Indicate your rating with an X.

[Total Recall]——————————————————————| [Zero Recall]

7) How confident are you in the accuracy of your rating?

    A) completely

    B) mostly

    C) moderately

    D) enh

8) You're sure?

    A) definitely

    B) probably

    C) maybe

    D) sure

9) You'll be back and in your new car in no more than 7 minutes. We promise. What's next?

    A) search the glovebox for your pistol we took

    B) search the middle console for your stiletto we took

    C) search the rear hatch for your Slippery When Wet CD we took

    D) search the ash tray for your Kennedy half dollar we took

    E) search the driver side visor for your St. Christopher medallion we took but then ended up putting back

10) Let's talk about something else. You look nice today.

    A) Seriously?

    B) Thank you. Your hair is cute up like that.

    C) You said 7 minutes. And I really gotta go.

D) Thank you. No one ever tells me that anymore. That's, you know, one of the things about all this. Not hearing that. There are other things, too, of course, and most of them are more important than that particular thing, but, yeah, that's a thing right there with that.

E) Thank you. No, wait. Fuck you.

F) Fuck you. No, wait. Thank you.

G) Fuck you. No, wait. Yeah. No. Fuck you.

H) Okay. Sure. I guess there's still time.

I) It's time to fit you with some new glasses then.

J) This is one of those paying it forward things isn't it? Like Oprah did for that whole final season of her show, when she ran around Chicago giving construction workers chicken soup and leaving long stem roses on the windshields of single people and taking an entire gradeschool of teachers out for mani-pedis and giving everyone in the studio audience a brand new car? It is, isn't it? Isn't it?

K) Okay. But let's not talk about when I was 9 and went to Montessori school and that girl who also went was out sledding with her dad because it was a snow day and not even the private schools didn't meet that day the snow was so bad, and that girl, she and her dad were in the park with her dad's Chevy Silverado and a sled just bought at Wal-Mart and almost a full foot of fresh snow and a towing chain and the flurries were actually big enough and falling fast enough to be really called flurries, and the only sound outside was that sound of the snow landing on itself one flake at a time, the whole sky the same color as the ground and no depth of vision for everything you can see. The next day, see, they didn't cancel school even though they really probably should have, because the girl, Maddie, she didn't come to school because she was dead and her dad was getting ready to go to jail, the wide swing and clanking sound of the tow chain and the splintered sled against the low concrete retaining wall. The news vans out in front of the school and first my dad in the morning and then my mom in the afternoon being asked by the reporters to comment on the thing that hadn't even happened there, but nonetheless was a thing that wouldn't have even happened had there been school the day before, on the day there wasn't any school, instead of the day the news vans were all there, which, of course, was the day there was.

L) The last person to tell me that just died. You do know that, right?

M) Indeed. Can we finally talk about how your company initially denied my claim?

N) Sounds good. What's your take on Meniere's Disease? Or is that a fiction too?

O) Let's not.

P) Sure. We had just got our 6 year old son a chinchilla before the accident. Our son named it Sarge. What happens every morning is our son gets up and says how the chinchilla is dying or has already died. So far Sarge has died from TB, prostate cancer, lime's disease, cyanide poisoning, hunger strike, hanging, and a botched organ transplant. Pretty much everything. Except hypothermia. Never hypothermia. Not one fucking time has it been hypothermia.

Q) Let's do. So I can tell you my theory about all those sequined jeans you see everywhere these days, the ones with the crosses and fleur de lises on the back pockets. The shortened version? Okay. It's this: those pants are for people who have no ass. Shall I continue?

R) Okay. Will you send me a ticket in Candy Crush now?

S) Yeah? Like what? And what specifically are you talking about when you say that? Seriously. What in particular makes you say that? You don't know me. Bitch, please.

T) You're too kind. What's your name again?

U) Take a good look at me right now. No, I mean it. Look. Just stop for a full 10 seconds and really look at me. I don't know what you see. I wouldn't tell you, either. More to the point, though: I certainly don't know what you want to see, nor do I think it's appropriate for you to try and put it off on me like this. This, what you're doing, it's way over the line. You can see that, right? How over the line this is? Wait though. Maybe you can't. Maybe that's why you said what you said, especially the part about how I look. You can't really see me. You think you can, but you can't. You're just guessing at what I really look like. I'm talking underneath. You don't and can't know for sure.

V) What the fuck do you mean by "nice"?

W) You're too kind but you're wrong. I look a mess. I should. This is what mess looks like. This. Me.

X) Heh. Sure, whatever. Nice ain't the same thing as beautiful now, is it? You can't really say gash out loud, though, ya know? Listen, I do understand. Don't worry about it. Really, it's okay. I get it.

Y) And you have greasy, stinky palms. Oh I'm sorry, did I say that part out loud?

Z) Don't. Just. Please, just don't. Just tell him goodbye from all of us.

Andrew Ervin and Ricardo Cortez Cruz
Yin & Yang

Mittersill • September 15, 1945

His son-in-law went to pick up a box of black-market cigars from some Negro cook, one of the countless G.I.s polluting Salzburg and the surrounding countryside with excessive noise and venereal diseases. The war has been over for four months, yet detonations still rattle the windows around the clock. From the veranda he can see smoke rising from the city, 60 km. northeast. Benno should be home by now. Webern, to put it bluntly, is desperate for a cigar.

In February, American airplanes strafed the train in which his only son Peter carried medical supplies to troops stationed in Yugoslavia. Shortly thereafter, Webern and Wilhelmine fled their home at Mödling on foot. They have come to Mittersill, to the upper Salzach valley, to be closer to their three daughters and their grandchildren. It is safer here, so much safer, though the strict rationing continues. They live with fifteen others in the crowded home of Webern's childhood friend Halbich. Every four weeks the entire household receives a mere 33 dcg. jam, ½ kg. butter, 1½ kg. flour, 6 kg. bread, 90 dcg. meat, plus the choice of ¼ kg. of fatty cheese or ½ kg. lean and every so often ½ kg. cane.

His eldest daughter Christine and her family have found other accommodations half a km. away at 101 Am Markt. They have invited Webern and Wilhemine for supper, a Saturday evening feast. Benno will be home soon.

It has been years since Webern last smoked a cigar. He spends the afternoon in the garden, waiting, meticulously and from memory copying lines of Rilke onto the staves of his notebook: *Who speaks of victory? To endure is everything.* The crumbling journal contains the first sketches of an unfinished cantata, one abandoned back in the spring. He has not added or erased a note since they received word of Peter's death. The music will not come amid the chaos, which finds him even here. He can see the entire valley, hemmed in by a crown of ice-covered peaks, including the majestic Großvenediger, which Webern climbed just nine years ago.

His cough worsens despite the healthy mountain air. His glasses slide down his nose. Only a few weeks shy of his sixty-second birthday, he feels the months of malnutrition, of dysentery, in the new lines of his face. His buttoned collar is looser now. He hears the steady rumble of machines, the distant percussion of gunfire ceaselessly echoing from the peaks. When the wind changes, he smells the pyres that burn all over Tirol. *To endure is every-thing.* The stench of fire upon flesh, human and horse alike, has seeped into his very consciousness, the rotting decomposition of the old order.

There are stories emanating from Poland and Hungary and Czecho-slovakia, illogical stories which he is prone to believe if only because of their absolute impossibility. Something important has changed, even all the way up here. Something essential. There can be no mistaking it. The masses must surely realize that things are different now. They must be prepared, finally, for the dissolution of tone, for the artistic liberation his friend and mentor Schoenberg first envisioned nearly twenty-five years ago. Has it really been so long?

War, if nothing else, has readied the masses for his twelve-tone sys-tem. It can save Vienna. Webern will be their champion, delivering hope and redemption, and returning the glory of that city's proud musical heritage. Twelve-tone composition will free music itself from the corporeal corrup-tion of the past, from the yin and yang of peace and war. The disarray of present-day Austria will lead to a new age, one that will embrace a new music as dissonant as its now broken spirit. No, not only a new music. Vienna will embrace an entirely new way of listening, of hearing.

Webern has lived long enough to welcome the epoch, not of harmony but of glorious disharmony instead. He looks again at the still-born music in his notebook and finds that the cantata, his third, now sounds profoundly different.

New York • October 30, 2002
(Warning: sound bomb)

Rap "Jam Master Jay" and his accompaniment "Black Peeter the Neigro" stand strapped and sulkily smoking in their studio room. Twenty-foe/seven,

Andrew Ervin and Ricardo Cortez Cruz

they're guarded, surrounded by security. All the same, these black men appear to have a fresh beginning in the high/rising tenement slums of the city built by a white man named Moses. Though Rap and the Neigro have gone through changes, these brothers seem relaxed now, content to listen to a mixtape loop Public Enemy's "Bring Tha Noize" while checking out their notes under a skylight. They look to have themselves together.

"Bass/base, how low can you go," chants Black Peeter, singing as soon as he opens his big mouth after counting wads of dirty cash. In love with green, he's more Ludacris than any sellout performer in the Garden. The only other activity that ever made Black Peeter happy was street hoops, which he quit after tearing an ACL and undergoing major reconstruction surgery. He didn't know how to be true to the game.

Rap stays quiet. He's a grown man living in The City, among residents that never sleep, with achluophobia (fear of the dark). Rap be cocky during the day but humble at night.

Black Peeter's been experimenting with rock and now he can't stop, won't stop. "Biblically and in Greek, my name 'Petra' means rock," he reminds Rap. Though Black Peeter swore he would follow Rap even to death, he's a dangerous liaison. He's a crackhead in constant motion pausing only to peep at the ornately framed picture of Cornell Barnes' *Last Supper*, the art showing Frederick Douglass, Marcus Garvey, The Honorable Elijah Muhammad, Malcolm and King as the disciples breaking off some bread for one another while in a friendship circle.

"I'm hearing those voices again," Black Peeter warns in a whisper, a caution that's straight-up more to himself than anything. "You know, table talk, the sound of those black disciples, their twelve-tone music filling me with rhythm and blues.

"My therapist says I need to stop playing," he adds.

After all, brothas had come up, arrived "like aliens taking over the planet," as Black Peeter kept noting earlier that night in a fit that was strange even for him.

"We the fiery Phoenix regenerated, recouped, after getting hurt and wounded by the enemy," Black Peeter argues, slangin' his words around like he was still gang-bangin'.

"We's reincarnated," Black Peeter says.

God had taken care of them. (Black Peeter swore.) Black Peeter was the first to observe how hip-hop had eventually exorcised/exercised Rap, pulling him out from the thug-or-die clique—the gangs and street wars that even pioneering DJs such as Bam hated.

"Rap's got a calling now," Black Peeter blurts in a manner to suggest his friends are already long gone.

"Seeing you this loyal to all yo' friends and family kills me," Black Peeter adds, collapsing onto the carpet. Because the Neigro refuses to take off his combat boots, he's tracked in mud.

Partners in crime, the two hear a car come to a screeching halt, horns going off nonstop. Charlie Parker blares "Out Of Nowhere," wrecking them with trauma.

Amid this dizzy atmosphere, Black Peeter inexplicably grabs a razor blade from the deep pocket in his Portfolio pants and starts slicing and dicing mess from the black market, cutting up on the floor. He gets down. On his knees. Dancing and swaying round midnight in Parker's mood. So lovely and free and easy. Until his belt unravels, maybe as a part of its own conspiracy and brass-knuckle effort to hang him high, this brotha trapped in the prison of his mind.

"This stuff's no good, son!" Black Peeter shouts (he lets it all out). "The place I normally hit is a little bodega on the corner where the Afro-Latino bad men burn garbage in the aluminum cans and do those sickening toasts."

Rap's a standup person but simply watches as the evil of reconstituted Cain/cane spreads and makes itself at home. Outside, ghetto birds are choppers, too. Planes from JFK strafe over them as if the war for civil rights ain't over.

Black Peeter pays no attention and creates a row. Then commences to snorting, the powder burning the flesh inside his nose to the point where he feels gassed and his sense is gone.

Black Peeter's a real monster in disguise, cutting up tonight the way he'd take out a civilian caught slipping in his territory.

"Hell, homey (he almost seems to say 'hold me'), I'm through with slavery," Black Peeter says, drawing the shit out before getting it off his chest for good. 'Cause now they can afford spending time doing nothing, letting musicians record for free. Since Valentine's Day, folk in the hood have embraced the space as a house in the street, with sweet honeys and fly girls from the Jamaica section of Queens gathering in the lounge like it's a kitchen.

In a classic(al) act of defiance, Rap makes an effort to compose himself. But, Black Peeter—slummin', tapping his leg but somehow maintaining and looking copacetic—offers him some primo.

Rap shakes his big head no, electing to skip the blunt. Only sixty minutes ago, his brother Rev. Run had just finished an important nationally-televised interview and vanished into thin air, singing "Elvis has just left the building" and what sounded like a cantata or some shit while gayly strolling down Merrick Boulevard. Nigga might as well been a gentile/gentle priest.

Fuck dis nickel-n-dime bag, Rap says softly. Everyone in the room, almost 20 moochers pulled together (as one might do roots to create dreadlocks), had fallen into a rut, and Rap didn't want that to be their m.o.

"Time for a jam," Rap says, an X premonition that occurs to him while posing at the window, by the bright lights of the big city, his eyes closely watching for traffic jams but the cushiony phones on his head stopping his desire to really listen anymore. "Biz'ness screams for attention."

"I'd like to finally throw down and wax some ass," Cuz (Black Peeter) bluntly says, amped, exhibiting 'tude by any means necessary. In adolescent excitement, he raises up.

For the record, rap interrogates everything. "What else could go wrong?" he asks the Neigro.

Enter A and B conversatin', hating on everybody, wearin' buck-wild fros and do-rags but steppin' up to the challenge.

"Boo, whass crackin, you little mark!" they yell to Rap. They're buggin' out, illin', snappin'. Suddenly security vanishes.

"You stoopid," Rap asks, "or is this a paper chase?"

"We hear/here for you," Playa #1 says. He showcases big lips, a notorious B.I.G. natural diamond stud in his ear, and a horrifyingly monstrous, wobbly, elliptical head to match. Watching him roll up on them is like participating in a creature feature at a drive-in theater. He gets up in Rap's face, all personal, jaws tight, and starts telling him a story. Tiny gangster #2, another ig'nant busta, funs along, follows the leader.

In this surreal moment, Rap hears Run in his ear: "Nigga, break out … before you get bumrushed!" Fleeing the scene is a routine he has down pat, but it's obvious that the terrible twos ain't hearing/having it.

"Deuces are wild," #1 says.

"Get up, stand up," #2 spits to Black Peeter.

"What go round come round," the first one with the big Shure stylushead says. He points to Rap's signature piece, some wrapped/rap lyrics under *Beatdown.* "That you?"

Rap says shit. So motherfucka, who rap assumes ain't gonna listen to reason anyway, performs the big payback.

"Ain't gonna be no scrapple in the Apple this time," motherfucka says. Wound too tight, Watermelon Head presses his entire body, his mouthpiece and his dick, against the back of Rap's receiving ear and kisses him goodbye, executes him. The shot proves so powerful that Rap feels the ignited powder blast his shirt and burn his dark skin. For good measure, they pop Black Peeter in the right ankle.

Soon as Rap realizes Watermelon Head has wetted/stained him, he slings/flings his papers (insurance policy etc.) to the hard floor, spilling murder ink (Murder Inc.), and even the dime he carries falls out.

Blood drops like water.

It wasn't long after the nigga, blowed, began to flow that that was all he (w)rote.

Mittersill • September 15, 1945

Benno returns without the cigars, and Webern tries to hide his disappointment. Benno claims that his dealer will be calling later in the evening. He says he will bring the cigars and maybe even some Kentucky whisky. Webern wants so much to believe that he manages to believe.

The valley has grown dark and he is very tired. Despite the exhaustion, he participates in the atmosphere of general hilarity, the kind only made possible by armistice and reunion. In the kitchen a goose is basting slowly in Gewürztraminer and its own fat. Webern rollicks on his hands and knees, playing Lippizzaner with the little ones. He even bangs out a few children's melodies on the hideously out-of-tune upright. The piano is an abomination, and yet he finds it strangely appropriate.

Soon he will return to his Vienna, where he will regain his musical life. He feels well enough now to travel, and has decided to accept the post of conductor for Radio Vienna. Wilhelmine simply worries too much, but even Webern fears that the days of Volksoper and festivals in the Stadtpark are gone. The map of the capitol has been redrawn into barricaded quarters. Those bold enough to violate curfew are shot on sight. Vienna is different, true, but it waits to be rebuilt on that unparalleled firmament of musical genius. There, he knows, his music will come. It will enter unto him and with it he will help revitalize the very nature of Austrian society. Twelve-note composition is the plaster with which Vienna can be rebuilt atop the rubble of Mozart and Mahler, Schubert and Strauss. Disharmony is the only rational response to the new world smoldering around him.

Some of the piano's black keys refuse to function and the children laugh when he substitutes silly, incorrect notes in the middle of his chords.

Andrew Ervin and Ricardo Cortez Cruz

Christine sticks her head in and calls them to the table. Webern marches the grandchildren single file to the kitchen, singing a *bom*-bom-*bom*-bom beat and swinging his fist in time until they take their places at the smaller table. Benno carves the goose and Webern offers a prayer for the eternal rest of their departed Peter and for the end of Austria's shed blood. He gives thanks for the unbridled joy of feeling in his arms once again the warmth of his beloved family. There are, unbelievably, potatoes and carrots, rolls of white bread, and a brick of real English cheddar. He takes a bottle of beer with his meal, a proper Austrian beer unlike anything he has tasted in an eternity, and then another. Benno shares a third with him, and even Wilhelmine accepts a small glass. Afterwards, Christine puts the children to bed and returns to the chore of making order.

Someone raps loudly on the door, and Webern and Wilhelmine retire quietly to the parlor, where the children have fallen fast asleep. Voices penetrate the room, earsplitting American voices. Christine enters producing a cigar from her apron. The voices continue but Webern does not hear them. The weight of the cigar in his fingers reminds him of a baton, as if he could conduct the entire nation from his high-back chair. The very tempo of Austrian society changes around him, his forgotten cantata now begs to be completed. To endure is everything. The American voices resound from outside like an angelic chorus. He wants to join them. Notes and tone colors now align themselves in his head. A half hour passes, maybe more. He can hear the cantata coming to life, reborn. When Webern can no longer wait he carefully cuts the cigar then strikes a match and lights it, drawing the first puff of golden blue smoke onto his palate. As he expects, Wilhelmine playfully scolds him and orders him from the room.

Webern stands. He carries his cigar and notebook into the foyer where he stumbles over his own discarded shoes. He steps outside onto the veranda and hears more American voices. There is shouting, a Jeep idling. To Webern's horror, Benno is being taken away, arrested, charged with dealing on the black market. Webern panics. He lifts his cigar and inhales too forcefully for his weakened lungs. The ember glows bright red, a small flare in front of his nose, and he begins to cough. At the sound, a startled American soldier leans out of the shadows, his gun drawn. The sound is certain to wake the children. Webern drops the cigar. Smoke curls around them both, embraces them like brothers, obscures the stars above.

New York • October 30, 2002

(Precipitation)

In front of the lamp posts was where he stood, his hands moving in the twilight while his body worked its way into the serious crowd, mixing with the *lumpen* proletariat, the lowest of the low, as he began to hustle. Life's a blast from a Hummer's hood. Nothing is like the criminal element—H2 (that dope new car smell) and OE (malt liquor). But because even his hair is laid-back in a fade, Rap hopes he can blow everything ovah using finesse. So brotha, sky-high and on the cover up, manages to segue into the building like it's nothing.

"Time to leave Mista Wind, Hawk, behind," he says. He moves the crowd outside, shouting "my Adidas" and talking about puttin' his foot up somebody's ass. Then he says "peace/piece," got himself togetha, and slides/eases toward the open door with the main thang botherin' him being the rain makin' waves, doin' pit-pat, F dis, F dat.

Crowd #1 tries to reach out for him and pull him back to reality but obviously feels skin tougher than leather 'cause it suddenly lets him go, releases him. Crowd #2, not particularly large, turns more hostile. A couple of niggas charge Rap, spit at his feet and hurl stones, hollering that he "talks too much." Rap strokes the rocket in his pocket in order to feel like a man, feel secure. Like Daddy-O always said, he could cap their ass, but you don't subsist on a diet of Sly and the Family Stone or Gil Scott-Heron and go out and kill people.

Inside the live studio, things heat up. The ghetto-fabulousness of Hot 97 shimmers through the loudspeakers, while a coal-blooded, black bee-yotch-chickenhead fresh from a 50 Cent concert affair tosses him a weak cocktail. "Do what you have to do," she clucks. "The ice is on you for a change." Baby girl only sports itty-bitty titty, but she has the nerve to swagger/sashay her fat ass, her tight jeans made by Phat Farm, into the next room full of ruffians. Hard not to pay attention to the trunk-thumpin'.

Rap watches as shorty/shawty squats in the lap of some muthafucka doin' a soul clap, singin' "Give It To Me, Baby" and "Happy." She hums along in an effed-up duet like Tina Turner following Ike's lead. They flirt/toy around with a Mortal Kombat video game and Def Jam 2, fighting for NYC until he suddenly snatches her by her good hair and takes over the second controller. The black Mad Catz controller: He insists that she submit. "Fish, right now," he demands, this cat in the hat climbing all over her with a hump in his back.

Andrew Ervin and Ricardo Cortez Cruz

"This bitch, she think she the queen of soul," dude says, looking up in the direction of Rap. When the woman raises up off of her knees, she moons him and quickly darts for safety.

Rap temporarily puts down his phones, digs out a pair of ice cubes, tickles the juice with his pointing and middle fingers, his internal affairs always on the rocks. Black Peeter the Neigro's fire/sticks embraces them as brothas, covers them with a dark cloud, almost promising "foe sho'" they'll git fucked up.

Yo, tell me somethin' good, rap whispers to the almighty Cut Creator. He feels blacker than Thou, so tired of all the yang, the nonsense. As if Rap's the Lawd's first creation, he leans back in his office chair to find some support. The soft, cushy leather protects him like a bomber jacket. He waits for something in The Big Apple to prove acidic.

Rap knows he's gonna git wasted, probably by some zipcoon or Staggerlee who recently migrated to Harlem hoping to get at least a dirty job. Because Up South, it's like that, and that's just the way it is. You can't last forever.

"Me and Black Peeter's become nothing more than black rat snakes in the city that never sleeps," Rap says to himself, livin' (at) large, full of prophecy, being as dramatic as the eccentric famous actor Christopher Walken. The King of New York.

"The black reign/rain's slowing down," Rap utters, noting that there's so much trouble in the world, getting wind of the grumbling in the distance, the children stirring it up and waiting in vain, wailing stuff, including boasts of how they shot the sheriff.

"You need to turn your lights down low," Black Peeter warns.

Niggas will only show(boat) (grandstand) to impress some pussy, according to the NYPD; that's their profile, period.

At first Rap panics, tries to hide so he won't end up discovered by Columbia U. rowers in the Harlem River. Then he turns 360 degrees, anxiously scratching the grooves of his black skin while in a New York state of mind, *piss on them.* Hotties around him nod for no reason or maybe just to go along with him, several rushing into the room barefoot, giggling, and tripping. Too bad Rap ain't going nowhere; naw ... he experiences a flashback while preparing for the next chump from Queens or mouthpiece from The Streets to bogart him. He wanna see somebody just try to bust into his place all fast and furious, smokin' like a Twista or Busta while full of (self) destruction. That sucker will get got, end up being dust in the wind.

Even when Rap takes a second glance at the nutty brown chocolate women, his vision is that of a holocaust—their panty hose torn and snagged into holes revealing dun flesh and ashy skin as if snatched from a Nazi's incinerator. Not realizing how they startle him, the women (often healers) smother themselves with Vaseline Intensive Care, then pretend to be superior.

Rap looks over to witness Black Peeter. The Neigro's gotten soft, thanks to the good life, but he's also not ready to be a martyr. The Neigro's become a caricature, stereotype, or spoof of himself. The nigga acts as if he's got everything but the kitchen sink shooting up his ankle and sending chills down his spine. He appears fake and bitter. Shoot, Black Peeter's a lemon now, strange fruit that Rap should've returned to the market.

Somewhere along the way, Black Peeter rotted.

Now the Neigro features a crooked walk and a back far from straight; he writhes in unnecessary pain. But, Black Peeter refuses to cry; for this man, one tear's still enough. Later, the guilt would lead Black Peeter to crack, alcoholism, death by drowning his own ass in a madd bathtub story, but this is now. Full of scarification, Black Peeter stares at the moochers; they get on his nerves. Black women get *the message* and run away from the Neigro, rebuking him and finding themselves cursed.

To Rap, they're dashing hopes.

"Yin & Yang" first appeared in *Fiction International.*

Andrew Ervin and Ricardo Cortez Cruz

William Gillespie

Risky School Shooting Cut Short by Suit Malfunction

David despised pretension, inflated diction, and experimental fiction whose formal risks were divested of emotional risks. He told us to write for Joe Sixpack, or Joe Lunchbox, or Joe Plumber, or the guys wearing ties who could be seen washing their cars on their lunch hours, who had "gotten their girlfriends pregnant," hapless guys he claimed were the real heroes. (Note that no other professor of English would ever say such a thing.) I got the sense with this that he was giving us his best advice—advice he had crafted for himself.

After the Challenger exploded, the shuttles were grounded, leaving only two astronauts on the Space Station to conserve resources. Two men instead of three. Why did they pick Hawking? Anyone else would have been cool but Hawking kept pushing and pushing. Wouldn't let it go. The timing for this mission was wrong. They needed three men. Now here he was blind with a ruptured dehumidifier, bulbs burning out, space junk hitting the hull, shuttles burning up over Texas. The neglect was infuriating. A space program was not something to cut corners on.

She wasn't allowed to touch a student. She could get in serious trouble for that. Some litigation-crazed parent would drop the courts on her head. Discipline was out of her hands. If three brickheads decided to pummel a gothrocker in her classroom she could only call security. It would take them ten minutes to get to the room. She could try to scream at them to stop fighting but if they ignored her it would undermine her authority even further. If a child was being hurt she could do nothing. Classes continued to expand and the distance between her and the students increased.

"Helmet." "Sealed." "Oxygen." "Flowing." "All systems go." "Roger Crusades. Over." Moving slowly in the pressurized suit, Hawking opened the airlock. A few silent specks of dust dribbled away. They unzipped the canvas bags and stepped out, drifting over the tables. Some of the kids looked up at them. One was amazed. Another laughed. One threw a carton of milk. Rock discharged his firearm. A wave of consternation swept the room. The recoil from the shotgun made him spin end over end until he came to rest entangled in the light fixture. "Careful of that recoil Rock." "Roger that. Let's teach these kids something." Skinny girl, down. Pretty boy, pop. The whistle of air blowing out of the depressurizing cafeteria. "Crusader this is Mission Control. We have a possible malfunction." "What the hell?" "What is it Rock?" "Something's going wrong with my suit." "I'm coming." "I'm getting warm. It's raining in here." Rock watched trickles of condensation inside the helmet wriggling away from the oxygen blowers, lit by the head-lamp. He raised the weapon to the visor and the sights wavered in the liquid sheeting his helmetglass. Jockhead fell forward on the floor, blood pouring from the back of his head. It was awesome, so red. "The collision with the light fixture maybe dislodged the oxygen feed on your suit." Hawking care-fully maneuvered around the tether to check Rock's suit. Rollercoasters of screams poured under them. It was comical, the way those idiots ran, wide eyed, elbows akimbo, hands to faces. Mr. Smith looked directly into their eyes for the first time in years as he pushed the door to his classroom shut. "Temperature's alright." The thump as a heavy table was pushed onto its side to barricade a door. "Am I losing pressure?" "You're fine. Your thermostat and barometer are malfunctioning. It's just moisture. Just hold still and try not to overheat. I'll try to finish the job myself." Two sharp retorts cast flash-es through the rivulets streaking the helmet. The shape of Hawking moved down the hallway. Lightning in a rainstorm. "Die." Crackle. That scream was unbelievable, a profound wail twisting from below. Had to be a teacher. An expletive and a bang. Red flecks. "How's it going?" "Under control. Sit tight. We'll get you back from cafeteria as soon as I've deployed the rest of these pipe bombs." "Ro- Ah! Mission control I'm being attacked. Hah! Wait. Okay it was just a kid tripping over my tether." Pop. "Copy that. Just try to sit still. Control your breathing. Even keel. Over." "What's going on Hawking?" "Well I'm trying to find the biology teacher. I was hoping to shoot his ass in the face. But he doesn't seem to be in the classroom. I just want to let this last bomb go in the library, maybe burn up some books. Then I'll get back to the cafeteria." "How are the sirens? Seen any action out there?" "Nothing but scared little bunnies Houston." "We're counting twelve squad cars with

William Gillespie

plenty of sirens in the air, more on the way. You'd better wrap things up."
"Roger. You wanna fuck with me? You wanna fuck with me? Huh? Scream.
Scream. Fuckyeah." Rock hung somewhere over the long folding tables. Who
could still be lurking in the cafeteria. Or who might be creeping up. Running
crouching below the window line, taking aim. Who might be behind him.
Rock considered cocking the firearm, taking a tough pose. Machismo failed
him. In some tiny corner of his head was the thought they could get out.
Too young for the death penalty. Fuck it. They were already famous. After
Mission Control releases the footage. Drop the gun, he could just drop the
gun. Nobody was going to shoot an unarmed eight year old in a spacesuit. A
broken spacesuit. They might smack him around but he was ready for that.
Might enjoy it. Like to see someone try it. "Rock I'm heading back down
the corridor. Looks like someone crapped their pants. You should have seen
me take out the library man it was totally vote. Can you see me? Over?"
"Seeing nothing but water. Wish I could have helped you with the library.
Over." "Fellas this is Mission Control we need you to finish up. On this
side of the school we've got a SWAT team on the roof. Over." "Copy that
Houston. Roger." There came a purling through the headset, some interfer-
ence. Distant music, rock and roll. Rock was on the beach. The sun was high
and warm. He lay out on the sand and watched people surf. He saw Hawking
out there, riding in on a slow curl. Something moved across the sun. A gloved
hand. Hawking was upside down, waving. "Ready?" crackled Hawking, almost inaudible beyond the polyglossia. The flame from the jet winked. He
felt a hard tap on the helmet and through the surf could discern a perfect
circle, the mouth of a barrel. "Copy that. Over and out."

Stacey Gottlieb

The Fall of Clear Ideas

David was as entertaining and quirky as he was smart—ablaze in his shaggy sportif, college sweats in loving decay, cotton headgear and a rotating orthotic or three; gallows humor in high gear; holding forth on canine hygiene one minute and Cartesian modalities the next. But what stood out most to the student writers in his midst was his respect and compassion for anyone equally awed and overwhelmed by the possibilities of this strange, shared tic of storytelling. Once, after talking to him about struggling with my work, he left a copy of Maimonides' Guide for the Perplexed in my department mailbox, flagging the part where the philosopher notes:

> At times the truth shines so brilliantly that we perceive it as clear as day. [At others] our nature and habit draw a veil over our perception, and we return to darkness almost as dense as before....like those who, though beholding frequent flashes of lightning, still find themselves in the thickest darkness of the night.

I took it as a kind of promise that, while the trials of the work were certain, they might be mediated, at least, by such occasional flashes of beauty and light. And it was just what I needed to hear.

This story starts not really where I begin it. It starts not with the ringing phone, not with the late hour, not with the voice on the other end of the line. It starts before that night altogether, with the year itself. Not the year's official beginning, that day of hangovers and resolutions, but rather with the fall preceding—fall, a season when, for many years, things were prompted to start anew, to begin again with a brisk about-face and a revived sense of possibility about the world.

Perhaps part of the problem was expecting this from the season still: a fresh slate, a clean bill, another chance to try again. Because while the year had reached this point when this story really begins, it was off to an onerous start. Not a thing was coming easily and even the easiest of tasks seemed tough. Though in many ways it felt like we were shrinking, shriveling from the weight of some fundamental unrest, I learned instead that we had started to expand. I read this in the *Times*. The earth, it said, had been expanding over the last thousand years by something like a hundredth of an inch. Just a hundredth of an inch, but still. You read something like that and you just know it can't be good.

That fall began with difficulty for a lot of people, though. While we had yet to experience certain tragedies, we were not yet recovered from those past. The markets were down. Inflation was up. Little things, like bums and panhandlers and dogs messing the sidewalks—they were all up, way up; you could see it wearing on people when you caught their eye in the street.

These difficulties achieved a kind of critical mass over the long, muggy summer that had just then drawn to a close—three months of humid, pestering heat and an almost spiteful amount of sun and so, in the early days of September, when fall's fresh newness appeared no closer to settling in, I began thinking more seriously about making a move. Of moving away. Of scrapping it all, cleaning house, clearing out. That's not to say that I had figured it all out. Not in the least. It's just that these figurings, these observations, they are this story's true beginning; they anticipate the place where I've chosen to start and so, for that reason, I set them out for you to see.

I think it also needs saying that while I had yet to fully discern the source of what it was that had been feeling so wrong, the idea that something or maybe everything had to change was, by this time, quite often on my mind. It was on my mind and, slowly, certain things were making themselves clear. It was clear, for instance, that I'd been standing still too long. Becoming stagnant. Stale. That like the very earth beneath us, I was starting to expand.

And so the call: the one that came in the middle of the night. That's where I had planned to begin, but even that is a somewhat false start. False in the sense that the description turns out to not really be true. You see, while I had thought that my senses were never more sure, that I was keenly aware of even the smallest details, my recollection of the hour when the call must have arrived was wrong or misremembered or of some murky nether-region in between. It was, in fact, impossible for the call to have been a *middle of the night* affair, given what was going on when the call came through. It's been an interesting lesson in the fallibility of perception: I'm positive that Leno was on when I picked up the phone because once I was clear that it was Kit on the line, I knew at least enough to put the show on mute. And because it was Leno that I placed on mute, the call *couldn't* have come in that late, as Jay's scheduled airtime was Copernican in its reliability, and middle of the night it was not. But it at least *felt* like middle of the night for the way I was rattled by the phone's unexpected ring, a tinny little whine that broke, unexpectedly, into my evening alone.

Also: I remember that the day had been notably gray, dispiriting in a way that they had all been at the time and so, in an effort to salvage such evenings from the disintegration I saw around me, I was trying to sit peacefully, quietly, in the hours before bed—a futile attempt to both wind myself down and perk myself up. It was in this way that I had come to rely on Jay. While I had no real interest in his show, I had discovered that his steady stream of amiable interviews with equally amiable, impeccably groomed guests, provided a calming foil of white noise toward this end. So that's what was going on when the call came in; when the phone rang, as I said, unexpectedly, and with what seemed like too much strum und drang for such a small device to make. It rang and I reached for it and I heard my sister's voice on the other end of the line.

Kit is older than me by only three years, but the gap between us has always felt generational. It had long been my suspicion that she regarded me less like a younger brother than as a parent might their difficult teen— an equation both dense and taxing, and one not necessarily worth trying to solve.

Kit had been living, already for many years, in a split-level ranch with an all-terrain car and a puffy-faced husband named Neil. I lived a short hour from them in the city, in a neighborhood Neil liked to say was *on the verge*. Neil dabbled in real estate, so I let the comment sit, but on the verge of what he never really said.

In any case, the forty miles between our front doors might well have been four hundred for how distance had become the convenient excuse for our inability to see much of each other at all. This was true even when our parents were still alive, when we had a more tangible obligation to make plans, but that's another story altogether. There is no use, I've found, in plumbing an otherwise vanished past.

I mean mainly here to explain that we were not, as a rule, prone to calling one another for a mere leisurely chat and most definitely not at an off-hour of the night. In other words, we had quietly made the choice not to be too much in each other's lives, tended not to pursue each other unless something was really wrong, and so I knew without asking that that's what this call had most certainly to mean. I think this sense also kept me from turning Leno off—led me to keep him on, if only on mute—as if to ensure that somewhere behind or beneath this conversation nearly guaranteed to bring bad news, there would be a small reminder that in some places, things were still okay. That said, such a premonition would have been a remarkably prosaic hunch to have had, something not particularly common for me at all, and so I am not sure that it, either, is entirely true.

It's Karen, Kit said, behind a wall of static—an air alive with strange, audible currents and codes. *Something happened at the meet. We're going up right away.*

Associations are funny things. I clearly hear my sister say these words, allow them to register and start processing what they mean, but I am equally engaged in watching Leno's jowls sway silently on mute. And maybe this is why I make my first gaffe, why the first thing I start to ask about is not what these words mean, what they must mean about my niece, but instead about what will happen to the dogs.

Kit and Neil's mutts are remarkably stupid, but so stupid as to be incredibly endearing, especially to me, who often feels like the least capable human in the room—particularly if it's a room in Kit and Neil's immaculate suburban ranch, a two-story split that sits on an equally pristine and manicured swath of lawn. The animals' care might have come to me just then because Leno has always struck me as the poor man's Letterman, a shabby imitation of a man not even worth imitating, a man plenty fine pimping dogs across his stage just to generate a modicum of audience support. But again, while this might be the reason why I *think* of them first, it still fails to account for why I *mention* them first—fails to explain why, before uttering an appropriate acknowledgement of the news she's just shared, I instead tell Kit, in an upbeat-as-hell tone, that I will happily watch the dogs.

Kit's response to this assertion is to merely to let the line collect with dust—more errant static and the trickle of a conversation filtering in from a crossed wire. This patient withholding, this non-retort retort, is one of Kit's great strengths, and it tells me all I need to know. It tells me that my reaction was inappropriate: inappropriate to have had, inappropriate to have shared; but also that it has failed her in some sharply familiar way.

Still, I know how much Neil loves those dogs, those stupid dogs that I too love, and so I know that while he regards me, generally, as good for very little, he trusts me almost completely with regard to their care. I can't recall

Stacey Gottlieb

an evening spent at their home as a guest, invited like any other, but I have watched their house, sat for their dogs, any number of times. I've watched them last minute, on simple overnight stays, but once for a longer stretch when, as they have in recent years, Kit and Neil gave themselves the gift of going off to one of those places they go to get away—places with names like exotic stones: Turkoise, Tortola, Málaga, Majorca. While I could have felt funny about the rather business-like relations this arrangement established between us, the truth is that I enjoyed very much these sojourns at their abode; took pride in not accidentally burning it down, in caring tenderly for the hounds; and derived a sizeable pleasure from how rendering this service allowed me, in my own small way, to both fill a need and fill it well.

But these are not things I've had time to say, not things I can, in the middle of this exchange, take time to explain. To explain in order to make less strange. To both make less strange my reaction to Kit's news, and to convey the feelings of support and concern that I mean to. Which I do.

At least the words I *do* say, the ones about the dogs, at least they come and go in an instant and, while I know for sure that they're not at all the right ones to have said, I know too that, in the end, they won't do much harm.

Of course that doesn't stop me from trying to adjust my mangled expression, starting predictably with, *I'm sorry*; moving immediately onto, *I just meant*; as in, *I just meant* that if they had to leave, had to leave straight away, that I could come. So they could go. And I would stay. But Kit hears none of this, I don't think; none of this at all. She is listening only for a pause, for a break in my monologue that will allow her to pass on the remainder of the details she's called to relay.

She does this gracefully, I believe, offering a segue intended to bypass my bumbling, but I cannot quite make it out, the static and other background noise growing loud again. I imagine, though, that it does the job, because Kit is good at that kind of thing—adept at moving even the most tortured conversations along.

Karen, their girl, their older of two, is also blessed with this skill but despite this, or maybe because of it, she is, apart from those dogs, the only member of the family with whom I've developed an independent sort of kinship, if you can use that word for someone who is in fact kin.

While at the time of the call I had not seen her in some time—the *up* Kit used in *we're going up right away* stood for upstate, where Karen had been *boarding* for school—I had begun, over the course of this particular dark span, an epistolary friendship with my niece that I had come to relish and that I was reasonably sure she enjoyed too. Not yet fifteen, Karen was smart and funny in ways I had always wanted to be, with a mordant sensibility I liked to imagine we shared by virtue of common genes. But my last reply, I realized now, was a good deal overdue, and this oversight suddenly seemed irrefutable proof of the many ways I fell short as a man.

But this was not the time to talk about such things, awash as we were in a sea of static—unable as I was to determine if Kit was even still there.

Kit? I ask tentatively, hoping that maybe we *have* been cut off, that maybe I will be able to start all this again.

But no. That hope is just one more kind of wishful thinking indulged in during this conversation that will later feel to me like *middle of the night*. Middle of no time. Middle of nowhere.

I'm here, she reports, though where that is, I do not know.

I do know that I have yet to ask any of the proper questions and so, in an effort to get a handle on things and with our connection, for the moment, seeming intact, I ask where it is that she is and she says in the car, and I say I know, I mean *where*.

This is generally how things go between us; like two people trying to hold a conversation under water, we see each other's lips moving but cannot for the life of us make out what they mean to say.

But then I wonder, what *is* Kit up to—in the car, all alone, driving in this worried state and at this hour of the night—so I ask what it is that she's doing but the opportunity has passed.

We just heard, she says. *We only heard just now.* She says this, I think, by way of an explanation, though of what I'm not quite sure. She adds, as if to clarify, that they're flying up at six.

I repeat my query, unsure if she can hear, and that's when she says that she's gone out. That she's gone out to get a few things—for the girl who's staying; at the house, with the dogs—so she's driving to the QuikStop both to get these things and to try to calm down.

I'm hurt, I'll admit, at the news of this girl, but I feel, at least, like my concern wasn't entirely off track.

And Neil? I ask, but again a beat too late. Something, maybe me, has forced a crack in Kit's calm and after getting out only that he is home, waiting for news, my sister begins to cry.

The first spell lasts for about a minute and while that may not sound like very long, it is in fact a pretty long time when you're listening to it on the phone. And when that first crying jag is through, another one begins, this time the sobs coming so fast and so hard that I begin to worry, really worry, since she is still, I know, somewhere on the road.

Stacey Gottlieb

Pull over, I instruct, as evenly as I know how. *Pull over and take a breath and take a minute to calm down.*

As soon as these orders have left my mouth, as soon as they float irretrievably through the line, I'm distinctly aware that I've heard them before; heard them directed at myself in fact, and certainly more than once. But this role reversal seems, miraculously enough, to have worked; my string of imperatives sufficiently effective because there is a sudden and somewhat dramatic decrease in sobbing on the line.

I'm running in now, Kit announces, her voice a shrill falsetto that bespeaks a shaky hold on even this much calm. *I'll call you back.*

While I don't immediately get that *run in* is short for *run in the store*, I don't ask because I don't want to excite her even more. Still, once this information has had a moment to sit, it does not, in fact, sit so well. It's a return, I decide, of my clarity of mind, and I am ready, thank god, ready for it when it comes.

In a voice much closer to our dead father's than anything of my own, I repeat the edicts I ought to have laid down from the start: that she is not to hang up, that I will wait here while she shops, but that she is to keep me—*does she hear me?*—keep me on the line.

And then—. And then Kit starts sobbing once more.

It's okay, I tell her, bolstered now by the authority of my own tone. *It's alright.*

Kit lets this pronouncement sit for a minute—enough time to suggest that she might be willing to simply take me at my word.

I'll call you back, she offers finally, sniffing and clearing her throat before she does indeed hang up the line.

And the rest? The rest is simple, or simple enough to explain: the line goes dead, dead quiet and still, though I wait there a few seconds just to make sure. I make good and sure and then I hang up too. I hang up my end and walk over to the kitchen to put some water on the stove. There will be a while of waiting and then another call, and in the interim I'll grow frightened, nervous and anxious with concern. I will tinker and pace, worry clinging to my side, and only sometime later will I think to miss the season—the one with the clear ideas.

"The Fall of Clear Ideas" first appeared in a slightly different form in *Quarterly West*.

Amy Havel

Here's What I'll Give You

...One comment David made about my writing that really hit home was that I was being "too nice". This got me thinking about what I was trying to give to the reader in terms of emotion, and he was right: I wanted my readers to relate to the characters, but in a "good" way, not in any way that would make them uncomfortable or sad or anxious. At the time, I was also in a snit about the number of recently published memoirs by writers in their twenties who had dramatically overcome issues with mental illness and substance abuse in a nifty narrative arc. (Maybe I was mad that I didn't have a proper issue—or too many issues?—that I could use for material.) So I sat down and wrote a character that was sick of having to tell a story that made everyone feel good or worked out in a neat shape. I wrote this story very quickly and without much revision, and it's one of my favorite pieces.

The story will be long but not too long, and not so short that I seem abrupt. She'll be just what you've been imagining all this time but could never picture. It'll start off slow, and there will be complications in her plot that will arise softly, subtly. Just enough so she's still mysterious and you still don't quite know what you're in for. But you won't be afraid; she won't be that unfamiliar. She'll give you the feeling that she's been there with you all along but you never knew it.

She'll have grown up in a small town, maybe rural south, or no, better, rural north, so you can imagine her tiny white body shivering against the cold of the long, hard winters, as she lay in the bed she shares with her two older sisters, listening to her parents argue. Maybe her father has a drinking problem and her mother is a whore. That's good, then you'll understand more when later in the story she develops her own addictions and wanton ways.

Just when you start to grow weary of hearing about the small town she lives in, and you've been supplied with quirky vignettes of the local personalities, and yes, a short yet somewhat violent episode of dirty abuse by an uncle, or a friend of the family, she'll leave that place. Let's say at age sixteen, though she could pass for thirteen or eighteen depending what you want. She'll head for the city, the big town, though getting there will be the long way around, a series of starts and stops as she runs out of money and has to make more. She'll hook up with a buddy at some point, a bad influence who will turn her on to the more fun parts of life. We'll call her buddy Sal or Sammi or Deedee or something. We'll watch them through a series of escapades, you know, girl stuff that's in the movies but doesn't really happen in reality: secret pranks, conversations about future love, dreams, etc.

But then Sal will start to get in over her head; the drugs get to her and our girl won't be able to handle her anymore. What's happened to Sal? She steals, beats people up, runs away. She dies. This turns our girl hard. Maybe there's a tearful scene—no, better—no scene, just one brushed-away tear as she packs up Sal's stuff in the apartment that they share. Giving all the stuff to Goodwill will make it seem like she's worked it out. Still, we know now she's different.

Our different girl tries to heal pain with more damage; you'll want to help her, you will, but you know she's got to settle it herself, so we'll let her get really messy and sick. She's dangerous to herself; she's dangerous to others. She passes out in a gutter.

At this point maybe we'll circle back to something from her past, to some kind of thing, some thing, some kind of object that she holds dear or has sentimental value. Maybe a locket? A heart locket? No, something else, why do I want to say a mitten? Maybe she remembers, in her soggy, druggy state, a mitten that she had as a child way up north; the mitten somehow has meaning to her, although she doesn't know right then what the meaning is; she's just thinking about a mitten. It's blue? It's a blue mitten?

I'll give you more dreamy mitten thoughts, maybe a flashback to sledding on a piece of plastic in the good old days, until you remember she's in the city in a gutter, for Christ's sake, and it's winter; it has to be winter.

So the sleepy blue mitten dream becomes the blue of a police uniform, as a cop helps her up, and he's a nice cop, he's only feels her up a little as he's hoisting her onto the park bench: asks her name and where she lives, radios a cab, pays for the cab, sends her home, neat as a pushpin.

Days of sleep and slug go by, and she looks at a snapshot of herself and Sal, and she burns it, and she starts to call home, and she hangs up, and

Amy Havel

she thinks about the cop and straightens out a little. Maybe gets a job down the street at a card store. A store that sells cards, greeting cards, has very little business but the old woman who owns it feels sorry for her. Our girl works in the afternoons while the old woman goes home to walk her dog, water her plants, have some tea or something.

Now is that where you'll come in, right then? Will you be buying a card and see her there at the counter? Is that when we'll get to tell her story, after you meet and offer to buy her dinner? After she says no, she couldn't, a couple times, until you insist and begin to patiently ask her questions: where are you from? What was your childhood like? How long have you lived in the city?

If that's the time, she'll tell you: about the winters up north, maybe a little about Sal, about how she used to have much worse problems than she does now. But the mitten. Will she tell you about the blue mitten, even though she doesn't know what it means?

Probably not. Instead, she'll tell you about a locket her mother gave her, and maybe, just maybe, show you the little picture of herself inside. She'll say her mother gave it to her with some wise words on her death bed. Oh, that's nice: death-bed mother words about the dangers of the word that she can understand now, so clearly and so nostalgically with you holding her hand like that. You'll be happy then. You'll have her, just the way you want her; I'll give you that. And when I give it, you'll think you've got it all: all her mysteries snapped tight in a clever story, snug as a cheap and tiny silver heart.

"Here's What I'll Give You" first appeared in *The Adirondack Review*.

Gregory Howard

Glaciation

I would talk and he would listen. Then he would talk for a while and I would listen. He talked about his own process and his own problems, though not too deeply, just enough to help me, but not enough to compromise his privacy. I remember apologizing once because every conversation was the same, apologizing in effect for wasting his time, and thanking him profusely for putting up with it. And I remember him brushing this gently aside by saying that he was getting as much out of it as I was. At the time I thought Dave was just being nice, but now I understand that he was being honest. He was saying that he wasn't a charity, that he was a complicated person with complicated motives. In other words he was just another person.

And yet on a northern railway line terminating at a certain coastal fishing village where a yearly festival is held in honor of the sea's glaciation, unexplained derailments had suddenly increased, leading to pronounced injury and, in at least one case, death. The railway company, JR Hokkaido, whose motto was, at the time, "Bringing You Closer", responded, under considerable pressure, with all the requisite urgency necessary to a public trust. First they sent mechanics, then engineers, then managers—all without results. Finally, after some debate, it was agreed upon by those same officials that video cameras should be installed upon both nearby telephone poles and the trunks of larger fir trees for the purpose of capturing, if not a cause, at least an explanation.

The cameras recorded for three months, during which time, once the footage was viewed, they captured, it seemed, only this: snow blowing through the gnarled branches, shuddering gently; a curious fox digging in the rocks between the tracks; snow settling on burnished iron rails and melting; the darkening sky of dusk; snow blown dizzy into whiteout; and the striated sky of dawn. But then finally, at last, after much viewing, there it was: another derailment. And upon close inspection of this particular footage an extraordinary scene was unveiled. The tapes, viewed by only the highest company officials, displayed unequivocally what could only be a murder of crows swooping down to the side of the tracks and then *actually working together* to drag nearby fallen branches onto rails. Their task complete, the birds then congregated in the nearby trees. For a long time the video showed only this: the black birds nestled in snow heavy firs, their attention seemingly fixed upon their handiwork, behind them a blur of branches, sky and perhaps, in the distance, the mountains. But then suddenly, inevitably, a train appeared and, just as quickly as it appeared, hit the branches and, bucking briefly, turned over, skidding off the tracks and sliding until it came to rest some ten to fifteen feet from the site of impact. It was terrible to behold. At least one official, thinking suddenly of words he had said to his daughter—displeased and disparaging words—his daughter who loved trains, who loved to stand on the hill near the tracks wearing costumes—she'd read about it somewhere—and putting on shows for the pleasure of the passengers, returning constantly to the hill, now a lemur, now a "gypsy", standing and posing there, he couldn't take it, she was so strange, withdrawn, her gnawed fingers and nervous eyes, standing on the hill—can't you do something natural for a change, he had said—standing there on the hill imagining she was riding, her head against the glass, to some place in the dark distance that would embrace her. Suddenly recalling his words the official is said to have gasped a little and stared dumbly at the hard taupe carpet of the JR Hokkaido conference room. Yes, it was terrible to behold, the footage, and the grainy soundless quality of the security cameras made it only more terrible. But it was not the most terrible thing. The gray footage and the crash. No, that was not the most terrible at all. Because the most terrible thing—noticed by the officials only on the second viewing—was this: there in the trees beyond the tracks the crows, much to the horror of the officials, in full view of the cameras, and only after the train had wrecked, had completed wrecking itself, seemed to caw in an uproarious unity and flap their wings. They seemed, one official later remarked quietly, to be celebrating.

After some debate, the officials finally decided to consult with distinguished ornithologists from several prestigious universities. The consulted ornithologists noted, not without excitement, that crows not only have the intelligence to recognize and interpret patterns, but that they also have what seems to be an endless capacity for game-playing, problem-solving, and self-entertainment. For example, they cited Eckers and Wilch, in which researchers placed a crow upon a metal table in a small white windowless room. There on the table the crow encountered on one end a clear glass soda bottle into which a bit of raw meat had been inserted and on the other small strips of wire of varying lengths. The crow, called in research documents subject B, but by the researches themselves in conversation and to the crow itself, Terrence, was, after only a few minutes, able to construct a hook with which to procure the meat quickly and efficiently. And they also cited Kuroki, Sugita, and Yui in which crows had been able to effectively win the sleight-of-hand standard, "cup and ball," roughly fifty-seven percent of the time. Not to mention, the ornithologists went on, Wallace and Kratch; Frederic Grayson; Lentino, Russo, and Schtutt; and certainly Taggart, Lee, and Westover. Certainly them. However, this situation, the ornithologists all agreed, was much different. Something of this orchestration, magnitude, and implication, the ornithologists marveled, had never, at least by the ornithologists themselves, or for that matter any other ornithologists the consulted ornithologists knew of, been witnessed before. It was, the ornithologists enthused, truly magnificent to behold. Further study, they proclaimed, was of course necessary. Perhaps it was possible, the ornithologists ventured, to send a train down the route more slowly so the phenomenon might be observed? Or maybe several trains? Trains without passengers, obviously. There would certainly be funding available to offset the costs to the company. Not insignificant costs of course. All variables considered. But this was, the officials decided, out of the question. What was needed, the officials said, what *they* needed, was a solution, a quick one, not more study, not more *consideration* and, when pressed for one, the ornithologists, after some reluctant discussion (pacing and hand rubbing) ventured that crows though intelligent are easily distracted and suggested that perhaps a diversion, another kind of game, preferably with objects both shiny and prone to mechanical movement, might be constructed to entertain those marvelous, intelligent birds elsewhere. Another kind of game. So after much consideration it was proposed by the president of the line, Sakuro himself, to build a small-scale replica of track and train deeper in the forest to the east of the line and through simulated corvid distress calls, a method pioneered by a small town in Bihar (Buhpathy, Azeez, Mukherjee; Singh: *Stolen Fruit and the Methods of Retribution: Expunging Crow Nuisance Utilizing Ethological Triggers*), lead the crows to the newer train and demonstrate its value so that there in the clearing the crows might entertain themselves.

The idea, Sakoro later explained in his defense, after the footage of the crashes had found its way, as these things do, logically, inevitably, to the internet and then the airwaves, hinged upon the understanding that because of the birds' intelligence and communication skills there was no way of knowing how many crows had actually learned the game and so simply killing crows indiscriminately would not suffice. Sakoro's casual use of the term "the game" to describe the crows' activities, a term that had become, in retrospect, unfortunate habit among railway officials in discussing the derailments, prompted immediate outrage with council members, media pundits, and public agitators—all calling for Sakoro's prompt resignation. The president—a compact man with a square, soft face and a lacquer of side-parted hair—however, was adamant. And instead of resigning, he decided to make a point to ride the northern train every week in full view of a television crew in order to demonstrate the safety of his railway and the soundness of his decisions. For a while, "Sakoro's Rides" became so popular that rather than airing as the promotional web video they were intended to be they were sold eventually to NHK and turned into a network special. Sakoro, with his combination of dignified rectitude and unbridled enthusiasm, cut an unusual comic figure in his broad attempts to convey the safety and luxury of the train, exclaiming to the camera "Now that's comfort!" whether he was taking a seat, drinking tea, or having just finished using the toilet. He evoked, one television theorist later recalled, a classic slapstick figure, the overgrown child let loose in the mechanistic, determined world.

The gambit worked. The public became so enamored with the figure of Sakoro that in hopes of encountering the man himself they began to clamor for tickets on the northern line like never before. Demand became so high that the railway decided to launch a weekly nonstop luxury train, which would make its way slowly to the end of the line and back over the course of a weekend. It was only on these special trains that Sakoro would ride. The luxury rides were an immediate sensation. Tickets for the first three months sold out, and the public watched with envy and delight as Sakoro, in all his genial oddity, interacted with the most fashionable actors, politicians, captains of industry, international delegates, and beaming pop stars of the moment, all attired in smart tuxedos and elegant gowns, smoking and sipping cocktails. What one fashion-and-culture magazine christened "The New Glamor" swept the trendy niches of the nation's trendy niche-filled cities. Bars and nightclubs held "Ride Nights" in which only those replicating the couture and postures of the luxury rides were allowed entry; while some clubs, formerly devoted to

Gregory Howard

dwindling popular subcultures (New Romanticism, Future Shock, Teddy Boy, Northern Soul, Gothic Lolita, etc.) went so far as to convert themselves fully into "ride bars," mimicking the décor and ambience of the train rides so closely that certain patrons preferred not even to watch the broadcast but instead merely pretend that they themselves were riding in the trains *at that very moment*, staring at the flickering projections of winter scenes on the clubs' brick walls—icy branches trembling, the slate sky over steel blue seas, several crows, like sudden strange thoughts, fly slowly past—the tendrils of floating nostalgia and melancholy webbing their minds, feelings accommodated and accentuated by a low soundtrack of mechanical muttering and the surprising but welcome sudden proliferations of celebrity impersonators most notably of course, Sakoro himself. For a while it seemed they were everywhere, these Sakoros. On television of course—in commercials, games show panels, singing at sporting events—but also in the fabric of every day life. Even in bars and restaurants not dedicated to the rides, the Sakoros would appear suddenly, several of them, standing in the middle of the room gesturing and pulling faces only to disappear just as quickly between removal of the soup and arrival of steamed meats, or be discovered sitting quietly at a counter, alone, bringing noodles messily to his unshaven mouth and staring dumbly at the menu from behind his face.

By the time Sakoro himself was captured on video, now a serious and brusque man, discussing with his producer the best direction to take the "Sakoro character," the public had already for the most part moved on to other entertainments, leaving Sakoro to take a leave of absence and then quietly return to a subordinate position in the company and the impersonators to find other celebrities they could enact or some other gainful kind of employment. It was one of these Sakoro impersonators, a young man by the name of Masaki O Abe, who bore such a striking resemblance to Sakoro himself that he needed no prosthetics only some old age make-up and hair powder to produce the illusion, who rose, after attaining and then losing a position as a financial analyst in what was later understood to be the second economic downturn of next decade, or The Gradual Collapse, to greater recognition as the leader—in this photograph see him in profile, robed and serene, near the bank a rocky, tree-crowded stream in the lush, labyrinth of Nikko National Park (on a distant hill also in profile a large, regal crow) his long, wavy hair obscuring partially his baby face, his eyes and wan smile, waiting, waiting, and the sky hazy behind him—of the Burisu No Ashi cult, famous for their visions of pastoral utopia, wardrobe of blue, interest in the miraculous power of certain animals, belief that only structures with rounded edges could bring harmony back to the earth's dangerously distorted polarity, and, of course, the deadly fire attack on the Conran Office Furniture factory, which Abe now claims was in fact perpetrated by a rival shin-sukyo, the Kōfuku Raiburari in an attempt to undermine the growing popularity of his own group, in whose practices devotees had found a persuasive and dramatic release from the anxieties of everyday life. And indeed, it was not unusual for a time to see in the countryside the long caravan of blue cars flanked by long-haired, blue-robed attendants, men and women, old and young, singing and praying, moving slowly through the countryside toward the next "aperture of discord" and there through certain physical activities redress the terrible imbalance. And nor was it in fact uncommon to see other groups, in the cities and in the country, lying on wooden boards or upon one knee, a decorative sword outstretched, or facing each other in public parks and watching warily, or in groups of only three, attired solely in black silk trousers, squatting and staring with contemplation at selected discrete objects. "In uncertain times," Abe—hair now shorn, close cropped, face thinner, drawn, eyes searching and watery—wrote of his time in the Burisu No Ashi and of the age of the cults in general "the best resource is often method, or at least, the most common."

Still it was years later, after all but the most affected had forgotten about the derailments and what had followed, that Sakoro abruptly resigned his post and disappeared, taking nothing from the house he still shared with his wife and daughter but an overnight bag carefully packed. For a long time there was only this: the rooms of the house, though exactly as they had always been, still somehow emptied of sense, the splintering of memory and desire, and Sakoro's wife and daughter, unable to live in this way, dusting fastidiously the relics of their life, retreated from one room after another, leaving them to their stillness, their calcification, until they simply put mattresses upon the kitchen floor and camped there. But then after many months letters began to arrive. Letters from Sakoro. To his wife's disbelief, they were addressed solely to his daughter. These letters did not explain his actions. They did not apologize. Instead, they spoke only of the crows. Despite what he knew of them, Sakoro wrote, he had never seen anything more beautiful than the image of crows nestled in snow-covered pine branches. He wrote that they seemed like temporary openings to another deeper something, that which was beyond the endless white. He wrote of returning to the site of the "the game," a clearing in the woods that bordered the actual train line to the east as the sea did to the west. He told her that he walked the ovular track "like a soldier" for three straight days "as if enchanted" waiting for crows to appear, the snow blowing through the branches and settling on the defunct train, the rusted tracks, but waiting in vain. Indeed, he told her, that upon reflection he felt perhaps he had lived his whole live waiting for these crows, waiting for them to do what they did, waiting for his own response, and that everything before and after seemed like a dream or someone else's memory. He would find them again, he wrote, them or something like them, other crows or wolves that work together in a hunt or the trembling of winter berries hung over a frozen stream—he would find them and he would know them; he would know them and return.

His last letter came after another long silence. It was short. The handwriting was shaky and cramped. What can be said now, he wrote, that the song is no longer a song? And then for the remainder of the letter he went on to describe a certain coastal fishing town, where, in February, if you stay for a week or two, you can watch the entire ocean slowly solidify into ice, which the locals celebrate as a bridge for the recently deceased to the spirit realm, and that they claim, the locals do, that if you stand there and wait, in the cold winter light, if you are patient enough and still—the light distant, opaque—you just might see where they are headed.

A D Jameson

Bonnie Raitt, I Am Coming to See You

… I never took a class with Dave, but I used to visit him during his office hours, and show him the stories I was writing, some of which ended up in my story collection Amazing Adult Fantasy. *He always had a lot of encouragement and advice, and I still remember those conversations fondly. But what most struck me was how no one else ever stopped by during that time. Dave commented on this once; he said, "It just goes to show, you can become a bestselling author, and students still won't come to your office hours."*

Bonnie Raitt, master of fife and drum, keeper of tribal unity, parent of a jogging Elvis, friend of an Estonian dog, attired in a British colonial jumpsuit, I am coming to see you. At my heels snaps the Headless Mafia. I have burned your music to disc; I burned all of your songs to one disc. In my hand I hold every song you've ever written, your number one hits and your dance remixes, your reggae beats and your lullaby favorites. I even have songs you wish you'd never sung, the songs you've deliberately forgotten. We will listen to those songs together, to all of your songs together, and I will tell you everything that I have waited to tell you. I will tell you that I recognize your voice even when you sing in Spanish. I will tell you that you are not a weirdo, and that you are tranquil. I will say that your music mixes all styles, and that you hold your talent in hand, like roses. You, Bonnie Raitt, will get bigger and better. You will master the art of ceramics, ceramic music. You will promise a bounty of aural simulation, and special surprises.

The Headless Mafia snaps; they pack a hunter's punch. They want my disc of your music for devious ends. But try as they will they won't find me, tucked away among this city's historic meat warehouses. I pick my way through fourteen-foot-tall revolving doors and get lost in this country's biggest mall.

Bonnie Raitt, although you are fifty-seven, you are hotter and feistier than ever. I packed with throngs of other music lovers into the Orpheus Theatre to catch you, to swagger at the sight of your silver-red mane of hair. You've made eighteen albums, wearing a purple velvet bodice. The crowd cried with one voice, "Bonnie Raitt, you are my idol!" You gave us something to talk about. You cut up the stage like an album. You know what it's like to battle alcohol and weight gain. You know what it's like to battle cancer; you battled cancer for eighteen years, wherever you could find it. You've been on the skids. You've been on the run from the Headless Mafia. They got pissed that you ran your trucks on bio-diesel, and that you boasted about this between songs. They got pissed at how you staggered about the stage with more sex appeal and energy than people half your age. They envy you your famous Broadway father. They envy you your leave of absence from Radcliffe. They want you to go back to Radcliffe! But you earned fifty bucks a gig, singing blues in local clubs. You had a down-to-earth charisma. You befriended an Estonian dog, a mutt who clapped her paws while you laid down your licks. Like you, this dog was raised a Quaker. Like you, she was active in Civil Rights. A lucky star shined the day you found this dog. She listened to hundreds of records, to every single one of your CDs, and picked the songs for your debut album on Warner. You followed her advice and haven't put down your folk guitar yet.

That Warner Bros. record had your breakthrough songs; it went to number one for eighty-one weeks. You had product endorsement offers, of which you took several. You endorsed the video iPod. It might be the best iPod yet, or at least the most popular. Your songs built its success. You endorsed a robot boy named Gizmo, a kid who could speak more than one hundred words, and play games and listen to tunes, some in Spanish. It could name the forty-seven presidents. Everyone wanted a Gizmo for the family. But sadly, Gizmo was only a fiction. Our world wasn't ready. Parents who couldn't buy Gizmo grew enraged. They responded in kind to these emotions. That was when you met the Headless Mafia: your fans took out a contract on your life. They wanted no more songs about an ideal robot boy, songs that caused only pain. They wanted to rend you limb from limb. Enraged, they threw sticks and stones at you as you played. But your beautiful music caused their aim to fail; they didn't hit you.

You turned your back on your fans and disappeared. You floated downriver to the Mediterranean shore. You went to Spain and disguised your voice with Spanish. You abstained from sex, and refrained from eating eggs. You sang, "What am I, some kind of weirdo?" Your Estonian dog brought you *dulce de leche* ice cream. The Headless Mafia followed, growling, snapping at your heels. You spurned them in favor of tender teenage boys. You grew restless. You simplified your style. You didn't look back.

You thought about money, and making more money. You thought about fame, and you thought about nothing but music. You hid out in the Andy Warhol Museum, a seven-story warehouse tucked away in the meat-packing district. That was the darkest time in your life, although you didn't know it. You thought it was a very exciting time. I saw you waddling among the museum's concrete-and-plaster setting, gaping at the folk-art illustrations. I followed you for seven floors, until we reached the deliciously narcissistic Silver Clouds room. You were at your most colorless, though you thought yourself brimming with color. You were colorless, but I sensed the potential for color. You were minimalist and proud. I needed you fiercely. I was at the darkest time in my life. I was battling cancer, and exploring the currency of celebrity. I was in my Pop phase. The museum stayed open till 10 p.m., and there was a bar. There was music by Winslow Homer and Degas. I asked what you were drinking, and you said, "DINO-mite." We bought seven bottles and went to the roof. You pointed at the moon and said, "That'll happen." You spotted a parrot monkey and burst into tears. I held you in my bird's-eye view. Slowly, you understood the larger picture. As dawn waxed, you realized the world needed different songs. Why long for a boy who could never exist? The world has other problems. It's losing its white Bengal tigers and tree kangaroos. You wrote a song on the spot lamenting that loss. You shined a spotlight on those problems. The world has patches of sand, tremendously large sand patches that do no one any good. You wrote a tune that highlighted this great problem. From the roof of the Andy Warhol Museum you shined a powerful spotlight onto the world's worst sand patches. You raised awareness. You perked people up.

I told you, in sacrosanct terms, about the cancer I was battling. I'd spotted the cancer last in Monkey Jungle, where I'd stalked it for weeks. But cancer is a skilled diver, and it escaped into dark river depths. Having failed to master swimming as a youngster, I was reduced to lobbing coconuts into its wake.

You at once grasped the situation. You knelt and crafted your most powerful spotlight yet; you shined an immensely powerful spotlight onto cancer. That spotlight wasn't stopped by cancer's evasive skills. It could follow cancer anywhere, even to the depths of lakes and rivers. Everywhere cancer went, people could call it by name. They could block it from the raisins and koala nuts it craved, and force it to slink back underwater. Starving, disgusted, it ran away, though not before vowing to return when "Bonnie Raitt was no more!"

Everyone heard this oath and recognized you as the source of the recent spotlights. They realized that they had misjudged you. They forgot your robot boy songs and embraced your unique, blues-tinged performance style. Your records returned to number one, and to numbers two through ten. Politicians gave you the Quaker Music Award, which a fair world would have awarded you lifetimes ago. The Andy Warhol Museum hung your ceramic discs on its seventh floor, among the narcissistic Silver Clouds.

The only downside was the Headless Mafia. Worriedly, your fans recalled the contract they'd taken out, and phoned to break it. But the Headless Mafia never remits a contract. They inherited long-term stalking skills from cancer, the dark lord that they serve. They swore never-ending adversity. But there wasn't that much they could do about you then.

After that we bought a two-story walkup at the Cocowalk. That's a Mediterranean-style shopping village in the country of Coconut Grove. It offers a more family-friendly nightlife than the one at the Andy Warhol Museum. You performed a variety of concerts, in styles ranging from trip-hop to jazz to quip, from bubble to squeak to flamenco. We lounged in a patio surrounded by specialty stores, admiring the human-powered rickshaws. We played graffiti with spray paints and planned a family. We ate *dulce de leche* ice cream. But suddenly you remembered the music you'd forgotten, back at our old haunt in downtown Pittsburgh.

I vowed to retrieve it. I stole away one moonlit night and without a backward glance returned to the Andy Warhol Museum, scaling its seven floors of Heinz boxes and super-16 films of frayed bohemia. In the room filled with free-floating Mylar balloons I found your ceramic discs, eighteen records ranging from doo-wop to gospel. I plugged in my video iPod and backed up your songs, then burned them all to one disc, every one of your songs, including the forgotten ones about Gizmo. Bonnie, they're wonderful songs. They promise a bounty of aural stimulation. I hold them in hand, they fit in my hand like roses. With your songs in my hand, Bonnie Raitt, I am coming to see you.

Brian Monday

Arbitrary Nimbus

...When asked what it was like to have been one of Dave's students—first in an undergrad creative writing workshop and then in a graduate lit course, where we read DeLillo and Gass and Gaddis and McCarthy—I recite the standard, now-iconic details about his do-rag and scruffy garb or his dipping tobacco in class or his militant stance on grammar and proofreading. But then there's the evening that stands out clear as an epiphany, when Dave read a lengthy passage from a manuscript of Don DeLillo's Underworld. *It was the only time Dave read aloud to us that I recall. The excerpt was the scene in which Father Paulus gives his charge, narrator Nick Shay as a young man, a lesson in the names of quotidian things: "Sit down, Shay, and tell me how you're doing. A young man's progress. That's the title of this session." I've since read this very scene aloud to my students, to teach them the same lesson Dave was teaching us and that DeLillo was teaching Dave and that character Father Paulus was teaching narrator Nick Shay. "A young man's progress." A fitting title for my few years at Illinois State. I'm no longer a young man, but I'm still in progress—thanks, in so many ways, to the impact of Dave's earnest and brilliant teaching.*

Dr. Wimund was less interested in diagnosis than aesthetics—the ominous clouds of a lit-up x-ray, the dark ribcage flickering on, the branching veins backlit like the tops of trees at sunset, the infinitely varied masses blooming. Of secondary concern was the revelation of this or that malignancy.

His earliest memories were of his brother cupping the shine of a flashlight in his hand or enclosing it in his mouth, to luminesce the blood. The blush of his own warm blood thrilled him. He imagined that, were one backlit by a bright enough light, standing on a hill in the early morning, the sun rising behind him, one might be made transparent with the bruises showing through. He thought of death, his patients' or his inevitable own, as a final irradiation.

A halo of blessings had fallen indiscriminately on his head, and among them were his wife and children, his education and career, his wealth and intellect. Most notable were his professional achievements and, though he may not have thought it, his paternal ones. He was a luminary in his field. The focal point of his office was a framed print of "Hand Mit Ringen," the first known x-ray image of Wilhelm Röntgen's wife's ghostly hand with one knobby knuckle, a large shadowy sphere that was her wedding band.

When Dr. Wimund first met his wife he saw into her more than he had any other person. She was clear to him, and he would examine her not to discover anything new but to verify what he had just seen, looking away and back again to make it true. As a child he would study things for hours, peering into their depths: a perfectly hollowed-out beetle shell, the gluey pollen-dappled stamen of a lily, the boundary between the bright, elongated trapezoid of sunlight lying across the bedroom floor and the blue shadowy edge around it. By the age of four the insides of bugs and animals fascinated him. His mother, a favorite photo of whom displayed a delightful corona around her coiffure, grew to accept these fixations after she recognized his extraordinary talent to draw out the essence of things with a diviner's sensitivity. He felt infused by the fundamental nature of objects around him, could sense the presence of metal with his nose, would test himself, eyes closed, to see whether any was nearby, the itch and anxiety at the tip growing stronger.

The night before the vacation he meticulously packed the boys' things, as he always did. Their luggage was oppressive. There was the milk bag and the diaper bag, the food bag and the toy bag, his book bag and hers. He packed two sippy cups filled with ice for the older boys, the same with the baby's bottles, one with formula shaken, the others empty and sanitized, their once-clear plastic now cloudy with use. The milk tote could hold one sippy— with flared base for stability and of a plastic that turned from green to purple when cooled, chameleon-like, or like the flush of blood to one's face—as well as one four-ounce baby bottle, two ice packs crammed in pouches lining either side of the tote, which was then placed into the larger and more general formula-sponsored food bag, along with granola bars, pouches of formula powder, boxes of raisins, corrugated bottles of purified water, and the specially designed blue and white brush for cleaning out the insides of baby bottles and their nipples. Next to the black food bag, set near the garage

Brian Monday

door where a collection of other gear grew, along with the bulky items of a stroller and pack-and-play—next to this he placed the diaper bag pregnant with size-four and size-one diapers, a slim dispenser of baby wipes, a travel tube of diaper-rash cream, sunscreen, and antibacterial soap. He was most fastidious in readying his own attaché case. Being caught without materials—on the chance he might have a moment to read, a moment to breathe, as when all three boys napped in the minivan in a mall parking lot while their mother shopped for perfume—was unbearable. So he prepared for such a chance as a celebrant prepares for a liturgical rite, envisioning the moment on the plane or early morning on the hotel balcony when his wife and his boys still slept—she on her curved spine and they on their soft-boned sides— though his were wholly secularist ends, the spurring on of one daydream or another. Any immediate, unplanned stimulus would do, whether an artificial or naturally occurring thing or a combination of the two, as in the play of light on the sidewalk, the entrancing synthesis of varied visual elements, but to be safe he carried with him a cache of ready-mades, mostly stylish advertisements clipped from magazines.

He had honed this procedure and packed out of a conviction in convenience and efficiency, which might mean freedom, a second to oneself, and was why he fed the baby at two in the morning knowing that if his wife did the baby fed twice as long and would have reticent burps and incipient gas lodged, and why he often put the two-year-old to bed with a near-religious fervor, and perhaps even why he had a profound wish the first days after his boys were respectively born for his wife to drop breastfeeding, which struck him as sloppy and inefficient, to convert her to the precision of the bottle over which he would have ownership and control. In the first days of each boy's life, she had briefly put them to her breast, collecting and offering to them on her earnest finger what little precious colostrum there was after they let go of their weak latch and they cried, nearly screamed, pushing away with their little closed and hateful trembling fists, their heads bobbing and weaving at her breast like nearly-KO'd boxers. He looked on at the untidiness of it all with skepticism and a horrifying desire to put an end to the entire scene. He meanwhile scanned the thirty-something lactation consultant and in a single visual burst rounded her breasts and hips with his eyes, then delved into the healthy bones and blood, the lucid and mass-free brain. What he saw and the self-awareness of seeing it added yet another layer of deep, nearly-psychotic aggravation for him, a subcutaneous itch that threatened to surface. He felt something of bile and spleen at the consultant's slow persistent efforts, at the newborn's frantic fight with the punching-bag breast, at his wife's guilt coming in like the tide as her milk went out to sea, at his own attraction to and repulsion by the consultant's beauty and obstinacy, at the even deeper feeling, one he was unaware of and would have batted down and dismissed had he even glimpsed it, of a confounding filicidal urge to barehandedly snuff out the life of this newborn, as if some oracle had prophesied his future.

That last fateful morning at the hotel, room 710, he woke exceptionally early. This very room would be available for occupancy only three days later, the next occupants none the wiser. He would take his last shower, walk down to the hotel lobby for his last cup of coffee; he would take his last stroll around the well-groomed hotel grounds, and finally, before returning to the room where his wife and sons slept, would witness a phenomenon of sunlight—a heiligenschein, or Holy Light—on his shadow backlit by the early morning sun and cast across the dewy lawn.

He was a man of routine, mostly, but for the last few months of increasing strife he was more and more a man of impulse. In these days he unwittingly partook of a succession of lasts: his last sweater worn at the tail end of spring, last drive in his Audi, last heartburn, last humiliation, last phone call home to mother, last ice cream, last ejaculation. As a younger man he'd once predicted this view of life, a countdown of final conveniences, pains, pleasures, and eked-out accomplishments, life converted to a series of numbers—18,252 sunrises, 18,251 high noons, 18,250 sunsets. This countdown of lasts reached far into one's past, prefiguring one's demise, like the earliest undetectable signs of cancer, some retrogressive genetic path branching back to a last first-love kiss, last fishing trip with father, last stuffed animal, last tricycle ride, last diaper. Every day of one's life, he thought, offered an undetected last.

The early morning was the only time that he felt unburdened, and he lingered in the shower, trying the showerhead settings. He then kneaded the skin of his aging face in the mirror with a high-end moisturizer for men. He brushed his teeth vigorously, shaved with a stealthy straight razor, put on the new aftershave and cologne that his wife had given him for their seventh anniversary, which they were here celebrating, and thought erratically about work, about his radiant reputation, about the just-out-of-college sylphid assistant with the lustrous arms, about the most recent and maddening arguments with his wife, about whether it was ambition or domestic distraction that forever held him back from complete fulfillment. He thought about his sleeping sons, about the hours of rocking them in a room bathed in the lambent glow of a nightlight.

Sandal-shod and with keycard in hand, he eased out of the hotel room. Since the birth of his boys, anxiety filled him as much out of love as resentment and most palpably when the boys slept. He would creep by their room, feeling in his heart each pop of the floorboards of their newly-renovated lakefront home, but the uneasiness followed him far from their fragile naps—even to his workplace and back again. He would have elaborate daymares, skirting their climaxes but fully sensing their ends: about his wife not waking up one morning after he'd gone to work and his boys stranded, the two-year-old crying more and more desperately in his crib, calling out Mama Mama, then Dada Dada, trying every nuance in the delivery and tonality of these words, growing more thirsty, more confused, thinking the world has ended, eventually trying to climb out of his crib, timid as he was more and more prone to say "I can't" when he used to say "I try"; and while older brother runs to the neighbor's house, finds no one and is finally lost down the street, middle brother manages to climb to the top of the railing and in a moment of unwitnessed, forever-unrecognized courage goes over and drops hard to the floor, recovers himself after more crying and tries to reach his kiekie and binky, which he's left behind at the far side of the crib, more crying at this defeat, but then a rush to find Mama in her bed, unmoving, perhaps her batteries run out, perhaps Dada can fix her; meanwhile, baby's cries are now a series of dry-mouthed screams that shake the bassinet, and on tiptoe the toddler peers over the bassinet edge and tries to see him, console him however he knows how, "That's okay, baby," thinks to go downstairs to the fridge for milk, is now able to open the fridge door, and lunges for a half-filled sippy left over from yesterday, sucks some down, then even sees and seizes a bottle for baby but reaches an impossible task when back upstairs, unable to reach baby, lacking the know-how, having reached the limits of his little problem-solving skill set. Eventually he cries himself to sleep on the floor next to Mama's bed, awakened later by baby's final frenzied cry before he falls altogether silent. He would recurrently play out other scenarios as he drove to work, or as he jogged through his neighborhood: about a man much more man than he breaking into the house in the wee hours, the boys utterly defenseless; about their plane going down, the boys' screams, the baby's silent tumbling through the air; about a house fire in the middle of the night, the boys suffocating in their sleep; about the menacing tree branch of their Siberian elm unaccountably breaking off and crushing his boys where they played below; about his errand-running wife crashing the minivan with the boys in it while he's home surfing the web on the sly, clearing out the history in the settings when done, individually deleting the incriminating names of remote unknown women—Olesja, Ruslana, Sveta, or Uli—already halfway fantasizing about a fresh start, a life with a different woman, catching his guilty self and minimizing the refreshed page to reveal the wallpaper photo of his boys' waterpark-logged faces.

But this morning his mind was at peace, and a slight euphoria came over him as he gently shut and triple checked the security of the door, having achieved this early solitude. He walked the length of the hallway, which was silent save for his sandals alternately padding across and slapping up from the ornately-patterned carpet. He went down the south-end stairwell and exited the hotel.

It was dark yet, the sunrise an hour off, and the outdoor lights bombilated in the morning air. He traversed the parking lot and joined a sidewalk that ran between the hotel and a stretch of affected landscape, where he stopped under the fluorescence of a light and stared at the unplumbed dark of squat shrubs and pines; then he turned back, passing again between the silent cars. The hotel balconies and windows were dark and curtained and unreadable. He entered the inactive lobby. Opposite the counter was a sunken dining room where an employee, an old lady, stocked and shined the continental breakfast bar with stern vigor. No doubt the boys would have eaten here, perhaps at the round table near the TV secured in a ceiling corner, and would have watched a second helping of Saturday morning cartoons—Disney's Playhouse—all the while adeptly managing their diverse little agendas, the baby in his high chair, bib'd and babbling, mauling a banana, the two-year-old making a tunnel of his napkin for his latest toy car, amused and chattering, stopping his play only to take automatic bites of a cake doughnut, and the four-year-old's attention going from his tenuously-held-together robot creation to the television and back again. The mother would have met each of their trifling demands as if they were grave necessities, she would have simultaneously continued the veiled argument with her husband, and already at this early hour her eyes would have begun to reveal the same residual frustration and fatigue. As it was, this meal would never take place, and the vigorous, stern old woman would not pick up the baby's dropped bottle or the middle one's toy car or the eldest's robot. The thought of this breakfast with his family and the inevitable and ensuing anxieties made the father's current coffee less rich, its steam less pleasant. Only one other hotel guest was already eating her breakfast, a woman in her thirties, near the dormant fireplace. The woman had tidy features and a complacency about her that was neither haughty nor smug but completely unconscious and all the more refined and alluring for it. He gave himself full leave to

Brian Monday

watch her and to imagine the tidiness of her life, and this leniency quickly gave way to fantasy. One had to be efficient and make the most of gaps in the routine, of respites from responsibility which daunted one and crowded out even the remotest wisp of intrigue in one's otherwise insipid existence. The advertisements he had collected, in both video and print, particularly those of high-end automobiles, tickled his lust for the posh and transported him to a stock fantasy—the glossy rain-glistened sleekness of bumper and black-top, the rounded curve of fender and road, the low glowering of sky and faceless driver, the rich yellow texture of undulating wheat and gear-shifting forearm, the monochromatic ambience of techno sound and sight, the con-tour of stitch and strand—all the artistic-seeming but oversold refinements promised the gazer. This woman, who would attempt to calm the doctor's hysterical wife only an hour hence, finished her orange juice, rose lithely from her chair, and walked up the few steps in her jogging suit and out of sight. He had surveyed his wife the first time he had seen her, but for differ-ent reasons. That survey was more substantial, more hopeful than this one, about real possibilities and personal breakthroughs; it was about discovering the depth of another person and curing loneliness, not about quick-release fantasies, two-minute escapes and lustful escapades of imagination. His wife had been lithe, as well, and complacent with the tidiest of features. During a recent fight, a few days before their trip, he had accused her of cheating. She didn't deny it, and he harassed her past midnight about it until she retaliated, bringing to light his inadequacies, his self-absorption and abstraction, his impotence, his distance from his family, this last what finally put him over. They lay in bed in the dark, taking turns delivering half-awake harangues, until this last blow. He reached over and grabbed her arm, both of them flat on their backs, and squeezed and shook it, controlled yet threatening, an unprecedented moment of violence, then sprang off the bed and out of the room, down the stairs, and slammed through the kitchen, down another flight of stairs into the basement where he finally huddled under a pool table, slapping and punching himself in the head, sobbing out of anger and guilt. A connubial cancer had manifested itself and was spreading, incurably. He had seen it coming, had detected it on the horizon one spring evening when the eldest boy was only one, the second just conceived. They were down by the lake. The cool wind swept through them like particles of light. His wife laughed at some expression on her baby's face, and it sounded like the flash-ing shake of a transparency thrown up and pinned to a light board. At that moment he saw through the relationship and the family and identified the unnatural growth sitting fat and Buddha-like, sending out its noxious tendrils.

On his way back from the lobby he carried a load of breakfast items in the pockets of his cargo shorts—a yogurt cup and mini-boxes of sugary cereal, a napkin-wrapped cake doughnut—and he balanced his coffee cup atop another doughnut in the palm of his hand. The sun was up now and other fathers were loading or unloading their minivans, this most pedestrian of American scenes infused by an aureate warmth. He crossed the parking lot again to walk along the landscape. A blind man tapped toward him. He wore no shades and bared his gauzy, unblinking eyes. The doctor slowed then stopped to let the man pass, who stopped fully as well and moved his head up as if looking at the doctor and parted his lips, about to deliver some prophetic words, some high-drama divination, then closed his mouth and shambled on, keeping to himself whatever prognosis he presaged. The father too moved on, only to stop again some yards later before a miniature valley in the landscape to listen to the sparrows nattering in the squat shrubs and pines and to watch them frivolously flit like cards in a trick from one to the other. He missed whatever significance there was in the nature of their flight, but the sun was warm on his back, and he was in the moment—of the landscape, of the dew on the freshly-mown lawn, of the birds acting real in this manufactured valley-of-sorts—some time before he became aware of his shadow stretching stilly out before him as if it had been waiting for him all the while. The morning sunlight came at such an angle, and played on the dewy grass in such a diffracted way, that the faintest backscatter radiance circumscribed the shadow of his head. Theologians at the time of the Renaissance would have attributed a deep spiritual significance to this rare vision, this heiligenschein, but he saw in it nothing symbolic or holy, though he was moved to his mental core by the sight, which represented a phenomenal synthetic display, an array of variables converging—the amount of dew, the cut and texture of the lawn, the angle and quality of the sunlight, the chance of his stopping at this moment, at this spot, and finally, the drawing of his attention along the length of his shadow-self up to the arbitrary nimbus. His trance was cerebral only and touched where aesthetic bliss resides.

At their door he carefully extracted the keycard from a pocket of his cargo shorts, quickly swept it through the slot and, the indicator light clicking green, gently pressed the handle down, all with his left hand; he then softly shouldered the door open and let himself into the room, which was nearly dark with the heavy curtains drawn, the first lights of dawn just beginning to make their way from behind. He placed his coffee and doughnut on a table near the door, slipped off his sandals, unloaded his pockets of the other breakfast items, and decided to risk crossing the room to open the balcony

Brian Monday

sliding glass door to sit out in the morning air—all of which he managed to accomplish without a single misstep, passing his wife in the bed nearest the door, the two older boys where they shared a queen-sized bed, and the baby in his pack-and-play breathing loudest of them all. He pressed on the balcony lock firmly so as to absorb any sudden sound it might make, cracked the door incrementally, then slid it on its track and disappeared behind the curtains, leaving the door slightly ajar.

Just another half hour was all he asked, even less would suffice, but a little more time to breathe the morning air and to absorb the sparrow's insouciant flight from railing (where swim trunks hung to dry) to branch—the fathers' loading of suitcase and sneaker below a part of this snug perspective from above, their jigsaw-puzzling out of this or that stroller or duffel, each subsequent selection from the brass-barred and in-demand bellboy cart a feat of planning and preparedness, a testament to man's logic, to the calculating mind of the engineer, the designer, the executive and the doctor, as long as all went well and no unforeseen and jaw-tightening piece with seemingly no comfy fit presented itself just as the entire picture was about to coalesce, such as the spill of coffee or the misplacement of keys or even the most trifling trip of foot over curb that could unhinge the swing of the spirit and wreck the otherwise flawless start to another much-needed day of vacation, what's been looked forward to for so long, planned for so particularly, envisioned by parent and child alike so vividly, the expectations and hopes for which elevated to such heights that fate itself is tempted and even the tiniest wrench unhinges the swing and curbs the cozy gratification and sets the whole family on edge, rippling from parent to infant, from high-strung dad who, in light of one more whine or complaint or accusation or allusion to that rawest of issues that cuts to the quick of marital strife, goes from agreeable leniency to sullen, fist-clenching and arm-wrenching lunacy, down to baby who settles into a jag of colicky inconsolability, after all of which only an hour of healing—of purchasing and eating and bottle-feeding, along with a stroke or two of luck: a short line for the ride or magic-show tickets still available—can things once again return to the copacetic state of domestic synchrony sought for in the vicissitudes of vacationland.

These periods of peace, which presumably should have induced a parental renewal of a nearly-spiritual sort, in fact had the opposite effect; instead of rejuvenating the father, they charged him with anxiety, gave him a taste of what had been lacking, what had been stolen. He so desperately clung to these spoiling moments—they were such a rarity—that the thought of the lull being spoiled by yet another trip out of bed and down to the nursery for yet another lullaby set him on serious edge, and the longer the break from the familial frenzy the more he was filled with anxiety and resentment when returning to it. Paradoxically, though, he spent what would seem a healthy portion of these reprieves reliving, even savoring the memory of a moment with the boys—as he did now, thinking about the first months after the boys were respectively brought home, how they slept on his chest so long their hair got sweaty and their cheek held the imprint of a shirt button when, at last, they stirred and lifted their tottering head and looked up at his face with an expression of sweet and matchless nescience, how their room had a rich, humid smell when he went back in to check on them a last time before going to bed himself; or thinking about some more recent memory such as their shivering bony joy at the waterpark the night before, then their awed excitement afterwards (after a quick dry and struggle into their clothes, after dinner at the hotel's restaurant, after his wife's bitter, nanometric weighing of the scales and his retaliatory accusations of infidelity) their excitement, that is, at the magician's performance, their glee, especially the four-year-old's, at the deft disappearance of the doves—and yet the thought of this or any such reverie broken by one of these very boys and his needs or fears was enough to make him grit and grind his teeth and stamp down the stairs and with formidable effort tamp down an emotion akin to rage, and yet again, once back in bed, after having rocked the baby to sleep or tucked in one of the boys for the fifth time, and after having calmed himself and pulled his own blanket up to his chin, he would be overcome with guilt at having felt and expressed such impatience and frustration and, lastly, would sometimes go down again and watch them sleep, even sit by the eldest and stroke his cheek. So it was not that he was devoid of gratitude, as one might guess. In fact, an intense appreciation for these fleeting days and of letting the fullness of them saturate him brought him at times to a near-catatonic yet epiphanic state of living in the moment (never, notably, of imagining their futures: their futures were a void to him), such as when they went to the beach and the weather was glorious and his wife agreeable and the boys rested and agreeable as well, vying for his attention: "My turn, Daddy. Toss me, toss me." But he was profoundly aware of the unremitting pounding his personal dreams took and the washing out of all conjugal coloring their once-vibrant marriage had held, leaving only dim vestiges, hollow bones fixed in a blue-gray glow; and increasingly aware, too, of the irradiation that children were on a marriage, a limning of what ailed the bond and a treatment that would heal if it didn't first kill; and finally aware, in his gut, of an inexorable Greek-like fate growing like a sinister phantom organ, drawing nearer like the beetling rim of a shelf cloud. So to keep that front at bay, or to stay just ahead of it, he

Brian Monday

stole back flashes of personal freedom, greedily snatched at the narrowest of breathing-whiles, fiercely guarded them, found himself taking on obscure and elaborate projects, grossly inconvenient but justifiable and curative diversions, whether domestic or professional, found himself engaging with unheard of serenity in inane chores and indulging in fantasies more and more involute and on-the-fringe, simultaneously so uneasy in these states that the slightest threat to them—an inexplicable battery of fireworks going up out of the neighborhood in mid-May, a motorcycle throttle opening up at the nearest intersection, whatever might wake his slumbering sons, or an unexpected request from, or engagement made by, his wife—would send through all his insides a rushing wave of heat that originated in his chest and spread out in every direction and that finally settled in his agitated hands.

And so it was that his baby, whose name was Aidan, began to cry.

He had been born, like his brothers, in the early morning. He was a fall baby, had blond wispy hair, and though it was premature to draw such conclusions, seemed to his father the most irascible of the three. His future features—what his toddler face would look like, his little-boy voice sound like, his grown-man handshake feel like—were indiscernible to the doctor, who didn't have a favorite, who in fact went out of his way to love the three boys equally but who nonetheless felt more remotely about each consecutive child, due he guessed to less and less time devoted to each as the family and its demands grew. Gauged by their relative six-month weigh-ins, Aidan was the smallest. Each boy had had more complications than the last, had fallen lower on the growth charts. For this, and for being the last, Aidan was the most coddled and the most indulged and so the least content. He was a week from nine months, weighed eleven pounds, well below the third percentile, and had just learned to roll over. His most charming attribute was his hair, which shone in the sun; his least charming was his wake-up wail, which he let out now into the otherwise-amniotic air of the hotel room, immediately stirring the two-year-old, Connor, who slid off the bed edge and high-stepped it over to the pack and play, then over to where big brother slept, barking, "Wake up, Brother," which prompted big brother, Ethan, who by the time he could say his first words was creating metaphors, pointing to his zipper and saying "choo choo track," to emit a deafening whine and pull his covers over his head, and mother, Maria, a self-proclaimed stay-at-home, decay-at-home mom, to rise slowly in her bed and offer a rejoinder of complaint at why her boys had to wake up always so early and why, today, so cranky, and to reach for the remote to begin the day with chaotic cartoons, the glow of unearthly colors and frightfully animated voice-overs filling the room—all the while the doctor standing in the balcony doorway, looking in at the scene and feeling that wave come like a pyroclastic flow billowing down the mountainside, a vast involucrum smothering any native dream of self-fulfillment or -actualization and petrifying a budding culture there for some archeologist to unearth eons later, to brush ever-so-gently the ash off of and to demarcate the site of and to wonder at the inner-workings of, such a distant and enigmatic mental milieu with its unfathomable infanticidal leanings and psychotic customs, its impenetrable glyphs—where its tortured, repressed inhabitants piled their waste, what they ate and what they worked at, what medical conditions ailed them and contorted their bones and twisted their teeth that x-rays would finally bring to light, what dictated their social orders and their marriages, and above all what king ruled over them and what constituted his aesthetics and what god, if any, he worshipped. Dr. Wimund drew the curtains back, letting the raw morning light flood in, and entered the scene, leaving the curtains and balcony door grossly agape behind him, walking by the looking-up baby, the spinning-round toddler, the sitting-up boy, the already-questioning wife and into the bathroom where he placed his hands on the cool lip of the sink and lowered his head. His wife shadowed him into the bathroom. She shut the door behind her and turned on the ceiling fan. The boys were oblivious to the argument brewing and the revelation their mother was even now delivering to their father. The four-year-old had discovered the breakfast treats and was inspecting them, ignoring the growing cries of baby brother, breaking off a piece of the doughnut for his toddler brother, then unwrapping the juice box straw and trying without success to jam the frail straw through the aluminum hole covering when his father strode by him to where his baby brother lay and picked up and cradled the baby, looking down at the baby for a brief moment with an unfamiliar expression somewhere between pity and disgust, if there were words to name it, and glided out onto the balcony, with a magician's stealth, and tossed the baby, whose cries were inexplicably silenced now, over the balcony railing, and then returned for the middle boy who thought Daddy was playing a game of chase and who ran the other direction giggling and trying to wriggle out of his father's determined reach, the four-year-old's mouth hanging open now and his eyes fully wide and circular and inert like Frisbees suspended in a fixed spin not knowing where to be caught or where to land, his half-eaten doughnut falling from his hand, the ceiling fan's whir part of the auditory backdrop now, part of the opposition effect or surge, and the sound of the middle brother's short falling puppy yelp just audible from the balcony, and

Brian Monday

finally, not the slightest hesitation in his step, the father's third trip back for his firstborn who stood immobilized and beginning to cry, his folded hands at his mouth and him saying, as his father hefted him onto his shoulder like a parent does when carrying a child to the car for a talking-to, "What's going to happen to me, Daddy?" The mother shut off the fan, perplexed for a second at some sound or lack of it that she couldn't place. She turned the corner just in time to take in but not fully register the baffling, split-second vision of her husband, Dr. Wimund, casually rolling over the balcony railing, doing so by securing one hand on the railing top and swinging his legs over the edge, as a hiker crosses a low fence or a diver goes over a boat's brim. She scanned the room—its beds and chairs, their covers and pillows—in utter panic. The room was flat and vacant and placenta-loose. There was only the sound and sight on the TV screen of some cartoon character throbbing purple. She staggered onto the balcony, wheezing now, and peered down at the ground where her boys lay on a patio in the shade, part of a primal tableau, a gilded triptych in which a bright glory of red collectively encircled their images and filled them with light.

Maria would have taken the plane that bore her children and husband home to Chicago, but this was not possible. Instead a friend flew down, then drove her home in a rental car. The entire ride Maria neither spoke nor cried but simply sat, bathed in intermittent sunshine that would have warmed any other passenger. At times she would look down around her, at the seat and floorboard, would rifle through her purse or pat her pockets or turn as far as she could, peering at the back seat or at the road stretching out behind them. Then, suddenly remembering what she had left behind, she would sit defeated through another state.

In the weeks to follow a chorus of "why's" pursued her. Psychologists examined the father's possible motives—environmental stresses of work and parenting, marital conflicts, revenge at his wife's perceived infidelity, perhaps combined with some touch of mental illness: impaired impulse control, lack of cognitive flexibility, unbalanced judgment, altruistic thinking: he imagined saving his children from some fate, from some suffering, stemming from some delusion system, melancholia, manic depression or character disorder—and cited historical precedents going back to Medea and her sons. He fit the profile, in retrospect. For one, he performed the act with his bare hands, which was typical of an infanticide. Others, the clergy and their laity, scrutinized the inscrutable for some symbolic order—it was, after all, from the seventh floor, on their seventh wedding anniversary, with a trinity of boys—and still others, a smattering of seculars, interpreted the calamity as the random synthesis of a thousand unfortunate variables.

In the end, coworkers, friends, and family all agreed that Dr. Wimund had been a loving and doting father, and at the funeral the wife even placed a bouquet of flowers on her husband's coffin, which comforted most everyone and helped them anyway to put the remaining obscurities to bed.

"Arbitrary Nimbus" first appeared in *The Klein-Bottle Boy and His Ontological Dilemma.*

Brian Monday

Scott Rettberg

Hands

I wrote "Hands" while I was a student in Dave's fiction writing workshop at ISU in, I think, 1995. I think Dave was getting a little tired of some of our attempts at postmodernist sleight of hand, and challenged us to try to write a story in which the word "love" could be earned as something other than a cliché. He suggested trying to write a story about a boy whose pet rabbit died.

Billy Haskins is a mute boy who is loved very much by his parents. They care very much for him and they wish very deeply that no further harm should come to him. Billy's parents know how little boys can be cruel, how they would make fun of the scars on Billy's throat and his half-severed tongue. Billy would be the boy who couldn't talk back, the boy who would be defenseless, the boy who could only make noises like a chicken clucking.

A tutor named Theresa visits three days a week, and Billy slowly learns sign language, gradually, step by step, gesture by gesture. Billy's parents pay very careful attention to him and provide him with toys, healthy food, and warm clothing, and they speak to him as they would to any child, even though he is mute. After all, Billy is a normal child. Just because he is mute does not mean that there is anything wrong with him.

Billy's parents love him so very much that they try to spend all of their time with him. They both do their work at home on their computers and they hardly ever go away from Billy. They take turns giving Billy lessons on history and art and writing and other things, and although he cannot speak, Billy is a very good listener, and he has developed a fine handwriting.

The house that they live in is a very nice house in the woods, on acres and acres of land, behind an electrical fence, very far from the nearest neighbor. There are birds and squirrels and stands of pines. There are the noises of the woods, the calming sounds of nature, which Billy can hear, because although he is mute, he is not deaf. Sometimes on summer evenings, Billy and his parents sit out on the porch and drink tall cool drinks, and listen to the woods.

But it isn't summer, it's Cleb's birthday, and that's the only day in the whole year that Billy's parents ever go away, to the place that Billy's Mommy says is a cruel place for children. Every March 15th, three years in a row, they fly there in the morning and fly back late at night. They are anxious when they leave, anxious about leaving Billy by himself with just the baby-sitter, although they trust the baby-sitter very much. They know that she'll look out for Billy while they are away, but still they are anxious, anxious about their son.

When the baby-sitter says it's bedtime at nine o'clock, Billy plays like he's sleeping until ten o'clock, then he gets out his penlight and looks beneath his bed and pulls up the secret floorboard and gets out the cigar box that has the hand in that made Cleb mad that Billy saw it before Cleb got sent away. Billy opens the box, to see how it has changed. The bones have gotten yellower, the tiny little fingerbones. He touches them. The stuff on top flakes off but under the flakes the bones are hard, really hard. It doesn't smell as bad as the last time he checked. Billy's parents don't know about the hand. Billy keeps it a secret, cause good brothers keep secrets.

* * *

Cleb is Billy's older brother. Cleb was bad and that's why he got sent away. Cleb was bad cause he hurt other children. Cleb was bad cause he hurt Billy. He didn't believe Billy when Billy told him he wouldn't tell anyone about the hand. Billy just wanted to play with his big brother, he didn't mean to surprise him, but Cleb wouldn't believe him. When Billy saw Cleb holding the hand he thought it was neat, and he told Cleb so, but Cleb said he shouldn't have seen it, that he was in big trouble. Billy promised not to tell. He told Cleb it was neat. He asked Cleb to show him more. Cleb let him hold it, but had a mean look in his eyes, and in the night Billy had a nightmare, only it was really real, cause when he woke up he was bloody and his throat was cut up, and his tongue was gone, and when his Mommy came in she screamed and screamed and screamed. Billy's window was broken, and the police thought a bad man had come in and did it until Billy's Mommy found Cleb's Swiss

Scott Rettberg

Army knife with some blood on it in his underwear drawer. She screamed and screamed and screamed and then Billy's Dad punched Cleb and then the policemen came and that is when Cleb went away to the special place for kids like him, kids who were mean to their brothers. Billy misses his older brother a lot. He was mean but they used to play sometimes and it was okay.

Billy doesn't think that Cleb meant to be mean. He just didn't understand that Billy understood him, that he wouldn't tell on him, that he knew that Cleb was his brother and that sometimes brothers are mean to their brothers. Cleb really messed up when he cut up Billy. Cleb cut him up, but that didn't mean he meant to hurt him. Billy knows that brothers fight sometimes, all brothers. It's part of being a brother. Most brothers just don't get so mean that they make it so you can't talk anymore with a knife. Billy feels bad that Cleb had to go away. He wishes he still had his tongue and the other thing like what the doctor said the thing that made his voice, the larynx, but even more he wishes he had his brother. You can learn how to talk with your hands, you can hear other people and talk back to them with your hands, but you can't replace a brother who gets sent away. Cleb knew things about the world that Billy didn't know. One time Cleb showed him the inside of a frog. You just can't do that kind of thing on your own, especially if you don't like knives. Cleb knew a lot, but Cleb was dumb that's what he was, dumb. Billy doesn't hate Cleb, but he knows Cleb was downright stupid for doing that. If Billy had a little brother, he would not cut him up. It's good to be a big brother, and it's bad to go away and leave your little brother alone in a new big house in the woods. Good little brothers don't tell. Cleb should have known that. Billy proved it to him every day. He never told nobody about the hand, and when he looks at it, he says to his brother, "See? See? You see now, Cleb? I never did tell, and I never will neither. I'm not the kind of brother who tells. Brothers ought to trust brothers. Brothers don't need to cut up little brothers to make them not tell." Cleb never answered cause he was away in the bad place, but Billy knows that if he were there, he'd have to nod his head and say, "I'm sorry Billy, I know you wouldn't tell. I'm sorry, Billy, I am. I'm sorry I cut you up." Cleb would say that, he'd say that when he got home, Billy just knows it, so he keeps the hand in his secret place, and someday he'll prove to his big brother that he never did tell.

Billy's brother is gone and Billy wishes he had friends. He's nine, and he doesn't go to school anymore, cause Mommy shook and cried when he told her he wanted to go back to school, cause there aren't any kids around the house and he wishes he could have friends to play with. Theresa is a good teacher, and she teaches him how to sign, and she reads him stories and shows him pictures of hands that make words, and he watches a big screen TV when his lessons are done, and he can play Nintendo so long as the games aren't violent, and Theresa is beautiful, and when in the stories Theresa reads to him there is a beautiful woman, Billy always imagines that the beautiful woman is Theresa, but Theresa isn't a kid, and she isn't a boy; she isn't like a brother. A brother can tell you things about the world. Theresa teaches him lessons and sometimes she gives him big fat hugs that make him feel all warm inside, but it's just different, and nobody can understand that. He tries to tell them, to sign it to them and to write it down, but his mother says there will be time for other people later, that he is better off right now away from the other boys. Billy has learned how to read stories, and the boys in the stories always have other boys around and do things with the other boys like playing ball and fishing and building rafts in the river and solving mysteries together and Billy feels left out when he reads them.

* * *

Billy's parents are home. Billy walks over real quiet in his pyjamas and watches them through his door, open just a crack. Dad gives Alice the baby-sitter some money and thanks her. Alice says that he was a good boy, no trouble at all. Dad says yes he's a fine boy isn't he and Mommy starts like she's about to cry and says he's such a good boy and Alice asks if there is anything she can do and Mommy says thank you Alice no I'm just, I'm just tired then she really starts to cry and Alice says she hopes everything is all right and Dad says it's fine just some pills for motion sickness you know from the plane she just needs some rest and Alice says if you're sure then I'll be on my way and then she leaves.

Mommy says Cleb, Cleb, Cleb what happened David why did it happen like that? Dad says I don't know Monica and Mommy says did you see him did you see his eyes they were just dead cold like he couldn't even see us any more and Dad says hush, hush, Monica, Billy's sleeping, it will be okay Monica it will be okay and Mommy says it's my fault you know I could have been there I could have stopped him and Dad says there was nothing we could have done to stop it and he puts his arms around her and says we didn't do anything wrong he just snapped there's nothing we could have done and there's no way to explain it and there's no point in trying to blame. I named him, Mommy says, I named him Cleb and Daddy says hush, hush, Monica, it will be okay and she says Cleb after my father in the war mother never talked about him I never knew him just a little girl he was away and then he died, it was just a name I thought, just a name and Dad says Monica, Monica, it was nothing we did, it's nothing we can blame ourselves for it was neurotoxins or something it was chemicals it was something other than us and Mommy says he was a beautiful boy he played and he smiled such a pretty smile if he was a girl he would have loved his little brother if he was a girl I would have understood her I could have told her things about the world and she would have loved her little brother she would have loved him and protected him and held him so tight I could have told her but I didn't know about boys how to get them to be … hush, Monica, hush … kind. We should have bought him different toys we should have never bought him that knife and Dad says I'm sorry Monica I'm sorry let's go to bed in the morning it will be better in the morning it will be okay and Mommy says every night the same nightmares David every night they come and I know it hurts you, I know it does David, but I just can't, it's not you I just can't anymore cause he came from me … I still love him David I still love him I do I can't stop even though I know that he went bad I can't shut it off I can't stop any of it what if Billy what if he goes bad too the world will come in I know the world will come in and Dad sort of shakes her and says Monica, listen to me, listen to me, Monica. Billy is okay, he's a good boy that's not going to change and Cleb well the psychiatrists think there's some progress and we're still here Monica, you and me and our boy, we're still here, Monica, we're still here and it will be okay. Mommy sort of nods her head, but the way she nods you can tell she's only sort of half saying yes and she says I need to see my baby and Dad holds her real tight in his arms and his hand is like a cradle on the back of her head and she's shaking and he says okay, baby, okay and he lets her use his shirtsleeve to wipe off her nose and they start to come up the stairs and Billy tries real hard to be real quiet getting under his sheets and he shuts his eyes real tight like he's been sleeping for hours and they push the door open and he can hear Mommy walking over to his bed and she puts her hand on Billy's forehead and says Mommy loves you, Billy, Mommy loves you very very much. Mommy loves her baby boy.

* * *

In the morning, Billy hears the thwack thwack thwack of his Dad's fists on the punching bag. He does it every morning. It makes a different sound when he kicks it. His Dad punches and kicks and makes groaning noises. Billy punches it every once and a while too and when he does it makes his hands get all scraped up and his Mommy gets mad and starts crying if she sees them scraped up like that and Billy doesn't like it when she cries so he doesn't do it too much. It's a heavy bag, and it's Dad's and his Mommy always tells him he ought not to hit Dad's things, so he doesn't do it very often and when he does he hits it sort of soft so it won't make the thwack noise and scrape up his hand so that Mommy will know and get all mad and sad. Dad hits it hard though, every morning, his knuckles are tough from hitting it. Billy can hear it even upstairs in bed and he likes the noise it makes when he wakes up to it. It's kind of like an alarm clock, only it's human, so it's better, it means that Dad is up and lively and everything is okay. His Mommy always sleeps later than that.

Billy pours himself a bowl of Cheerios and pours him some milk in it too. His Dad makes the thwack noise in the basement in a rhythm that Billy likes, and he tries to get the spoonfuls of Cheerioes in his mouth in just the same rhythm: spoon up thwack crunch crunch crunch spoon down spoon up thwack. It's like he and his Dad are making a kind of song together.

Billy finishes his cereal just as his Dad comes up stairs smelling that kind of salty sweat smell he smells whenever he gets done with the punching. His Dad comes up behind him and tousles his hair and asks him if he's gotten all his homework done, and Billy signs that he has and signs if he can play outside until Theresa gets there which will be 9:30 and it's only 8:15 which means there's more than an hour and Dad says sure, son, sure, just don't get dirtied up and be careful out there, huh? and Billy signs that he will. Theresa taught Mommy and Dad how to sign too, and they can understand it, but they're both kind of clumsy at doing it, which is okay cause Billy can hear them anyway so there isn't really any need for them to learn how to sign, cause even though Billy is mute he is not deaf.

The back yard is a good back yard, it's big and there are pine trees, and a sandbox that Billy never plays in cause there's only so much fun you can have in a sandbox when you're all by yourself and it only makes him think of Cleb and how much more fun it would be if he were playing in it too and he's too big for a sandbox anyway, it's not the kind of thing that big boys do. It's a big back yard though, his Dad says four acres and there's the fence around it which Billy never goes near cause it's electric and Billy got shocked by a toaster once when he tried to get a piece of burnt toast out of it and that was no fun at all cause it hurt his hands like all get out and Billy's hands are very important to him cause they are the way he talks so he keeps a good distance between himself and that electric fence. Billy really hates that fence, when you get down to it. It is not the best thing about the big back yard. The pine trees aren't either. They smell good and all and make a nice home for the birds, who are finally coming back, which makes Billy glad, but they aren't the best thing of all either.

Scott Rettberg

The best thing of all is the pond. It's not a very big pond, big fish don't grow in it cause it's not deep, but little fish do, goldfish do and tadpoles do too. Today is the best day, cause Billy can finally see the tadpoles, just beneath the surface. Some of them will grow up and in the summer they will be frogs. Billy thinks about Cleb and how he's missing it, and he thinks about what Cleb would do. There probably aren't any tadpoles where Cleb lives now. Billy looks back at the big house and there's nobody in the windows watching him, which is good cause Billy has a secret.

Real quick with both his hands, he swoops down in the water and scoops up the tadpoles, three of them, maybe four, he gets them in his cupped hands. He closes his eyes and feels them swimming in his fingers. They feel slimy and good as they swim in his hands. It tickles him, and it feels so good that Billy laughs. It is like they're talking to him, speaking to his fingers, talking to his hands. The water drips out and Billy lowers his tadpoles back into the pond. Billy likes to touch things, even if Mommy says that it's dangerous. The tadpoles swim away. The tadpoles are a secret, a secret that is good.

Billy wipes his hands on his jeans and then he hears something rustling in the dogwoods. He walks over by the bushes and squats down with his hands on his knees and listens for it and he hears it again and then he sees it moving around underneath some dead leaves. Billy sees some fur and he knows it's an animal and he loves animals so he wants to touch it. Billy is real quiet, real careful cause he knows that animals get scared and he doesn't want scare it away, he just wants to touch it. He creeps down and slips his hands in the leaves and then they all come flying up it's a rabbit scrambling up from the hole and running away. It's a good-sized rabbit with fur that's kind of funny cause it's brown but it's still got some white hairs in it like bunnies do in winter and Billy scrambles up and starts chasing it. The rabbit's real quick and it's running quicker than Billy but Billy's pretty darn quick too and he knows the woods and he thinks he's lost the bunny but then it comes shooting out from behind a tree and Billy tries to cut off its path but then it cuts to the right just near Billy's foot and Billy nearly touches its fur with his finger then he spots it by the biggest pine at the edge of the woods and Billy goes diving for it and lands on the ground on a bed of pine needles and realizes that his hand is empty then he hears a big sparking noise like and he looks up and sees the fence and the rabbit on it kind of bouncing around like it's hanging on it and Billy gets up and walks over and he sees that the rabbit has caught its paw in the chain links. Its paw is caught and it hurts the rabbit it makes little noises. Billy gets a stick and knocks the rabbit away from the fence and it just lies there. It looks burned around its paw. The air smells funny and Billy feels kind of sick in his tummy. He picks the rabbit up and looks at it. Its eyes are all burned up too. It's warm but it isn't moving at all. Its fur is soft. Billy pets it and he feels sad. He sits down on the ground in the woods and cries cause it is dead now. Billy is hurt inside cause the rabbit got hurt and died and it wouldn't have died if Billy hadn't chased it. Some blood comes out of the rabbit's mouth and Billy hates blood. He hates blood but he loves the rabbit cause he knows the rabbit, knows what it was like to be the rabbit. The rabbit didn't do anything wrong and a bad thing just happened. There's blood spilling out all over the rabbit but Billy doesn't even think about his clothes and he hugs it real tight. It's warm and limp and it can't feel a thing.

Billy knows that he should just leave it, that he should keep it a secret, but he can't, cause it's so bad, and even though he knows that bad things happen sometimes he can't understand why, even though he's not stupid. He knows that it's bad that he's holding the rabbit and he knows that it's bad that he chased it and he know it's bad it got killed on the bad fence and he knows that sometimes the world is just bad but it hurts, it hurts real bad and he can't understand why it needs to hurt why the world is so bad that things need to get hurt so he walks right up to the porch holding the rabbit to his chest, his fingers all wet and sticky with warm blood, and he can't stop crying like a big boy would, like Cleb would tell him to just shut up and act like a big boy, but he can't and he walks up to the sliding glass doors and he sees his Mommy standing there in her flowery robe with the curler things in her hair and her coffee cup drops out of her hand as she opens the door. Billy walks in crying and he signs with one hand Mommy, I killed it.

Mommy she just stands there for a second with Billy standing there holding the rabbit and the coffee in a big brown puddle at her feet and she looks down at Billy and he thinks she's going to hug him but she just stands there and then she reaches for his hands and grabs ahold of his wrists and squeezes them real tight so tight that it hurts very much so tight that Billy has to drop the rabbit and it falls on the coffee-soaked carpet and Mommy is hurting his hands when she looks at him and says Bad. Bad. Bad. You have been bad, Billy. You ought not to hurt things, Billy. To hurt things is bad. Mommy, Billy wants to say, my hands hurt Mommy my hands. Mommy says you hurt little things. You touch things and you hurt them. Why do you hurt things, Billy, why do you need to hurt? And Billy signs Mommy and he can't think of what to say and he signs Mommy I don't mean to. Mommy says the world Billy the world comes in and you go bad. Keep it out. Can't keep it out. You can't. You go bad. Billy can hardly feel his hands any more and Mommy lets him go and says bad, bad, bad. Boys go bad. Mommy lets go of him and she reaches down for the rabbit and she picks it up and walks with it over to her rocking chair and she holds it to her shoulder and rocks and says you need to know how to hold things, Billy, you need to how to hold them so they won't get hurt. You need to not hurt things, Billy. You need to not be bad, Billy, you need to not be bad.

Mommy rocks in the chair with the bloody rabbit in her hands and she starts to hum. It's a song that Billy knows, a song that he remembers. Mommy hums the song and holds the rabbit to her chest, and Billy feels sad cause his Mommy's eyes look like they are somewhere very far away.

Billy walks over to the chair and puts his hand up close to his Mommy's face. Even though his hands are bloody, he touches his Mommy's cheek, and she tilts her head into his hand and looks up at him and she smiles and mumbles something but Billy doesn't understand what she mumbles and then she mumbles it again and then Billy understands what she means and he knows that he will remember it. Mommy says love, Billy, love.

Suzanne Scanlon

Final Exam

In the first class meeting, he went through the syllabus. I noticed Richard Rodriguez's "Late Victorians" on the syllabus; it was one of my favorites. "It makes you shiver," he said. It had and it did. It was one of those bits of writing that you felt in your stomach, which is what he was always emphasizing. He wanted writing to be interesting, to be grammatically correct; but more than that, he wanted writing to hit you on a visceral level.

A Moody Story

The day after D- dumps her at Denny's 24-hr Family Restaurant, M- finds herself in the office of Dr. Alda Moody, the psychopharmacologist she has known almost three months, and whose particular compassion and interest in her care has never been particularly apparent. She knows not to take this personally of course; these are the days of in-and-out check-ups, managed care, and don't-call-us-we'll-call-you!

"How've you been?" Moody asks, friendly-like.

"— " M tries to say, but instead begins to cry, and it doesn't stop for a long time. Moody's nice about it, gives her a Kleenex.

M tells her what's going on.

"I am...and...he...."

Etc.

Until finally,

"He was my Professor."

Moody adjusts her jacket, with a look of compassion, and M is more relieved than she'd imagined possible with the Moody, who, after all, she can afford to see only once every few months. Her relief's so remarkable, as the mostly one-sided conversation continues, that she doesn't even mind where Moody takes it next:

"It's sexual harassment, you know."

"It's not." M tells her .

"I mean—we *talked* about it. About *that*. I mean he *knew* it."

"Of course *he knew* it!" Moody blurts out, projects incredible disdain: "Everybody *knows* about it, *now*— "

"It doesn't matter." M says finally, and hoping to end the discussion in these specific terms.

It comes out a little angrier than she'd expected.

"Yes." Moody says, nodding, and again M feels grateful for the Moody.

"Well. I'm not suggesting you initiate a lawsuit."

In spite of herself, M is buoyed and comforted by Moody's rhetoric— indignant, protective. It's unfortunate, she thinks, that the women most able to offer her this sort of sympathy seem to be overfull with their own agenda.

It was one—an agenda—M shared, or liked to think she shared, at least in practice or *theoretically* speaking...but right now it seemed—too easy? She wasn't sure. All she knew was that in *practice*, she found herself in this sort of position too often.

Pop Quiz

Q. If A, a self-identified Feminist, sleeps with, and falls-in-love with B, a self-identified Misogynist, is A *really* a feminist or just:

    a.   lonely

    b.   angry

    c.   sad

    d.   typical

    e.   hungry

    f.   there

    g.   all of the above

Q. If B, S.I. Misogynist, eventually does humiliate A, S.I. Feminist, how might A feel?

    a.   tired

    b.   broke

    c.   stupid

Suzanne Scanlon

d. nervous

e. hungry

f. all of the above

Q. Why does B choose A? Is it because A is:

a. hot

b. sexy

c. a feminist

d. there

e. all of the above

f. hungry

Rhetoric

Not *angry*. No. Not at all. It's not my thing. Not the type to play the victim as it were. Not in my nature. I am fine.

Q.

The emotional dissonance, now between us—is the state of our present re-lationship—that bothers me. It bothers me. Not a strong word, right? But neither is it neutral. I have a sound, definite stand on the matter; I'm capable of considering such things rationally. It is my sense—and hence the crux of my bothered state—that he might (should) have been blunt on the matter, and from the outset. For a man so aware of his own complicated emotional palate, his inherited *imago*, his *psychic shit*, a man who has been in countless 're-lationships' before this one—surely he was capable of doing the right thing, surely the considerations crossed his mind. How many times did it cross his mind, I wonder, and how did he confront such oppositional (to his lust, that is) thoughts? Did he say, oh who cares if she's my student, I want to get laid? Or did he not even articulate so thorough a rejoinder as that? Were his selfish self-deceptions occurring on a level beneath his consciousness? Is that how he managed to deceive me, to lead me on, 'put the rush on me' so thoroughly?

Q.

He should have been frank—and beyond the should have, I'm guessing (not having access to his psychic structure/interior solipsistic discourse) that he was able to be frank with me, and from the outset. That is, I believe that he was so aware of the complicated, compromising professional restrictions on our relationship, to have considered—and as suddenly as he felt certain carnal attractions to me—that this might be an absolutely ethically wrong thing to do. To pursue, for personal interests, a student. Ethically wrong indeed because students undeniably carry certain transferred emotive baggage. Toward a professor, that is. Thus, the student—having slept with the Professor—might (and very likely would) feel a number of things, the vagaries of which he could not imagine, given his lack of certainty re how long the relationship might last.

Q.

You want an example? Okay fine. For example, Professor B. might have said to me—putative attractive female student enrolled in his Sp. 2001 Nonfiction Workshop—might have said for example: "I'm going to give you some options, given my attraction to you and desire to seduce you. I've considered the obvious complications of such a relationship, and too the subsequent complications and hurt feelings given various potentialities. Various eventualities. None of which might occur, of course. But it is only fair that I—given my position here, and taking your own into account (I recall being a student myself, not so long ago)—consider such things, and pose them from the outset. It is the only way this might work, in my considerations of the matter. The only way to avoid such ugly eventualities, ranging from hurt feelings to ugly malevolent exaggerated lawsuits. I just want to be frank here. I've encountered the juggernaut of 20th c. Malevolent Separatist Feminism. So I just want to be clear. Because the fact is—and this is it, really—the only thing I need to say and wanted to say—I think you're hot. Damn hot. Fine looking. Gorgeous. You hear me?

Okay. So we're on the same page. We're on the same page. So I want to lay out the options here. I want to pose them for you to consider so to speak.

Option number one is that we date—the connotative meaning of 'date' in my lexicon is—I'm being frank with you here, see? Meaning is: *to have sexual intercourse*. Certainly there is more to it, including financial transactions, but that's usually where it all leads, the transaction—the what shall we do? Where shall we go? What night? What time? Okay? Okay I'll pick you up, etceteras. It's about—not entirely but in my experience reflectively it's more or less effectively so—getting into bed together, our bodies touching in a myriad of delightful and even unexpected places, my body wanting to have intercourse with your body—your body hopefully reciprocating —I'm admittedly going out on a limb here, see? Hoping for yr. reciprocal desires. So OK? So that's the first option.

Q.

Well I'll tell you that I don't know. I never know. In such circumstances, and you're smart to ask because the reason I bring it up at all is because you are my student and I think it is wise, given the potential for professional complications, hurt feelings—

Q.

Yes, yes on your part. But on my part too. Do you not think my feelings might be hurt in this whole thing? I have feelings too—I may be in your eyes the master teacher, professor, famous and successful writer, I might seem all this in your younger, less experienced eyes—

Q.

Of course you have experience. What I am saying is that I am not, in my own eyes, I am ashamed, I am no better than the next guy, I am a—and you'll forgive the heaviness—sinner. This is why I am trying here to avoid repeating past mistakes, past sins if you will, by so to speak laying it on the line for you—this is not something we can ignore, and if we do it may come back to haunt one of us sometime down the road in the future—

Q.

No. No I'm not trying to scare you—and I don't mean to even imply—what I want to tell you is that the first option, which is definitely in my opinion the more desirable option here—there are no guarantees, is what I'm trying to tell you.

Q.

Don't look like that. What I mean, and maybe it's too soon to talk about this—maybe I shouldn't have brought it up in the first place—

Q.

No just that it could end in some state of—and it might not end in any state, it might go on for a long time who knows you never know right? I go in, and I'm being straight here, I've learned this by now, with no agenda. I don't have time. I'm too old. So what I'm saying you never know. Sometimes yes in my experience it's been one or two weeks—Tina you've heard me mention our thing, which was really nothing at all—and sometimes it's you know a year. Two years—I don't know is what I'm saying.

Q.

How often is it one week? Is that what you're asking me? I don't add these things up.

Q.

Yes, okay, more often it is less than a month—less than a week. Yes I have one night stands. I don't like to—I'm not proud of it—that I'm almost positive is not what I intend our relationship to—

Q.

Now you're not saying anything. Why are you quiet? I don't know what it means when you get quiet all of a sudden. Are you mad?

Q.

No I—well sometimes when I'm quiet it's because I'm mad. Look. I shouldn't have brought this up. I'm sorry, maybe it was a big mistake once again I'm trying to be different for once to be honest to begin with honesty—you know to avoid problems, and necessitating further dissembling down the road. For once I wanted to try it and now I've made it worse. I'm just going to say—

Q.

Yes I was going to tell you that. The second option. Of course. The second option is that you remain—we remain teacher and student—an artifice, which works in certain respects, but necessitates certain severe boundaries. But we can do this, if you'd like. We can remain; keep *so to speak* what we have now.

Q.

I can see how it might be better for you at least—you might you know wonder about asking for my help, my recommendations down the line—I should tell you that our dating—first option connotation et al—would not obviate these potentialities however. You would still be able to get my help...I would still support and encourage etc.

Q.

Yes you might not want to. I can see that. But it would be for your own reasons I assure you and not because I would change my high opinion of you as a student —and yes I see it might be worse for you given certain eventualities (i.e. see option one) and yes. That is why I'm laying it all out for you here huh? Okay. Even if it was a bad idea probably. I'm sure now I've made everything more complicated than it ever might be. But those were my intentions here as I said to be honest for once. That's what I mean.

Suzanne Scanlon

Q.

Excuse me—I'm having a problem here. This is my monologue—my interview, is it not? My interview. What's going on with the subjective voice here? This is about me, my point of view. I'm having a problem.

Q.

I'd like to speak, please. I'd like to be the author of this narrative. What I mean is that I don't want to hear him—I don't want his voice—even his authorial voice—invading this text in any way, not directly, nor symbolically. And yes I understand I have invoked, created as it were this very problem…I realize this…through the form and yet—

Q.

What I need to say is that I am—it bothered me. I mean. It hurt. I know that doesn't sound like much. I know it's really very pathetic at this point. I know too that I was warned, regard readily my severe repetition compulsion—

Q.

From my mom. From my—when I was a little girl.

Q.

My understanding—post her death—of why she died. My child-logic, which lodged itself as Truth in my Psyche during that sensitive/fatal period of pre-adolescence, and thus has become the symbolic *bête noire* of my adult life.

Q.

That she died *because* of me. That it was my fault—that I was somehow a bad—an undeserving person—that I somehow caused her to leave me. Inspired rejection.

Q.

And thus, in my adult intimate relationships I manipulate events to somehow prove to myself again that this is the Truth of me. So to speak.

Q.

Either by getting involved with someone who, you know, *can't* be there—or someone who you know, is *very likely* to reject me, or someone who isn't but in that case manipulating events to sort of make the person leave me. To give the person some really good solid reasons.

Q.

Well it may be. But what's wrong with wanting to control it? It's my story.

The Sense of an Ending

Q. How does it begin?

A. Over coffee. In a diner. They share war stories. He's like her, she thinks, only more so. Insists aggressively upon his dominant position, physically and rhetorically. It's fine with her. She hates him but is drawn to him. Decides it's out of her control.

Q. How does it end?

A. One night in bed. Guess who is on top. She makes the mistake of Talking In Bed—feeling too completely in that space *so far from isolation* and still unable to find words *at once true and kind, or not untrue and not unkind.*[1]

Q. How does it end?

A. a. see *The Sense of an Ending* by Frank Kermode

   b. see *The End of the Affair* by Graham Greene

   c. see *Liars in Love* by Richard Yates

   d. see *To the Lighthouse* by Virginia Woolf[2]

Dating the Dead[3]

For so long it bothered her—and so much really that she could not deal with it and so had eventually forced herself to place two of his books (and later a third) in a box which she put underneath her bed. It was too difficult to consider actually dating him *and* having the books in her apartment (even if that's where the books had always been). Not that she would necessarily read them, nor open them, nor refer to them ever again; but she was not about to get rid of them, either. No date was worth that.

---

1 See Larkin, Phillip. "Talking in Bed"
2 Especially see: *"If we had not this device for shutting people off from our sympathies we might perhaps dissolve utterly: separateness would be impossible..."* V. Woolf.
3 *"The dead living in their memories are, I am persuaded, the source of all that we call instinct."* – W. B. Yeats

Beyond the books however, there existed too her past experience of having read them and having been moved, perplexed, intrigued, provoked, and bothered by their contents—in a wholly admiration-filled way for the author. The books then, even in their mostly unopened state along her bookshelf—represented to her, or *signified* something *very large*—something directly connected to the Author of the books, however Dead he may be.

And so she could *not deal* (was how she put it)—now that she was getting to know the writer, and thus the Author, alive, of these very books—she could *not deal* with having him in her head, or her life, or (most difficult of all) her apartment along with (at the very same time) the large signifiers of the dead Author himself, too. She decided pretty quickly that the two—Author, Real Person vs. Author, Dead—were in *no way* related, and would have to remain that way. That is, there would be no references to the writer, Real Person, when referring to the books of the Author, Dead thing. Or vice versa. This did not mean that she didn't *at the same time* understand how very related the two were: and this raised another whole set of ontological problems along the lines of: *Would it be more honest not to have any of the books on my shelf, or to have all of the books on my shelf?* The latter choice seemed too sycophantic, even if it was probably more honest, required less dissembling.

On the other hand, the former option seemed offensive, and blatantly dishonest—because in fact, she *had read the books,* and *did own them,* and so to hide them would be, you know, mendaciously going out of her way to protect herself from the vulnerability she's feeling now, given the 'connection' so to speak, of the man she's dating to the Dead Author himself, whom she so admires and whose talent and prose have moved her many times to states of out-loud laughter, deeply-felt identification and sheer delight. The books have articulated for her (more than once) worlds she would not have known were her very own worlds, without having read them there, in a voice not her own. There were things which might have come from her mouth—but never would have, had she not lived in the world of the book, and traveled with it, and found a comfort in the utter identification to its entirely separate world.

She took one of the books, the big one, and put it under her bed. Another she put on the bottom shelf of her bedroom bookcase (least available to his immediate perusal). She took another and placed it rather prominently out of place, in the main hall bookcase. She did not concern herself with the periodicals and essay collections that contained his work alongside the works of other dead authors. (Though among these were two *Paris Reviews*, two *Iowa Reviews*, one *Best Essay* collection, and one *B.A.S.S.* collection.)

After all this, it still didn't feel right to her that she was dating someone who was so nearly *related* (which was as far as she could explain it to herself) to the Dead Author who'd made such a lasting impression on her. It didn't feel right (she came to understand and finally admit to herself), because she suspected herself (but could not identify it, or *did not want to* identify it) of feeling an attraction based largely upon the very experience of having been so deeply moved, provoked, delighted, and made to laugh out-loud by, if not the Dead Author himself, then some *extremely close relative* who wrote the books now placed on her various shelves. And at one point she came to know pretty surely, unequivocally so, that if this Dead Author was not exactly the same person as the someone she was dating (who happened to be a fiction writer) then he was at least that extremely close relative.

There were clues. Maybe it was the night he tried to convince her that the woman her ex-boyfriend was now dating (whom he had dated some months prior) was an amputee. Maybe it was an accumulation of things: things she came to identify as certain aspects of her attraction. She could identify, for instance, the way that this man, who was something very much like her favorite dead author, was an extremely smart man. She loved that about the dead author—the demonstration, in an occasionally show-offy way, of an exceedingly high intellect. His books offered, without fail—one after another word to add to her New-Big-Word list (words she would note and immediately or later on look up in her *American Heritage Fourth Edition*), which she been compiling for years now. Her favorite dead authors were the ones who could offer her words for this list. Maybe the list began with Nabokov. She was young, reading *Lolita* and keeping a list in a notebook with every word she promised herself to later look up and incorporate into her vocabulary. It embarrassed her a little to look at that *Lolita* list now—ten-plus years later—and to see how deficient her vocabulary had been. It was as embarrassing to see how many words she could define, and yet had never quite incorporated in the manner prescribed by her ambitious if confused 18 year-old self.

She had found herself delighting in Nabokov's easy use of undervalued but crucial words, and she can see herself underlining and highlighting. She can even recall parts of the list she had memorized (if not incorporated) that summer: "acridity, manqué, coeval, perineum." Some she memorized in context: "a glorified *pot-au-feu*, an animated merkin." There were other phrases: "inveigled fructuate" or "such coruscating trifles" and "a favonian week" or "her phocine mama." They were wonderful words, you could taste them, eat their syllables. Words she would long recall in these Nabokovian incarnations.

An orchideous masculinity.

She's thinking now of *Lolita*, pt. 2, chapter 3—and too, still (madly) of the dead Author she is somehow dating. It was at the University last Spring, in the class he taught, that she came to know what she had expected (having read the close relative/dead author): that he had an exceedingly high IQ, and, too, an extensive available knowledge of vocabulary, syntax, and mechanics. His intelligence, as evidenced in the class, was revealed especially in his rather long considerations (mostly epistolary) of the workshop material of the week.

But also in class (something which made his intelligence nearly secondary she thinks) was the human incarnation of the dead author, complete with the understanding of and insistence upon the certain impossibility and pain of human relations—the heavy knowledge of *what it means to be alive*. Something Nabokov himself knew, she guessed. Because he was, as evidenced in the class, a human being simply and absolutely—under pressure and not always able to hold the knowledge that one day one will die—and it solidified the attraction she felt to him—who he was in her imagination.

On the other hand, she feels false, trying to break down the reasons and aspects of the attraction this way.

Eventually it ends. Like that.

And because it ends, it becomes less clear. Her former knowledge of what it was begins to fade.

While it is happening—nearly from the day they meet, and certainly from the day she sits next to him in class, and feels him next to her, hears him breathing in her ear and inside of her, below her stomach she feels the attraction—it has nothing to do with these things she is able to consider now. Now that it is fading. She considers them now because it is no longer in her body.

While it is happening—from that first day she is able to be close to him to the last day that they spend together—the whole thing is in her body. When it is over it becomes less alive in the body. Slowly it begins to live in her mind, until eventually it is not in her body at all (even if she can occasionally recall the utter visceral feel of how it did live there) but is now in her mind, which is why she can do things like this: break down the attraction; break it down physically, intellectually, and replete with references to Nabokov. She can do this because it is leaving her. It is *becoming something less alive* in her body.

As it begins to live in her mind, it becomes a question: why was she attracted to the Dead Author, and thus to the live incarnation and/or extremely close relative (who seemed to possess many if not all of the qualities of the Dead Author)?

Sometimes she will want to answer the question. She will want to say that the attraction had more to do with something pure toward the man she is no longer dating, who happened to be the closest living relative[4] of the Dead author. And sometimes she will want to say that it had not so much to do with the Dead author at all (or her theoretical, acknowledged attraction to Him).

In the end, it will be difficult to know the dead thing. She will think it was the person himself, she was seduced by him, the living person—but she will also think that it was troubling (as seduction can be) to be seduced by him, the living person. It had been this way, she will think. She will think that she was flattered and *drawn in*, or *toward*; she will think she was offended. Who knows what she will think? For a while, she will try to answer this question and others. She will think about the now dead thing which for a time both drew her in and pushed her away—and then she will come to an ending, or the sense of one, and she will neither think about the Dead Author nor those books on her shelf at all.

---

4 Even this she knew was not a precise enough description of the relationship— that is, the living writer (as alive now to her) vs. the Dead author of the books on her shelf—yet she could go no further, and this seems to be the closest she'll allow without actually admitting that the person she was dating was in fact *one person* with the Dead author, if not exactly the same person. Sort of like God and Jesus? But that raised.

Suzanne Scanlon

Ben Slotky

Dear Retarded Black Kid

See? And that was better than I thought it would be. It went well, it went well, [looking out, slowly shaking head, slowly, slowly at the light, so bright] and I can hear you out there better than I can see you, and it went well, that did. [Looking at book, smiling, looking up, walking] You know, and the pressure's *on* with a name like that, with a name like *An Evening of Romantic Lovemaking*. Because, I mean, that seems like a lot, right? A lot of lovemaking? An entire *evening's* worth? An entire evening's worth; the bar is set *high*. Isn't it? High in the sky, and I don't know if I'm ever going be able to live up to this. How *could* I; what could I *do*, really, in this? There's no way I'm going to be able to live up to this. [Looks out into light] I'm going to fail, right? Aren't I going to? I have no choice *but* to fail; an entire *evening's* worth? First of all, and let's look at this, an evening's worth; that's a long time, ma'am, to be doing anything, right? And by doing that I've really, I've hamstrung my efforts? Is that it? Ham-stringed them? Like a Gilbert Sorrentino character, and that'd be something if it wasn't anything, and ma'am, could you google "obscure?" I see you're on your phone; could you google 'obscure' for me? Could you google 'pretentiously obscure?' Thank you, and I mean I'll be *here*, like where I am right now, and you just do that, right, and get back to me. Like google 'pretentious literary reference,' thank you, I'll be right here. And I have a bit later on about Google, honest I do. This will tie in and I guess now I bracket something? Ma'am? Do I put something in brackets? Because that seemed like a good idea before, but I'm not sure it is anymore, and an evening of any kind of anything is a long time, right? But an evening of *romantic lovemaking*, and let's, right, exactly, *romantic lovemaking?* Romantic, ma'am! A specific *type* of lovemaking!

Heretofore!

Forthwith!

Romantic lovemaking? Did my voice crack? Um, I don't know about *that?* I mean, and I'll say it, I'm not into making love. No, I'm not, it's not, I'm just not interested in it. Not really, and not like it's not like I'm, whatever, you know? I mean, it's fine, that's fine, lovemaking is, and there was a time where I was really interested in it. Not really, but I think a lot about gay guys, and not, and [laughs, looks around, surprised] and what happened? No, this isn't, and I see where this is turning into a, no, hear me out. I'm not gay, but I think gay people, like gay guys are really excited about things; you know how that is, ma'am? About gay guys being excited about things? And not *all of them,* I know, but that's the stereotype about them, that they're all like "AAH!" you know, [waving hands] and "Confetti!" and "Mustaches!" and "Flailing hands!" Right? "Party!" Right, and I just think are they *that* excited? I mean, what would I be that excited about? You know, as they are about guys? About *guys?* What guys? I don't know, so anyway the title of this book, and we're just at the title now, I've read like one story? We're still talking about the *title?* This is going to be a long *time,* ma'am. Like I don't see how we're ever getting out of here [laughs], I *don't.*

Do you have a baby sitter a home?

Like how long do you think this is going to *take?* Because it's taken years to get *here,* so if you think you're going to get out in an hour? [laughs, shakes head] I mean, no, oh no. And I'm laughing because it's funny and I'm shaking my head because I just said I was and you might want to call *home,* you know? Before we even get started, you *may* want to call home because this, this is not, we're going to be here for a while, so get comfortable. Get as comfortable as you can, because I don't think we're going anywhere for a while. No. No, and I'm laughing and smiling, and sometimes it hurts to smile, and I'll just put this out there, because of these sores I have in my mouth [sips bottle of water, pretends to spit], like I'm getting these *sores,* and can I just talk about this for one second? [Sips, pretends to offer it to crowd. No response, shrugs [[It's going to be important to stick with this even though it seems like it could quickly get a little too precious]]] And then we'll get started, we will. I have these *sores* in my mouth, and I'm kind of whispering now, because they *hurt.* I have them now, but they're going away, but I have had them.

Sores, ma'am.

Mouth, ma'am.

My, ma'am.

You ever have *sores* in your mouth, ma'am? You know how you some-times get *sores* in your mouth, like *canker sores?* Oh my gosh. They hurt so bad, I can't talk, which is bad because all I do *is* talk, or think about talking, or talk about thinking, whatever. I have sores in my mouth that prevent me from talking about thinking. You ever have that? You ever think, where's the stage direction gone? So I'm like I've got to do something with these sores; I've got to write my way out of these sores, you know? Because, and let me clarify ma'am, because I can't tell if I've made these things happen by talking about them. It's a mess, ma'am, it's a mess, and a whole evening of *this?* [Looking around, squinting into light] What's romantic about *this*, ma'am? And what's worse is that this is a set-up to a *joke*, like I'm doing all of this to tell a joke? Waving hands,[waving hands,] and this is a long way to go to read a story about *lozenges?* This one here? That's what I'm doing, though. That is exactly what's happening. This is the set-up to a joke from a story that's not even in here, not even in this book. Can that have happened? [Looks around, wide eyed, confused]. I mean, that could have happened; see this is what happens when things aren't labeled, ma'am. You *see?* [Looking out into light, wiping forehead with mic hand]. I mean, I know there is a bit about lozenges in here somewhere, something about lozenges and sores in mouths, something I am gong to do. A thing I will do later and this isn't from here, that isn't; it's from *The Hill I'm Going To Die On*, which is not this book, not this book at all. I'll tell you what I have on that, on this here, and it's [Head down, pulls papers from back pocket of Nice Titty Jeans, reads] about a guy giving a speech about lozenges. [Looks down at papers, one hand held out] A little background. These lozenges are selling well, exceeding expectations, but causing sores. He's speaking, the guy is and it's bright outside, but nobody seems to be com-menting on how bright it is. This is important, will be important, later on, the being bright will and maybe the point of view changes from person to per-son. It starts out with the main character speaking and then shifts and shifts, bounce, bounce. There and back, from one person to the other and this is all in the meeting, ma'am, from the story that's in the next book I am writing. [Looks up] Just so we're clear, ma'am. About what is happening; this [waves papers retrieved from back of Nice Titty Jeans] is not this [taps book]. These are two different [smiles, eyebrows raised, head titled] things. [Head down again] And it's the agenda, maybe? There's this idea of a story being told in the form of an agenda, a corporate agenda; maybe this is that. And I said 'there's this idea of a story' on purpose; this isn't my idea, it's an idea that ex-ists, that is labeled, codified, written down somewhere, that I am just relating.

And there's a lot of hemming and hawing and bouncing around and the story is shifting and bouncing, too as the meeting agenda never lights on the facts, never lights on the bright reality of the situation. And that fact, the one thing they can't get around is that these lozenges are causing sores in people's mouths. These lozenges are doing exactly what they are not supposed to do and everybody seems to be OK with it. One person who's speaking is thinking how he is getting too fat for his pants; he is feeling his belly press against his pants-band, his waist-band. Is it waist-band? Teenage waistband? [Looking up] And I'm asking now, and it's shifting, all the time, shifting, so it's important to stick to the facts.

Facts are, around table.

Facts are, bright lights.

Facts are, lozenges and sores in throats. Everything else is conjecture and irrelevant. Everything else is taking up everything else. [Looks up again, small smile] And that, what that was, what all of that was has nothing to do with what we are here for tonight, which is an evening, ma'am. An evening of romantic lovemaking.

And let's get into it, [puts papers in back pocket of Nice Titty Jeans, picks up book] so let me ask you people, is it racist to not get that show "Black People Eating Popcorn?" [Walking, sipping water] You know that show? "Black People Eating Popcorn?"

Ma'am?

Back?

Because I don't get it. I will say that right now, I don't under*stand* it, [pointing out in the audience]. Like I don't *understand* what the show's about. I don't understand what's going on. Do you? Do you understand what's going on? I mean it looks to *me* to be about black people eating popcorn. That's what it looks like to me. To me, ma'am. Like from what I can tell, and I want to say I've watched seven or maybe eight episodes of this show, and is he angry right now; that's you talking, and from what I can tell, I mean, all that it *is* is; and I don't mean that like *all that it is, is BLACK people eating popcorn*, clenched teeth, under breath. I don't mean it like *that*. I mean it like it's about people eating *popcorn*, like that's what it is, that's all it is. And you go "So, oh, it'd be *different* I guess if it was about *white* people eating popcorn?"

No.

It wouldn't. [Shaking head]. No, it would not.

It would be the same. It would be ridiculous. So it's not just saying that these people are black, that's not the point, the point is that it's ridiculous.

Ben Slotky

It's ridiculous that this is even on, I don't even understand why this is. [Shuts book, looks out]

See that's what this joke is in the beginning. This is fun, this is funny, explaining a joke is. See at the beginning it's one thing, and then it becomes a joke about race, that story does. See, nobody's racist. I'm not. I said I didn't understand what the deal was with that show "Black People Eating Popcorn." I don't and there is no show, is there ma'am? I made that up and I'm smiling at you now, smiling as I walk to the other end of the stage [smiling, walking across stage]. Black people are called black people because their skin is darker.

"Well, technically it's not *black*..."

No, I get it. Like, I get it. Some people are black. They are, ma'am, whether we want to admit it or not. To ourselves. Some people, and I'm saying this to you know, to all of you, some people? Are retarded. They are, they are. Mentally. Physically. This is something that happens. And I prayed that my newborn son wouldn't be. Retarded, ma'am. Prayed, ma'am [pointing]. Pointing, ma'am. I prayed because I don't know what I'd do if he was. I don't know what I'd do, I don't know how I'd do it. I don't know if I could handle it for a lot of reasons, one of which is because I've been so afraid of this my whole life. Of retarded people. Because they're terrifying, aren't they? Making those sounds and running around? You ever see one? And this isn't funny, I know, even though it is. It *was* funny earlier, though; popcorn and black people, and it will be again, soon, but a part of me thinks about this all the time. A part of me thinks it's going to take this, something like this. And when they say what's the thing that does it, does it for me, what did it for me, that could be it. Because they're going to have to ask, aren't they [looking into light, making menu face]? Don't they almost *have to* ask? Because this didn't do it [waving arms, looking around], none of this did. All this did was make this, right, this evening that we're sharing here tonight? This lovemaking ma'am, all this sweet lovemaking [smiles]. But what I choose to do in the face of that, in the face of this that's about to happen next, will be a reflection of who I am. Then and now, and I'll admit [small laugh], and you caught me there, I was lost. [Laughs] And I'm laughing because I had no idea where I was just then, none! But can you blame me? I mean, look around. [Looks around, pauses, starts again]. And sure that's a long way to go about a story about a retarded black kid, of course it is; admitted, admitted, but if you have a better way to do this, then you do it next time. [Grins, smirks, reads].

And I guess I'm going to start out by apologizing right off the bat. I shouldn't be writing this letter, I shouldn't; it's pointless and doesn't make any sense. It's like a new pencil, this story is; it has no point, and that isn't my joke, that one about the pencil isn't, it's my friend's who looks Jewish but isn't. It's his, not mine. It's his, not mine, and it's also probably crossing a line, maybe a couple of lines, and I don't want to be doing that, not with you, not with anybody, not anymore, so maybe I should just shut up and stop. I need some help, though, and I think you may be able to help me. So I am asking for help. But you know what?

No, I'm not.

Fuck you, black kid.

That's right, fuck you right in the big black retarded face. Fuck you, fuck your black skin, fuck your huge head, fuck the two apples you've got sticking out of your ears.

Fuck your blowing effs.

Fuck the whole thing and I know, and I know, and fine. Fine, and let's take a minute if you want but I said it and I meant it and I'll say it again. And I don't want any fucking any-thing about this, any clarification or explanation or anything because I know what you're thinking and you're wrong. This isn't some joke. I'm not trying to be funny and I'm not trying to be shocking even though I am and this is, I guess, whatever, move on. This isn't that, though, it isn't. This isn't about that, this is about me making fun of a retarded kid, a black retarded kid or a retarded black kid, either one, doesn't matter, same thing. And it isn't a social commentary and it doesn't question values or morals or mores or mention John Moreland, this kid who lived down the street from me when I was growing up; that kid ended up getting drunk and killing some other kid. This doesn't question moray eels or morel mushrooms. It does not. This isn't that, this isn't questioning that. It questions none of those things because this is about me making fun of a retarded black kid, you, the kid I'm writing to, nothing more, nothing less and fuck him anyway.

You were sticking apples in your ears. You were making a sound like this FFFFFFF. You were blowing that sound through your teeth. I mean, Jesus fucking Christ black kid, what am I supposed to do with that? I mean, come on. *Fuck you*, retarded black kid and I'm saying this to *you* now, saying this to your enormously, retardedly black head because what else can I do. Because who do you think you are, anyway, standing there, blowing effs, apples sticking out of ears? What is this, what is that and what am I supposed to do with that, with the that that's right there, right ahead of me in line?

Ben Slotky

And before this gets too out of hand and before I say something stupid, let me explain something even though I shouldn't have to. I love black people; everybody knows this because it's known. I love black people, love them! Even retarded people know this. Seriously, you would have to be totally retarded or totally black not to know how much I love black people and that was a joke right there and it's OK. It's OK, because it's like this.

When I was in junior high school, there were two twins, still were, still are and by that right there, I mean I'm clarifying and I know I don't have to. I am saying that it doesn't matter that I was in junior high school, that this part is irrelevant, new pencil, let's go. Me being in junior high school or senior high school or any kind of school doesn't make any difference to this story, what I'm saying, what this is.

This is what this is.

They were brothers, the two of them were, and they were retarded. Jeff and Zack. Two retarded twin brothers. They were ugly, they were poor, they wore glasses. And nothing that I just said is wrong and by wrong I mean mean or inaccurate. The things I say about them, about them being ugly, poor, and glasses-wearing, those are all true things and none of these things says anything about me at all even though you think it does and how dare you for thinking that about me, me who has never done anything to anyone anyway.

Anyway.

Everybody was horribly mean to them, to these retarded kids. They would tell Jeff and Zack to eat things that they shouldn't eat, like boogers and pencil erasers and chewed up gum. We used to call that ABC Gum. That meant Already Been Chewed. Anyway some kids, anyway these kids, they would throw books at Jeff and Zack. They would yell. This is true. I a did anything bad to either one of these kids in my entire life. This is true, too, I asked. One time I asked somebody about this.

Here is what I said:

Let me axe you this. Can you remember any time when I, specifically, was mean to either Jeff or Zack? Outside of making fun of Jeff when he died? This is crucial, I think.

And I wrote this and said axe instead of ask because I want people to think I am clever and interesting even though I don't care if they do.

This person said no she didn't think I ever said anything mean except for that one thing, that one thing that wasn't mean.

Retarded Black Kid, here's what happened. I made fun of a retarded guy who died in the trunk of a car. I made a joke about him dying after locking himself in the trunk of a car. Is that bad? Is that, and I'm asking you as a retarded person here, is that a bad thing for me to have done? I don't think it is, because here's why. The story was this. The story was that Jeff or Zack, one of the two retarded twins, one of them used to break into cars and hide in their trunks. That is a thing he did, one of them, whichever. They did that, he did that; he would lock himself in a trunk. So one time he is locking himself in a trunk this retarded kid is. Just up and about, locking himself in a trunk, an evening of trunk-locking-in-ing. He's doing that, and he does it, he locks himself in a trunk.

Kerplunk.

Spelunk.

These are the sounds of a trunk locking, Black Retarded Black Kid, that's what those are, those were, those sounds. A trunk is being locked and there is a retarded kid in it. And he is feeling whatever feeling he feels when he locks himself in the trunk. Whatever feeling that is compelling him to lock himself in the trunk, that makes him do this, that makes him *want* to do this, even though there is screaming and light and noise that is telling him not to do this, saying no Jeff or Zack no don't do this you can't do this this is dangerous don't you see and they are saying that and Jeff or Zack is hearing that and he is doing that anyway he wants to do that anyway this is what he wants to do you want to do this and that is what he is doing that is the feeling he is feeling as he hears that sound, as he feels himself feeling that feeling that feeling that he wanted that he needed this is the feeling this is the feeling that he is having you know that feeling, that feeling ma'am, that is what he is feeling and that feeling stays. And stays.

And stays and stays and now he is feeling something else, Jeff or Zack is, he cannot breathe. There is no air no air in this trunk and it is dark and it has always been dark ,dark in the trunks, but now it is dark now Jeff or Zack *knows* that it's dark *understands* that it's dark and as he is in the dark and the air is gone and he understands this the last thing he thinks the only thing he thinks is boy am I fucking retarded. You know? I mean, *what am I doing?* That is who I am, I am the type of person who makes this joke. This guy, this kid, this dead retarded guy never did anything bad to anybody and I made fun of him, of him dying. That is who I am and this is who you are.

Retarded Black Kid, one time I saw a sign that said A Woman Is Raped Every Six Seconds. It was a billboard for I think the YWCA. I was driving by and saw it.

A Woman Is Raped Every Six Seconds it said and I said the same woman? Like that, like a question. The same woman? That's my first question, right there, I said. Because if it's the same woman.... I mean, that sounds wrong, even to me. I DO have to ask what she was wearing though, I said.

I shrugged my shoulders.

I mean, that's only fair. I said this, Black Retard, I said this all out loud to myself. That was a joke. People don't like rape jokes, I know, but that is pretty funny, I think, and I also think it is why people don't like me very much, because I say things like that. Plus I raped all those people.

Let me axe you this, Black Retarded Blacky. What song do you like better, the King of Carrot Flowers or the Queen of Cans and Jars? What's that? Not a real question? Maybe not and maybe it isn't, but that's not the point. The point is, you may as well've been wearing a goddamn cape in the supermarket, Black Kid. You were untouchable like Costner, unstoppable like a Denzel train. You and that guy who got his arms ripped off in that combine. I've talked about him before, to you I think and if I haven't, here it goes. Act surprised, Black Kid.

Once upon a time, there was a guy. The guy lived someplace up north, like a Montana, like a Minnesota. Like a Dakota, South OR North, because when you think about it, and believe me Black Kid I have, when you think about it, South can be pretty fucking North, it just depends on where you are. So he's there, this guy is, up and North in wherever and it's cold and he is going out to do some work on his farm. He is a farmer, did I say this? Would you know if I did? Anyhoo, this guy goes out into the cold, into the North, into the farm, to work, to work. He walks out to the field and it's far from his door, from his front door. It's maybe a couple of hundred yards, I'm guessing and if it isn't, it was still pretty far, I'm not sweating it, because who am I talking to who, here? You. Yeah. I'm pretty sure the second you pull those apples out of your goddamn ears you're going to fact-check the shit out of this. Again, and please stop interrupting, it's rude, and the reason I said shit and goddamn earlier was to demonstrate that this is an act, a character, like that guy in the Dakota or Montana. He is a part of this story I am telling even though he is real just like that character narrating this story is an act, a character even though he is real. That guy is going out in to work in the cold North farm and he gets an arm caught in a machine. It's a thresher, it's a combine. It has turbines and steel and blades and it is spinning, gears and blades are spinning and his arm is caught. Caught in the machine, caught in the North, caught in the cold. It is caught tight, he is enmeshed, ensconced, enveloped, his arm is. His arm is en-everything'd by this machine, the machine is ripping and tearing his arm off. This is happening, happening in the cold North snow. And he screams and watches his arm being en-everything'd and he screams and he tries to pull it out, his arm, because that is all you can do. That is all you can do when your arm is being destroyed by a steel machine in the cold North snow; all you can do is try and pull it out and stop it from happening and that is what he does Black Kid. He tries to pull it out and I know. And I know and I know and even you know, you with the apples still in your ears, you know what he does. You all know what he does. He tries to pull his arm out with the other arm and you know what happens, you know, you do. You know his arm, his other arm gets caught. You know this because this is what happens, what has to happen in this story. There is nothing else that can happen in this story, Black Kid, apples in ears or not. And he tries, Black Kid, he does. He puts his other arm in this machine and the machine, I'm imagining, is making noises now. I am imaging because I am assuming, Black Kid, and I know the saying. "You know what happens when you ASSume? You end up incorrectly describing the potential sounds that could be made when a man tries to free his arm from the spinning gears of a combine or thresher with his other arm." Of course I know that saying, but that's not with this, this is not an assumption. And I'm not a detective, not good at detecting, but the machine, by definition, would have to be making noise. Because the machine, whether it's a thresher or a combine or a whatever, doesn't matter, whatever it is, it was not designed to mangle arms. This is not an International Harvester Arm Mangler. This is not a John Deere or a Komatsu Arm Mangler. This is not supposed to happen so the machine is making sounds, I'm guessing, chipping sounds, mangling sounds, wet and clogging sounds, and the man is making sounds, screaming sounds, pleading sounds, what is happening sounds, and all of this, I'm guessing, is in the middle of the sound of snow falling down which even you and I know doesn't sound like anything at all. And this is going on Black Kid, this is happening and has already happened.

And I'm imagining blood is everywhere, red blood in the white snow,

Ben Slotky

blood so red it's black on the snow, black as your head, black as your apple, and he is dying. His arms are being ripped off and he is dying and he is dying and there is ripping and there are sounds and then it is over, it is over, he is out, out of the machine. He is out, and I don't know how, doesn't matter, but he is out of the machine, Black Kid, and I am whispering and it is over and both of his arms are gone, ripped off. They are in the machine, they are in the still spinning machine, and he starts to crawl. He starts to crawl through the snow. He starts to crawl through the snow on his belly to the house in the North in the snow and I'm guessing the machine is still spinning, still chugging and working. I am guessing he can still hear wet gears gnawing his arm parts, flesh and bone and tendons, parts and muscles in metal gears, spinning spinning and he hears that, right? He has to hear that, doesn't he? But, and I think I'm right, I think he only hears this for a while, because he is crawling, crawling through the snow in the cold in the North on his belly. And that quiet that was so quiet just a second ago, was this just a second ago? It seems like forever. That quiet is so loud now.

Now.

Now that quiet is all there is, this sound of the snow falling, this sound of the him breathing. This sound of the him crawling, that is all there is, that is all there is anymore. And he crawls I don't know how fucking far, Kid, you beautiful child, he crawls all the way to his front door and he crawls up the front steps and he crawls I don't know how into his house. And all of this happened my son, all of it, every word, every word, and he crawled into his living room and he knocked the phone down off of the cabinet where it was resting, knocked it to the floor, and he dialed 911, kid. He grabbed a pencil off the floor and dialed 911 with his teeth. And the ambulance came.

And he lived.

And he is alive today.

And this is what happened.

And I am asking you, kid, I am asking you how it is possible to ever say anything to this person ever? A word, how could you say a word? I am asking you this. I am asking you this, because if anybody would know, it would almost certainly have to be you. How can you say a word, how can you complain in front of this person? How can you do anything in front of him, ever? He has become invincible, untouchable. He is like you. I cannot say anything to you, standing there, standing here, in line, in front of me. I cannot say anything to you, making FFFF noises with your mouth and teeth, two apples in your ears. I can't say this to you, what I am saying, but this is what I would say. I would say and don't think I don't notice you have no parents with you right now. There are no parents anywhere around here; I am the only one around. My fourth child will be born in April, Black Kid. I have one, two, three boys already. I am afraid my fourth child will be retarded. That's what this is, Black Kid. I am afraid that child will be you. [Looks up, exhales]

Powerful! Thank you, that's a good one, that is a really good one. [Drink of water, wipe forehead and head.]

Sweat.

Smile.

And if you guys don't mind, I'd like to start this again. [Laughs] Like this whole thing [points to book with one hand, waves in air with other], this whole thing; do you mind? [Looking out in crowd] And let me explain, I mean this opening, how I opened this, [pointing toward book], this here in the front? That's not right. [pacing, looking down, hand on head]That wasn't right, it was *good*, but it's not where that part goes. This part should go there, [flipping pages, stopping, pointing], yeah, *this* goes at the beginning. This should be the beginning, so let's [stopping, smiling] let's start like this.

Ben Slotky

Nonfiction

T. Louise Freeman-Toole

Heading North

I learned more from Dave than just the craft of writing. When I was in a class he co-taught with Doug Hesse, Dave wrote me a letter taking me to task for being too harsh in my assessment of other students' essays. "I believe empathy is the very most important capacity in an artist," he wrote, "and I mean not gooey, 'I love everybody!' empathy but hard-headed imagination, the ability to vault the wall of Self and occupy, even temporarily and speculatively, other human lives. What I am speaking of, of course, is 'spirituality' as it applies to 'art.' To the extent that I can get past Self and Self's immediate reactions and can attend truly to Other and Other's reality and needs and emotions and wellbeing, I am enlarged rather than diminished." These words have stayed with me over the years, reminding me that showing generosity of spirit—not only toward other writers but toward every individual—enriches my life immeasurably.

When I asked for a room at the Mush-on-Inn for two nights, the clerk responded, "What's the matter, your car break down?" No one who doesn't have to spends forty-eight hours in the dreary little town of Tok, Alaska.

"I'm waiting for the mail plane to Eagle," I explained.

The woman had the doughy skin and bleary eyes many Alaskans have by winter's end. She just nodded, not inquiring why I was going to the isolated community just 122 miles from the Arctic Circle, well before the start of tourist season. If she had asked, I wouldn't have known what to say. It was unclear to me why I was being driven to go north, ever farther north.

Tired after my long bus trip from Canada, I immediately went to my room and took a nap. When I awoke, I lay in bed wondering what I was doing in this lonely crossroads, far from my home and family in Washington State.

Two long and boring days later, the pilot picked me up at the motel. As square-jawed and jauntily confident as any WWI flying ace, I could easily imagine him in a leather flight helmet with a dashing scarf around his neck. He drove out to the airstrip, threw a couple of bags of mail and my baggage into the back of the Cessna, and the two of us were off, with me sitting in the co-pilot's seat. We flew for a long time over snowy, jagged mountains that continued in all directions as far as I could see, untrammeled wilderness stretching all the way to Canada. The pilot shouted above the roar of the engine, "There's your first look at the Yukon River." I stared out the window at the broad frozen river heading, like I was, directly north.

We followed the graceful curves of the Yukon over islands of dark spruce until the plane finally banked and circled over a cluster of buildings set on a high riverbank. A toy town, with a tiny church, a white schoolhouse, and a scattering of Lincoln Log cabins. It nestled at the foot of a promontory of rock thrust into the river. I peered out the window, forehead pressed to the glass, enchanted with the place before we'd even landed.

My feeling for Eagle was to become not just a simple infatuation, but a conviction that this was where I needed to be right now, never mind that my real life existed 1,500 miles away. It wouldn't be merely a beautiful setting and a picturesque little town that made me want to stay, but also a solitary fur trapper—all gentle hands and soft beard, smelling of wool and wood smoke—whom I came to love with a passion so dazzling in intensity it became an obsession, consuming my life, destroying my marriage, and bringing me to the brink of insanity.

I hadn't spent more than eight consecutive weeks at my home in Eastern Washington in the past six months. I missed my kids, although my older son, Emlyn, was away at college and my younger son, Ambrose, was busy with his rock music and earning his GED. I had to admit I didn't miss my husband, Thomas, and his constant emotional turmoil, which all too often erupted into anger directed at me.

Normally a homebody, I had been hopscotching from one writing residency to another, from Sitka, Alaska, to New Hampshire, and back to Alaska, this last time to Skagway, a town of five hundred people at the far end of the ferry line that sailed from one isolated community to another along the Inside Passage. I'd arrived on the ferry when winter was still spitting sleet into the wind that blew constantly down the narrow valley wedged between the mountains. I stayed until spring carried in the influx of young summer workers, each looking for his or her own Alaska adventure.

T. Louise Freeman-Toole

My grandmother Smokey and her husband, Scotty, had lived in Skagway during the 1950s, before Alaska gained statehood. I was there to work on a book about her life. Smokey was fifty-seven and Scotty was sixty-one when they moved to what she called a "crazy little almost ghost town" of empty cabins and boarded-up storefronts, populated by an assortment of oddball characters. Smokey and Scotty had met at a diner in Manhattan Beach, California, when the waitress mixed up their breakfast orders. Scotty was an old sourdough who had lived in Alaska Territory since the 1920s but he was working, at the time, as a taxi driver in Southern California. Smokey was captivated by his tales of life on the Last Frontier. Six weeks later they were married. She couldn't wait to experience Alaska herself, and it wasn't long before they moved north, living briefly in Sitka and Juneau before landing in Skagway. In the past two years, I'd traveled to all the places they had lived in Southeast Alaska, searching for clues about Smokey and why she, a middle-aged widow, would have suddenly re-married, left her elderly father, son, and grandchildren behind, and taken off for a life of adventure in the far north. If I could figure that out, maybe I could ascertain why I, too, was drawn to Alaska despite all my ties to home.

By the time I was two, Scotty had retired from his job at the Skagway power and telephone company, and he and Smokey had moved to the bush, finding their "haven of peace" on Thimbleberry Island, thirty-five miles from Ketchikan. After five contented years there, they started feeling their age and relocated to a cabin a few miles from Sitka. The secluded cove was accessible only by trail or boat, which suited them just fine.

It was a special occasion whenever one of Smokey's long, detailed letters arrived in our mailbox in Redondo Beach, California. My dad would read it out loud to the whole family after dinner, all seven of us children sitting at the table, rapt. She wrote about the deer and squirrels they tamed to eat out of their hands, the wolves they watched cavort on the beach over on the mainland, the bear that kept coming into the cabin clearing, and the nifty bush plane that landed on the water just yards from shore, bringing mail and groceries.

It wasn't just my grandmother's life in Alaska that fascinated me: it was Smokey herself, although—or perhaps because—I only met her once. She and Scotty came down to Redondo Beach to visit my family when I was ten years old. While my friends' grandmas had their hair colored and coiffed and wore dowdy print dresses, my Alaska grandmother wore pants and her straight, steel-gray hair was cut short like a man's.

I thought Smokey got her name because she had a husky laugh and her breath smelled like cigarette smoke and her clothes like wood smoke. But when I grew up, I learned that she became "Smokey" when they moved to Alaska, because her paintings sold better if they were signed with a masculine name. She sent us a painting each Christmas, often of a cabin beneath the northern lights. The scent of wood smoke wafted out of the crate when my dad pried off the lid. It smelled like Alaska to me.

During Smokey and Scotty's all-too-short stay, I hung on my grandmother's every word as she narrated an exciting tale about the search for a plane that had crashed near the island, or a legend told by an old Tlingit hunter who happened by in a boat and stayed for a "mug-up" (the local term for a cup of coffee). Smokey would pull a cigarette out of a silver case, pick up her long ivory cigarette holder shaped like a polar bear, and put the cigarette in its gaping mouth. Gesturing with the holder in hand, she'd continue her story, laughing loudly and often. I was enthralled; she seemed so exotic and larger than life. And so unlike me.

Throughout my childhood, I didn't venture far without one or more of my six siblings. I felt safe in the crowd. I was small for my age and prone to nervous stomach aches. My parents treated me like I was fragile, and I grew up to think of myself as weak. Piano lessons were a torment since I was too shy to speak a word to my teacher, a French WWII vet with a disconcerting blind eye. Despite years of swimming lessons, I never swam far out in the ocean, fearing the rip tides would sweep me away. I clung to my older sister at Girl Scout camp—a terrifying experience among all those strangers—and refused to ever go again. I'd rather stay home and read. I loved our family camping trips to the Sierra, where the gentle soughing of the wind through the pine trees suited me more than the crashing of waves on the beach a block from our house. There was something about the mountains that emboldened me. I clambered up rocks, ventured into rivers, and went on exploring expeditions with my little sister. But back at home, I retreated into my role as the timid one, the sensitive one.

I felt I would never grow up to be like my brave, strong, adventurous grandmother who lived in the wilderness, shot guns, and cooked venison on a wood stove. I realized even then that my fearfulness of new people and experiences meant I was to live a circumscribed life. I read about adventurers and explorers, scientists and inventors, and knew I would make no great discoveries, explore no new places once I was outside the family's fold. Aside from an occasional trip to the mountains, I envisioned I would spend my life in libraries or curled up by the fireplace, reading. It didn't sound like a bad way to live, but it wasn't the stuff of stories like Smokey's.

I did, indeed, spend much of my adult life surrounded by books, working at a variety of libraries: a friendly small town library; a city library frequented by homeless people; a university library where I descended into the dank underground stacks to retrieve obscure tomes; a health sciences library where I checked out real skulls to medical students. But over the coming years, my life was to take some unexpected turns, and I found myself following in my grandmother's footsteps more than I could have imagined as a child.

I had received a writer-in-residence fellowship at the Klondike Gold Rush National Historical Park in Skagway to work on the book about Smokey. When my allotted month was up, in early April, I couldn't bear the thought of going home. My ears were full of the ghostly sound of Skagway's wind, my eyes were full of the underwater-green of the northern lights, my heart was full of the wildness that was Alaska.

I rashly decided that my husband and the boys could wait. I realized it was selfish to put my needs above theirs, but when was the last time I had done that? I'd put my family first for so many years that I hardly recognized—let alone acted on—my own desires anymore. Perhaps it was the moment to do just that. Emlyn was enjoying his sophomore year at college in the western part of the state. Whenever I talked to Thomas, he said, "Ambrose and I are having a great time together. He doesn't need you." My youngest was just seventeen, and I didn't want to believe he no longer needed a mother, but I took my husband's word for it.

When I called Thomas, he said, "I miss you. When are you coming home?"

"Maybe in a few weeks. I want to go someplace farther north. Everyone says you haven't seen the real Alaska until you've been to the Interior—the area up around Fairbanks. It's huge and practically empty except for some villages out in the bush."

On previous trips, I had only been to southeast part of the state. There the mountains were lower and the ocean was a protected passageway; the fact that most of the towns were on islands made me feel claustrophobic, unable to get in a car and head out in any direction. Smokey had loved the sense of self-containment to be found on an island, but it was not for me. She had never been north of Skagway, but I wanted to experience the vast expanse of Alaska's Interior. I realized that it may not be the wisest thing to do. By stretching our separation, I risked losing what tenuous connection remained between my husband and me. Thomas reluctantly gave his okay and then hung up, as usual, without saying goodbye.

For the past year, my friends had started asking me why I was gone so much. My answer was always, "I'm researching a book. I need somewhere quiet to write," which was true, but there was more to it than that. When I was away from my home in Pullman, Washington, for extended periods, I was usually more at peace, especially here in Alaska. I always felt alone, whether I was at home or hundreds, even thousands of miles away. Thomas and I had slept in separate rooms for years. We were still intimate, but in a disconnected way. We came together, then separated, each retiring to our own private space. We told each other it was because we liked different sleeping environments: he preferred the heat turned to eighty, the fan on high, and the TV going; I needed an open window, a light quilt, and silence.

Travel was not only an escape for me. The Alaska I had imagined as a girl had begun to materialize before me, becoming clearer with each trip—six in all now—I made north. My far-away grandmother, who had died before I'd gotten a chance to really know her, was becoming clearer, too. My friends asked, as well, "Aren't you getting a bit … um … obsessed with your grandma?" I knew my consuming interest in Smokey had started to seem a little strange, so I joked, "All biographers start to identify with their subjects." But I could trace my obsession—if that's what it was—to the spring I graduated from college.

For a graduation present, I had asked my parents to send me to Alaska to visit Smokey. At last I would get to meet, as an adult, this figure who had fascinated me since childhood. I imagined myself sitting in her room at the Sitka Pioneer Home, listening to absorbing tales of her adventures. I'd hear more about the island, her encounters with wildlife, the risks and rewards of life in the bush. She would even tell me about her childhood and what my father had been like as a boy.

But Smokey died just three weeks before I graduated. I was devastated. My only opportunity to get to know my grandmother had vanished. I had no idea at the time that this missed encounter would alter the course of my life. If I had been able to meet her, much of my curiosity would have been satisfied. Perhaps the reality of the aged, infirm woman before me would have dispelled the almost mythological status she had attained. And I would have gotten the answer to the question I longed to ask: Why did you move so far north from your family and everything you'd ever known?

When claiming Smokey's belongings, stored in the basement of the Pioneer Home, my dad and I discovered a treasure trove of trunks and boxes full of old journals, photos, memorabilia, and letters going back as far as WWI, all meticulously organized and labeled. I shipped the stuff home and, over the years, read every bit of it. Sometimes I had to use a magnifying glass because as she got older, she stopped keeping a journal and instead noted their daily activities on a calendar, squeezing as many as eighty words into a one-by-one-and-a-half inch square. This was how I got to know my grandmother—through her writing.

I discovered details of Smokey's early life that even my dad didn't know. (He spent most of his childhood at boarding school and said he barely knew his mother.) She was the only child of a wealthy newspaper publisher and stockbroker. Her first memory was of crawling around on a polar bear rug by the fire in her parents' Chicago apartment. By the time they moved to proper and prosperous Pasadena, California, she'd become an irrepressible tomboy, tearing her stockings climbing trees and artfully escaping the watchful eye of her governess. She later attended a private school, the main purpose of which was to prepare girls to take their place as society women, supervising their large households, attending teas and balls, and raising money for various charities. For the school newspaper she wrote a tongue-in-cheek advice column under the name Madame de Schnitzenheimer. She once delighted in thumbing her nose at her mother (the former owner of a stylish millinery shop in downtown Chicago) by advising one girl how to make a picture hat for less than six hundred dollars using only two wooden mixing bowls, pink crepe paper, orange and purple silk ribbons and four pampas grass plumes dyed Irish green. I was glad to learn my grandmother had always loved books. While waiting for the cross-town trolley, she used to sneak into the public library to peruse collections of fairy tales, which her mother—disapproving of such nonsense—forbid her to read.

When the U.S. entered WWI and college grew dull with the departure of her male chums, all of whom enlisted immediately, she dropped out of the University of Southern California to become a reporter for her father's newspaper, loving nothing more than an exciting night of ambulance-chasing. One of her many beaus wrote at the time, "You want to do everything that anybody else ever did, even if it was a boy that did it." In the roaring twenties, she made a terrific flapper, dancing her way into the arms of a blonde-haired playboy—my father's father. They moved to Carmel, California, a bohemian coastal community, all free love and bathtub gin. It was only after that marriage ended in divorce and her next husband died in a car accident, that she finally met the love of her life: Scotty. Wouldn't anyone find a woman like that worth writing about? Still, it was the last three decades of Smokey's life—her Alaska years—that had captured my imagination. There was something that had drawn her here and had grabbed hold of her. I felt that pull, too, and wanted to understand why.

Whatever the reason I was in Alaska, I found that it allowed me the space to try to figure out what to do about my troubled marriage and the chaotic, noisy environment our household had become. Thomas made his living by giving private music lessons at home, and the sound, which I had once enjoyed, was starting to drive me crazy. In an effort to get us out of graduate school loan debt, Thomas expanded his studio into a music academy that had gradually taken over most of the house. All the furniture—except the piano—had been moved out of the living room and the dining room. Chorus took place in the living room, the kiddy orchestra rehearsed in the dining room, and music theory classes were held in the family room. I felt trapped in my bedroom, where I was trying to write. I ended up working at night when the house was quiet, but then I couldn't sleep during the day, and I became groggy and irritable, especially with Thomas.

Once our children grew too old for playing in the backyard, it had become my private refuge. The music coming from the house was just a distant, pleasant sound as I tended my garden. But the students eventually invaded the yard, swarming across my patch of wildflowers and fighting noisily over space on the trampoline. My life, once safe and predictable and fairly comfortable, had started to spiral out of my control.

Sitting on the steps of the park rangers' housing where I'd been staying in Skagway, I studied my Alaska map, looking for a place to go. I set my sights on Eagle, a town of 135 people on the banks of the Yukon River, 500 miles to the north. There, I learned on the Internet, I could have a cabin for a month, rent-free, if I volunteered part-time for the historical society. Perfect.

It was not an easy—or cheap—place to get to. From Skagway, I caught a ride across the Canadian border to Whitehorse in the Yukon Territory, 110 miles away. There I spent the night at a hostel before taking an eight-hour bus ride to Tok. The only way to get from there to Eagle at that time of year was to fly on the twice-weekly mail plane. There was a road—a largely unpaved track that led 170 miles over the mountains—but it was closed for the winter, which, this far north, lasted from October to April. When I arrived in Tok, the Taylor Highway was still covered with wind-blown drifts of snow and wouldn't be plowed clear for another month.

The "bus" from Whitehorse to Tok turned out to be a battered van the size of an airport shuttle. The passenger door was held closed with a bungee cord. The only other person aboard was a red-haired, freckled Scotsman named, predictably enough, Angus, who said he was on his way to Fairbanks where he intended to make his living playing the bagpipes. He had been invited to play at a local bar, some kind of temporary gig; he was sure this indicated there was a pressing demand for bagpipers in the Fairbanks area.

I asked what his previous occupation had been in Scotland and he said, "I'm a deerstalker." I had to ask twice, unsure if I'd understood his brogue.

"What is that, exactly?" I asked.

"Well," he explained, "it's very like your hunting guides here." He was the personal deerstalker for a British viscount on the Isle of Jura off the northern coast of Scotland, a place the Vikings had called Deer Island. He looked out the window at the rocky outcroppings, bogs, and stunted trees of the passing landscape—perhaps not too unlike the Isle of Jura—and said in a melancholy tone of voice that Alaska made the wilds of Scotland seem very small.

I asked Angus what his job-hunting strategy would be, imagining it might be hard going making cold calls to restaurants and hotels, trying to sell them on the idea of hiring a bagpiper. He pulled out a letter of recommendation from the viscount himself. It bore an impressive-looking letterhead, but the text consisted of a single sentence, neatly centered in mid-page.

"We had a bit of a communication problem," Angus confessed.

I nodded. "I can see that."

He read out the couple dozen words, which attested to the fact that Angus had been in the viscount's employ as a deerstalker for a period of two years. The Scotsman folded the letter with an air of great satisfaction, as if it had been quite a coup to have wrested that one line from the taciturn viscount.

I asked Angus if he wanted some beef jerky, which he recognized as a food of the American frontier. He chewed it with a thoughtful look, as if he were tasting pemmican straight from Kit Carson's parfleche.

Two days after bidding good-bye to Angus and wishing him luck, I caught the plane to Eagle. When we touched down at the gravel airstrip, Nancy, the head of the historical society, was there to meet me. Short and efficient-looking, she was stronger than she appeared, handily throwing my baggage into the back of her truck. As we drove into town, she said, "We don't get many visitors before the road opens. What brings you here? You couldn't have come all this way just for a volunteer position." I told her I was writing a book about my grandmother's life and wanted to see what it was like to live in the bush—the same answer I'd given Thomas, though somehow, it seemed more plausible here. Nancy nodded, as if one excuse for getting out of the Lower 48 was as good as another.

In my travels around the state, I'd heard people give many reasons for moving to Alaska. Some were short: "The Army." "A guy, what else?" Others were more elaborate: "My wife left me, so I sailed solo from Japan to Alaska on a thirty-three-foot steel sailboat. It took seventy-seven days." "My great-great-grandfather came up in 1898 to strike it rich in the Klondike Gold Rush. Seventeen years later he went back to Boston, still broke, and gathered up his wife and family—they'd been waiting for him all that time— and brought them to Ketchikan." Even a simple explanation like "a job" was likely to have a story behind it: "I answered an ad in the Seattle paper for a waitressing job in Anchorage, one-way ticket included. When I got up here, I found out it was at a topless bar. That was back in the seventies when the pipeline was being built. The oil workers had tons of cash and cocaine. I had a great time."

Nancy took me on a tour of Eagle, driving up and down the small grid of streets, getting a wave or a sign of acknowledgment from everyone we passed. I noticed a large hand-lettered sign telling drivers to observe the speed limit, which kept the roads safe for pedestrians, bicyclists, schoolchildren, and sled dog teams. The truck puttered along accordingly—at fifteen miles per hour.

The whole town was little more than a scattering of log cabins amongst the trees, along with a general store, laundromat, gas station, post office, and a pool hall that had sat empty for years. We drove past the library. A boy banged out the door and went on his way with an armful of books. Nancy explained that the library was run by volunteers, whose tasks included splitting kindling, keeping the fire going in the wood stove, and making sure there was toilet paper in the outhouse. With the restaurant closed in winter, the library was the only gathering place in the community.

As Nancy drove past several restored historical buildings, she recounted a bit of Eagle's history, dating back to its heyday during the Klondike Gold Rush at the turn of the twentieth century. She pointed out the tiny log cabin city hall, which was still in use, and the well house, built in 1903, where the residents still came to get water in five-gallon buckets. I admired the handsome old courthouse and the customs house. The latter was necessary because of Eagle's proximity to the Canadian border—six miles away by land, twelve by river. Going through customs these days was conducted on the honor system. In summer, people floating down the river from Dawson City in the Yukon Territory were supposed to stop in Eagle at the boat landing and use the phone there, which automatically connected them to the customs agent, who lived nearby. He walked down to stamp their passports.

A few of the buildings were remnants of Fort Egbert, the army headquarters established in 1899 to bring law and order to an area full of rowdy miners. Eagle had swelled to 1,700 people, over ten times its current population, before the boom went bust and the miners moved north, lured by rumors of fortunes to be made in Nome and Fairbanks. Saloons, dance halls, whorehouses, and other businesses that had catered to them closed, and in 1911, short-lived Fort Egbert was abandoned. Eventually the sternwheelers that had brought gold prospectors, settlers, and freight stopped running from Dawson City, seventy miles upriver, and Eagle languished for decades. It remained isolated until the 1950s when the Taylor Highway was carved out of the mountains, finally connecting Eagle by road to the world outside.

The town was so quiet now—so blessedly quiet—that it was hard to imagine it had ever bustled with people and commerce. Nancy pulled up in front of a one-room cabin with an outhouse in the yard. This was where I would stay, undisturbed for an entire month. After unpacking, I walked back through town and climbed the hill above a huge barn that had once held dozens of army mules, and I looked down on the old military parade ground. The long open length of it, leading to the river, now served in summer as a grass airstrip for local pilots. Two small planes—one bright blue, the other bright red—sat, noses up, to one side.

The late afternoon sun threw corrugated Eagle Bluff into high relief, showing every ruddy crag and crevice outlined with snow. A tree-covered island sat gracefully in mid-river. Behind me rose the wooded flanks of a mountain. Before me, across the wide Yukon, lay a great expanse of forest that stretched to far-off snowy peaks in Canada. The impression was of both vast distance and sheltered space. I'd never seen a more beautiful place in my life. I stood in the cold, taking in the view for a long time. As dusk fell, warm lights appeared in the cabin windows below, and all of Eagle seemed safe and welcoming. I walked down the hill, returning to my own small cabin with the feeling I'd stumbled upon the one spot in the world that might cure whatever was ailing me.

T. Louise Freeman-Toole

C.S. Giscombe

From *Into and Out of Dislocation*

I caught the Greyhound back to Seattle, and the next morning at 5 I got on the city bus for the long ride out to SeaTac to catch the 7 AM cheap flight to O'Hare. The bus was packed with people going to work—it was jolly, everyone knew each other, most of the passengers were black. Some ways into the trip a friendly man sat down next to me and we talked about this and that for a while and he asked if I was on my way to a job. I replied that I was on my way to Illinois to get my car and then to drive it back here and then on into Canada. "It's a ridiculous story," I said, feeling oddly apologetic as I imagined—maybe there on the bus for the first time—the many huge states I'd soon be driving across for days. We were near my companion's stop and as he gathered himself into his coat and rose he reminded me that I had to do what I had to do and that, throughout it, I should hang tough. "And we'll see you when you get back," he said as he got off the bus, blessing me and my ridiculous story.

Seattle had been, as usual, warm and humid; Chicago was harsh—a slate sky and that wind. Out some distance from the main terminals at O'Hare is the interface with various types of more public transit—the subway, the buses. You have to walk outside, into the wind, to get there. I was headed for the subway and asked directions of a black man in a uniform of some sort—he was standing out at the end of a concrete pier over parking lots and bus stops, over a basin of vehicular activity. Many of the men and women I'd been with on the city bus in Seattle had been wearing uniforms similar to his, generic uniforms, the kind likely to have your name sewn in above the breast pocket. Frederick Douglass once described the poor fabric of his own clothes as "negro cloth." Nearby a group of black boys, eleven

and twelve year olds, was running for a bus—"Hold the goddamn motherfucka," the fat boy called to his friends who were closer to it, "hold that
motherfucka!" His voice hadn't changed yet, it was shrill and loud, the shriek
of a child. Everyone on the pier turned and looked. "You know that's the
Projects bus," the man in the uniform said, classing us off, separating himself
and me from the boys.

I went down to Union Station and got the *Texas Eagle* back to
Bloomington. My friend Ron Strickland met me at the Amtrak depot in
Normal—Bloomington's twin city, the municipality across Division Street—
and helped me, the next day, get through some errands. I bought the Swede
an oil change and a new Sony radio; I tried to buy a block-warmer but Süd's,
the local dealership, didn't carry them—"There's been no call for 'em around
here," the service manager said, and assured me I could get one "up there
where you're going." By 3 o'clock I'd done all the car stuff and was almost
ready to be on my way again.

There was the typical confusion about drugs—my wife and daughter were already in Fort George and my wife was going to need prescriptions refilled and soon—so I spent my last moments in Bloomington at the
Osco Pharmacy counter reviewing the rules for the international shipment
of medications. The pharmacist and I divided the pills up into several little
bottles and I put some of those into a FedEx envelope and, on the way out
of town, dropped it in the collection box near Stahly's Truck City. It would
get to Fort George before I did. I swung out onto Veterans Parkway then
and took it across town: I'm usually out there on its eastern route but it
loops west too, around the southern edge of Bloomington and out to the
interchanges on the far side of things. The sun was beginning to set when
I got on I-74 and headed north and west across the prairie, crossing the
Illinois River at Peoria and getting through that town's hills and back up onto
the flats before it got totally dark. The landscape would change again at the
Mississippi River and Iowa was on the other side of that. Fort George was
days and plains and mountains away, almost unimaginable. Still in Illinois, in
the dark, I pulled in an NPR or Pacifica talk show from out ahead in Iowa
City—there was a long segment on a group of women, nurses I think, who
ministered to homeless men who were dying of AIDS in some city, somewhere in this country. Guys different from me, guys who had nothing. Some
were reticent, some were very needy. Some could be courted—out of their
reticence, out of their embarrassment at their situation. One woman, speaking haltingly, said she felt a strange kind of honor or privilege—a feeling
she'd not expected to encounter in herself when she'd begun this work—to

be out there at the hour of someone's death with that person, to be able to walk the guy out to whatever was out there, she said, to walk with him right up to the gape of the edge.

January 1995, a little teary-eyed, alone in the car, on my way to Canada.

...

The country changed a great deal in the days it took me to get across. It was dark by the time I made it over the Iowa border but during the next day—the drive from Des Moines to Sidney, Nebraska—the landscape grew more and more desolate and, after Lincoln, the traffic thinned. From Sidney I bore north and crossed the mountainous bottom of Wyoming all in one bright cold day; I-80 follows the Amtrak route and I chased the *Pioneer*, a train I'd taken four years before, for an hour or so, losing it when I stopped for gas. I went inside to pay and use the facilities but the john was closed, the attendant said, the pipes having frozen, and I should just go out back. Out back was a tumbledown three-sided cowshed attached to the tumbledown gas station and I peed into the straw; it was bright and very cold but out of the wind. Around me were several nests of shit and toilet paper but there was no stink because of the temperature. I was heading toward winter's homeplace, Fort George, but it was winter everywhere. Later, just past Green River, I got off the highway and went a mile out into the actual purple sage on U.S. 30 before losing my nerve—taking the two-lane would have cut some distance off the trip but it was near dark and this was the winter and the road was utterly deserted. There'd be enough of that coming up in B.C., I figured. I got back on 80 and made it through an unpleasant, icy canyon into Ogden and the next day drove across a corner of Idaho and on into eastern Oregon, stopping at Pendleton. I'd kept pace, through Nebraska, with a tiny woman in a huge, new Dodge truck from Pennsylvania; in Oregon I kept passing and being passed by a woman in a rattly Subaru with those green Vermont plates. Out-of-state license plates are rare in Bloomington—I don't know that I've ever seen a car from Vermont there. From Pendleton I went up into Washington and crossed the Cascades on I-90—Snoqualmie Pass—and got to Seattle at rush hour. I was coming in though, from over the mountain, and everyone else was heading out toward the eastern suburbs: it was raining, a bright grey day, and I sailed smoothly past the stalled traffic in the oncoming lanes. (I saw a few Volvos in Ogden and Des Moines but not a single one on the interstates between Bloomington and Seattle. In Wyoming the roadsigns had said "Watch for Game," but no animals had crossed the road there or anywhere else during the trip. I ate in Chinese restaurants every night except in Sidney where I had to settle for Pizza Hut—in Ogden I flirted a little with my waitress at the China Pearl, a young woman with two kids, returning to school; she was the first black person I'd seen for days.)

. . .

I set out again for Fort George the next day: at Bellingham I got off the highway and went northeast on a two-lane toward the border crossing at Huntingdon, B.C. from which it's a hop, skip, and jump to the Trans-Canada. I'd stay in Hope that night, I figured, and do the rest of the way in daylight the next day. Hope's where the mountains start, where the Fraser River turns north, and where the road divides into three strands, like a braid coming un-done—one strand zig-zags east, another (the new toll highway) goes north-east, but I wanted the one that heads straight up into the Fraser Canyon, the Gold Rush Trail highway, Route 1. This was the turn inland: the road would go over the mountains and through the desert and up into the forest of the Cariboo, where Fort George sits—it's in the heart of the forest, it's deep inland. A drizzle had started in Bellingham and it was still drizzling when I arrived at the border. The fellows in the Customs house were friendly as they shrugged over my documents and wished me well and a few minutes later I was on the Trans-Canada and at six o'clock I pulled into Hope. It was dark then, and still raining, but I didn't feel like I'd put in a good day of traveling— I'd started late and hadn't covered much ground. And, as I poked around Hope, half-heartedly looking for a place to stay, I began to think about the incredible Chinese restaurant I'd discovered three years earlier in Boston Bar, this on my first trip to the north; I was on my bicycle and had arrived there in the dark at the end of a long day and the restaurant had been an unexpected reward—it was called the Charles Motel Coffee Shop and it was in an ec-centrically rambling building that also housed a tavern and the rooms of the Charles Motel itself. I'd bought a room in the Charles Motel and gone into the Coffee Shop anticipating some sort of basic mountain fare, meat and potatoes, and had been surprised to find a menu that featured a number of Chinese dishes—my soup had been exquisite, my main course delicious. I re-alized that I could do it again—stay in the Charles Motel and eat good food. I drove out of town and got on Route 1 figuring I could make it to Boston Bar, 40 miles north, in an hour.

Twenty or so minutes later—at Yale, B.C.—the road narrowed and a few miles after that I began to encounter patches of snow and an icy, ambigu-ous fog came up from somewhere. The road is gated in a few places—some-times winter closes it—but the gates were all up so I went on, still thinking about wonton soup and a peculiar halibut and vegetables dish that I'd seen on the menu and wanted to try. The Fraser River had become a presence—the road began to follow the river's curves and about ten miles later, at Spuzzum, I crossed it on a high steel deck bridge. By this time snow and slush were real presences on the road and soon after the bridge the road surface itself disappeared. The fog got thicker. It wasn't fun but then a couple of trucks came up behind me fast and sat on my bumper—the one in front flashed its lights at me and I could hear the bellow of its engine brakes. I was being urged to more speed, I suppose, or to pull off to let them by; but the road was too curvy and slick and the rocky side of a cliff was hard on my right, just across the shoulder which had seemed so generous when I was cycling here. There were temporary signs up, AVALANCHE DANGER DO NOT STOP, but there was no place to stop. The road curved and I curved with it, tapping the brakes for the man behind me but letting the transmission govern my speed, cursing not having stayed in Hope; finally a rest area appeared and I skidded off into it and the two trucks barreled past in a big cloud of white and headlights. I sat there in the turn-out until a couple of others went by and then ventured back onto the road, hoping I could make it to Boston Bar before someone else in a hurry appeared in my rear view mirror. The Volvo's good in snow: it has that low center of gravity and it's fairly heavy and I can take it through anything as long as I can go as slowly as I need to go. Back on the road I found myself alone; a few trucks went past in the southbound lane—the one that's right above a fatal drop into the river itself—but I got to the long China Bar tunnel without anyone rushing me and then there were the lights of Boston Bar. I pulled into the slush of the Charles Motel parking lot, got out of the car, and discovered my knees were shaking.

The Coffee Shop was still open when I staggered into the building. It had been three years, though, and things had happened: the restaurant was under new management, the Chinese menu was gone, and the best I could do was order the steak and the french fries. The potatoes were greasy and meat was tough and tasteless. Mountain fare. A bottle of A-1 sauce helped.

Next morning, though, the breakfast they served was better and indeed the whole day went smoothly: the highway was clear and there wasn't much traffic and I made good time. At Lytton I left the Fraser and followed the Thompson River along northeast through the desert, slowing down when I went over the pass where I'd ridden through the aftermath of a truck accident back in 1991, on the cycling trip. That trip had been my introduction to this country and, this time through in the Volvo, it was still very much in my mind as a series of overlays and comparisons. (I'd driven this road once since that—a later trip in a Budget rent-a-car, but I was with my wife and our daughter then; this was the first time I'd been up here alone since biking it and alone's an important designation for me. It's not better, necessarily, but it's different, profoundly itself—there's alone and then there's everything else.) I left the Thompson at Cache Creek and drove up the hill to Clinton and on through 100 Mile House and when I got to Lac La Hache at two o'clock I was conscious of the end of this trip looming before me and felt the pangs of that. Just north of Lac La Hache is where I'd met another solo biker—he was very young, in his 20s, and he was coming south from Alaska, heading for San Francisco, chasing the good weather; I of course had been finding the climate just fine—this had been a beautiful fall day, bright and about fifty degrees. "Why'd you wait so late in the year," he'd asked me, "to start your trip?" I'd not been looking for the spot where he'd swooped across the road to speak to me, it just came up—a sudden memory—when I got to it. But on the short steep hill out of Williams Lake I did look, without success, for the Sasquatch carving I'd seen out in front of a taxidermist's shop. Stories of the Sasquatch—the Woods Man, Dzonoqua, "Bigfoot"—get told all through British Columbia and have been told there for a very long time. The tracks tend to be the palpable thing: the creature itself—if there is a creature, if the creature is something other than us or our imaginations of it—is glimpsed very rarely and most often, it seems, at a distance. If there's a creature out there in those woods it's beyond us somehow: inaccessible, unfindable, mute. The carving I remembered having seen had been chainsaw art, but it was unusual—the being that had emerged from the block of wood had been startlingly lithe and had had more human features then we usually fancy Bigfoot as possessing and I was disappointed when it wasn't at the place where it had been before.

Previously published in *Into and Out of Dislocation* (North Point/ Farrar, Straus & Giroux, 2000, out-of-print).

C.S Giscombe

Doug Hesse

Teaching with Dave

In fall 1996, Bill Woodson, then graduate director at Illinois State, asked if David Foster Wallace and I might want to co-teach a new graduate workshop in creative nonfiction. Dave was getting weary of graduate fiction workshops even as students understandably were clamoring to study with him. I came later to understand what was at issue, as he had only one speed in working with writers: full throttle and exhausting. He'd cover paper drafts with comments and write multi-page letters about work in progress, often highly critical and even a little mean, though I came to understand that this intensity came at a personal cost to him and that most meanness was a function of his unswerving commitment to writing.

Given his role, Woodson obviously wanted Dave to teach grad students and thought two things might appeal to, even energize, him. One was a shift in genre. Until then, the creative writing workshops in the department were traditionally cleaved into 447.01: Fiction and 447.02: Poetry. Dave had been publishing a lot of magazine pieces, some of them collected in *A Supposedly Fun Thing I'll Never Do Again*, so perhaps he'd find it interesting to work with this kind of writing rather than fiction. The other was a chance to co-teach. My primary scholarly interest had—and has—been creative nonfiction, especially the personal essay/memoir tradition, and Bill thought teaming a writer with a scholar would play well. He also thought that I might handle some of the course's bureaucratic elements and that dividing responsibilities would lighten things for both of us. Of course, I leaped at Bill's matchmaking. I'd like to think Dave did, too.

Prior to this time, Dave and I were more friendly colleagues than friends. I'd been at ISU seven years when he arrived and was given an office directly across from me, his Stevenson 420C to my 420D. Because I had administrative responsibilities directing the first year writing program and its 50-some TA's and faculty, I was generally in the office from 8:30 to 5:00 or so. Dave would mostly show up in the late afternoon, as he often taught in the evenings. Indeed, his office hours were frequently at night, including from 9:00 to 10:00 pm the first time we co-taught. We'd talk about the news, about department events and politics (about which he cared fairly little and which seemed generally to mystify him), and about students we had in common, but I picked up that he was there for his official faculty roles, not to chat. Occasionally, I'd comment on a piece that he'd just published, but he made it clear he didn't like that. A few years later, after he published his "Present Tense" essay in *Harper's*, I said that I'd read and liked (but disagreed with) it.[1] Without speaking, Dave made a gesture of feeding himself with one hand and wiping his butt with the other, implying with enacting that cultural taboo that one shouldn't mix writing with talking about the writing. In his office, he'd keep off the overhead light, relying on lamps. Students would come by, sometimes for mundane queries, sometimes for intense conversations.

During fall 1996, Dave and I mapped the first offering of 447. The first third of the class we'd spend discussing published works while students were busy drafting for the last two-thirds, which we'd spend in traditional workshop. I wrote the introductory framework for the class (D.T. Max speculated, erroneously, that Dave wrote it), and Dave wrote the directions regarding the workshopping portion. Together we devised the topics of the reading weeks: I choose the readings for weeks two and three, Dave the readings for four and five.

We put out a call for applications to the workshop, which would be capped at twelve students. Prospective students needed to give us a piece of their writing, and we'd admit the most promising ones to the course. Only, as it turned out, we didn't need to turn away students, as the course didn't fill.

---

1 One semester Dave had asked to teach English 244: Applied Grammar and Usage for Writers, with which sophomore English education students could fulfill a requirement. He was a stickler for language, to put it mildly, and he really thought that right teaching could fix things for students. He came away disillusioned. During part of that term, he was off giving a talk or reading, so I taught a class meeting for him. I got the clear sense that most of the students had no idea that their intense professor was a famous writer.

Doug Hesse

In fact—and I then and still thought this odd—none of the creative writing graduate students at the time cared to enroll, as they were no doubt interested in their poetry and fiction. Instead, there were several PhD students who were working in rhetoric and composition: Kirsti Sandy, Scott Herstad, and Todd Travaille. Another doctoral student, Jennie Trias, drove over from Macomb, where she was teaching, and the rest were masters students in various areas of literary studies: Maureen Corcoran, Sarah Gelberg, Angela Staron, and Bill Weakly. The class star, at least for Dave and he wasn't wrong, was Louise Freeman Toole, a quiet and studious mother-of-two MA student whose husband was finishing a doctorate in conducting at the University of Illinois. That Louise had an impeccable sense of grammar and style endeared her to him, and that she wrote precise, spare, and evocative realistic narrative won him over. (At least in the classes we taught, he was much less interested in anything experimental than he was in lucid narrative and analysis.) Dave and I co-directed her thesis, *Standing Up to the Rock: Essays on a Snake River Ranch*, later published by the University of Nebraska and winning a couple of awards. Dave's jacket blurb reads, "A moving and very very fine book."

He was oddly—and to some extent, falsely—deferential in planning the class, though I don't think he was intentionally posing. He would repeatedly say, "You're the expert," when it came to what readings we might choose and what framework we might follow. He put a lot of stock in people who had PhDs as having read—and read about—more literature than he had, presuming some capacious historical, contextual, or theoretical knowledge. As if. Right or wrong, he attributed to me a pedagogical expertise that he didn't have; after all, I was Director of Writing, someone responsible for teaching TA's how to teach. Moreover, my professional domain was "rhetoric and composition," a field historically identified with teaching, especially first year writing (and often resisting that identification). In contrast, Dave cast himself as "just a writer." What he knew about teaching, he knew from being a student and, very most recently, as an MFA student. Now, of course, Dave knew plenty about teaching, and if you'd asked him about pedagogical theory—Piaget, for example, or Dewey—I suspect he could have recounted and critiqued it.

He could maintain that deference only so long in the classroom. Fairly often we'd disagree on the advice we'd give a student, and he'd press his point eloquently and hard. Part of it, I think, was competition and wanting to win. Part of it was that he was just so smart and could think of four ways to argue an interpretation and six ways to revise when any of the rest of us might best devise two. Part of it was at some deep level an insecurity manifesting as the need to prove himself. He detested anything that verged on cloying or that struck him as sloppy. Class could get uncomfortable at times, and every now and then I'd find myself defending a student writer perhaps more than I'd wanted simply because I thought things were verging on humiliation. This was challenging because I wanted Dave's approval, too, and I had insecurities about my own judgment held against his.

I remember one class in particular where I felt his opprobrium. I'd had us read an essay by Willie Morris, "The Ghosts of Ole Miss." Dave found it alternatively nostalgic, sloppy, racist, and plain offensive, and he was having none of my arguments about authorial stance and technique. Sensing blood in the water, the graduate students in the workshop joined the attack, and pretty soon I gave up, joking my way out of the conversation with a sort of "what was I thinking" posture. Later I came across the copy of the essay that Dave had marked up for the class. The bibliographic information was across the photocopy in my handwriting, and you could see his marginalia getting more and more heated. At the top of one page, he asked, "Did Doug pick this as model of jerkiness?"

Out-of-class meetings were charged only when we disagreed about the quality of something. A student in one of our two classes was a fairly weak writer, and Dave wanted to give him a C. I asserted that a C in grad school was pretty much an F, and this student's writing, while undistinguished, wasn't that bad. He begrudgingly deferred to my experience, and we went off separately to determine grades. The next day, he gave me a marked copy of the student's essay with a B followed by a long trail of minuses, which extended to the edge of the page where there was an arrow "over," the minuses then trailing to the edge of the back, too.

After that term was over, we worked together on various teaching-related projects. We co-directed a couple of nonfiction theses, and we served together on a few others. (One memorable thesis defense was over Maureen Spizzirri's Growing Up, My House was Gray: A Collection of Fiction and Nonfiction Exploring the Blurring of Genre; Dave protested at vehement length the dangling modifier in the title.) Otherwise, we talked very little shop. He'd come over now and then to play poker, and we'd meet regularly to watch X Files, sometimes grilling out. He'd ask about our younger kids, Andrew, who was a high school tennis player, and Paige, whom he'd tease until she'd kick his shins. He'd talk about writing with my wife, Becky, herself a writer with whom he'd previously taught a fiction course, but I didn't ask about his work, and he rarely volunteered.

We reprised the course once, in spring 2001. I'd stepped down as writing director by then and had also served a term as grad director. Ron Strickland asked if we'd co-teach again. Even at that late date, Dave preferred channels other than email, and so we faxed back and forth.

August 2, 2000

To: Dave, Fax 915 729-3456
From: Doug Hesse, Fax 309 438-5414

Dave, I'm glad you got my message about the 447 class.

This class would be INSTEAD OF the lit class you'd talked about with Ron, not in addition to it. We might be a little heavy on graduate contemporary lit courses in the spring.

I think there would be good student interest in the creative nonfiction 447. I think it would be a cool course to teach with you again, and Ron is agreeable.

So, let me know if doing the 447 (instead of the 487 or whatever that course is) makes sense to you.

We set up the class the same as before; this term was the spring of the ill-fated Willie Morris essay. One change over the previous offering was that creative writers signed up for the course; perhaps nonfiction had accrued more credibility among them in four years. Perhaps they wanted every opportunity to work with Dave; I sincerely doubt I had much to do with it. Even at that, the course wasn't full, the roster including Brian Budzynski, Tim Feeney, David Marshall, Tom McCulley, Mike Perillo, Donna Reinking, Suzanne Scanlon, Mary Timmins, and Julie Jung, who had just joined the faculty. We met Wednesday evenings around a large table in the conference room off the English department main office. Dave would chew during class and always kept a red Solo plastic cup at his side, into which he'd now and then spit. He apologized about this many times, and you could see it genuinely embarrassed him, but it was part of his way of dealing with things.

Dave's dedicated intensity/borderline hazing again manifested itself during this course. At the end of a five-page, double-spaced response to one student who had turned in a strong first work, Dave wrote (handwritten revisions marked by underline and strike-through, open parentheses and spellings ["jewler"] retained):

> 3. 447 will be unpleasant for you <u>if you do this again</u>. I may not say much this time—maybe you were rushed—but if you EVER turn in something this sloppy again, I will harp endlessly on the errors in <u>class</u> discussion, talk about nothing else in my Letters of Response, and will, if necessary, use grade-leverage (threating you with a low grade in the course, for example [don't think I won't, Hesse] to force you to take exquisite line-by-line care ~~with other work~~ and to learn basic usage-rules you have either not been taught or have not taken the trouble to master. I will have no ethical qualms about doing this: all other areas of this essay are so terribly sophisticated the line-by-line fuckups stick out like carbuncles; I will not permit a writer as fine and smart as yourself to demean your work by passing in something so error-ridden. [NB: PROOFREAD. Professionals do. Which does not mean looking it over quickly or running it through a <u>computer's</u> Spellcheck. It means poring over the final mss WITH A FUCKING JEWLER'S LOUPE. [And note <u>that</u> handwritten corrections are fine—neither workshops nor magazine editors have a problem with them if they're neat; in fact they make it look like the writer cares. Which is important. <u>NO?</u>]

He goes on in this vein for several sentences, ostensibly trying to defuse the vehemence with his characteristic smiley face in the margin. His shout out to me ("don't think I won't, Hesse"), reflecting our practice of sharing letters with each other, illustrates his generally belief that I was considerably less fussy about proofreading than I should have been. He closes the letter with "Ave Atque Valle," signing it "David Wallace" and jotting his home phone number.

At the end of the semester, we invited the students over to our house for a celebratory cookout:

English 447 Folks,

By Wednesday, May 9, turn in the following:

a. a copy of all the letters you've written to classmates this semester.

b. a copy of all your drafts that were marked by Dave and Doug.

c. any revisions. Append to each revision a brief paragraph explaining the nature of changes you made.

Photocopies of these materials are fine and, perhaps, preferred. Please note that, given the short reading time before final grades are to be submitted, our responses to the portfolios will necessarily be brief.

By far the best way to turn in your portfolio is to bring it to the final soiree Tuesday night, May 8. Should you need to turn it in later, you will need to give it to either of us directly. Note that Doug will be out of town May 9-11.

On Wednesday May 8, we invite you to a last class/party at 204 William Drive in Normal. Travel east from campus (toward Veteran's Parkway) on College Avenue. At Anderson Park, turn left (north) on William Drive. 204 is atop the hill on your right. 454-7175. Arrive at 5:00, leave when you need to, though we do have some writing to discuss. We will supply food and drink; you need bring nothing.

Dave brought about six two-liter bottles of pop and several bags of chips, his usual contribution to events like this. We grilled burgers and sat around the picnic table. At dark, when people started drifting away, we went inside, and I asked those remaining to stand for a picture around a coffee table, their pile of portfolios stacked where Dave and I would stay long after everyone left, reading and discussing the work. Dave is beside me, doing rabbit ears. A few days later, we met to discuss final grades; he told me that I'd have to assign the grade for one student because something personal had come up, and he gave me a piece of paper scrawled with his assessments: B, A, A/A+, C-, A-, A/A+, A----, I. (That A-4minus was for a student he wanted to give a B and he knew I'd argue for A.) The grades were in blue marker on the back of a piece of ISU letterhead with typing on the front. I hadn't paid it attention until going through class materials for this essay, when I recognized it as lines of dialogue toward what later would be made into *The Pale King*.

Photo by Becky Bradway

Doug Hesse

Curtis White

The History of Sadness

For David

Such griefs with such men well agree,

But wherefore, wherefore fall on me?

—Coleridge, "The Pains of Sleep"

It may be strange to say, but I think that one of the evolutionary advantages we humans have over the other animals is that we are the "blue" mammal, the dismal, glum, morose, rueful, woebegone, *mesto*, dolorous, woeful, and down in the mouth mammal. In other words, everyone knows that the strength of our brains is a great advantage, but an important part of that strength is our capacity to be sad.[1]

---

1 Oh hell, I can already hear it from the animal rights people about how they have documented the case of a cocker spaniel that grieved over the loss of a master by making ululating wails, or the obligatory ten days of mourning observed among the Macaque monkeys, or how a legendary African gray parrot once gave a funeral oration that lasted fifteen minutes. Actually, I grant all that. I have had parrots for many years, and when I die they will cover themselves in ashes, pull black scarves down over their heads, and utter woeful lamentations (if for no other reason than that it will be difficult to imagine another "owner" willing to fork out $30 for a container of Nutriberries or, as Peter Sellers said in the film *The Party*, "birdy numnums"). What I don't grant is the idea that on some desolate morning in early adulthood an animal will wake and for no reason think that it ought to kill itself. I know what my parrots would say to that: "If I kill myself, who will chew all the colorful wooden blocks in my cage?"

Others have weighed in on the subject of just what the animals are capable of, and I think we ought to take their opinion into account. For example, the great if bewildering French composer Eric Satie wrote, "Michelin has modestly stated that animals are our inferior brothers, that is to say, that man is animal's superior

In broad outline the case goes something like this:

Premise one: Most people have a biochemical tendency toward happiness. Or, better said, they have a general satisfaction with their world as they find it barring outside impingement in the form of poverty, famine, disease, or being beaten upon by others of their own species, whether in South Chicago or some utterly God-forsaken country in Africa in which if you happen to be out when local insurgents call, they will leave their message not on a calling card but gouged into the skulls of your wife and teenage daughter. But other than that, such folk are predisposed to cheerfulness and satisfaction with things as they are, however that might happen to be.

Premise two: once chemical destiny kicks in for the depressed person, she experiences a sort of inescapable pain that has no explanation (she is not poor, she can eat what she likes, she was not visited by insurgents, etc.). She is almost envious of those who can blame their sorrow on some outside thing. She is even more an emotional wreck than those poor souls, but, to her shame, she has no reasonable explanation for it. We now call this sadness-without-cause a mental illness, but can something so widespread, so common, really be a disease? Doesn't it suggest normalcy? And if it is a normal part of being human, just why is that? What health-giving evolutionary advantage does it present?

Determined to understand this pain, the depressed person begins a process of analysis. Something must be wrong, and she would like, reasonably, to know what it is. She wants to explain it to herself. So, first, she becomes skeptical of her immediate reality and everything she thinks she knows about it. (This is the depressed person's *epoché*, her Cartesian moment of "universal doubt.") She begins to wonder, for example, if the people who love her best, her own father and mother, aren't responsible for "ruining her life." Or the depressed person wonders whether her perfectly affable husband isn't the cause of her pain.

Premise three: At a more advanced level, the depressed person embraces the "hermeneutics of suspicion." Everything that looks like home for the normal person begins to look like a conspiracy to the depressed person, a

---

brother. Well, we don't have animal's opinion on the subject. What we do know is that animals are natural citizens in good standing, that they have rights and duties, and that their intelligence is considerable. Some animals are referred to as 'Domestic.' Why? I don't know. Painters and sculptors have often depicted animals. But animals, for their part, totally ignore the plastic arts: we know of no painting or sculpture by an animal."

Curtis White

conspiracy to make people like her unhappy. The government, corporations, religious fundamentalists, gun owners, the media, the military, and just generally anyone who seems responsible for running the place comes under the microscope of this suspicion. At its extreme, the depressed person assumes that the above are conspiring against her happiness, are the enemy, and are the cause of the depressed person's pain. Her only confusion is why *everybody* doesn't understand this. After all, they're destroying the world! It's *depressing!*

Nobody understands the urgency of the depressed person's discoveries except for two or three depressed friends with whom she shares an intense infatuation with certain rock bands (with some crazy depressed name like Olivia Tremor Control). Often, the lead singer of the band will actually commit suicide, or at least give it a good faith effort. This cements the bond they feel with the band, and further corroborates the suspicion that only they and the band are not either fascists or slaves to fascists.

In none of this is the depressed person wrong. Her parents in all likelihood were strong contributing factors in her sadness. As Philip Larkin put it, "They fuck you up, your mum and dad." But not everyone who is "fucked up" is depressed. Some can laugh about it, with a genial sigh, while having Thanksgiving dinner with the parents some twenty years later.[2] And, frankly, in most cases the husband or wife has some share in the misery too. (I won't go into that; I'll just let you fill in the blank. You've got plenty of your own details, your own actionable grievances.) And of course there is no argument about the role of the miserable, squamate people responsible for government, religion, media, and the military. For the depressed person, the rank corruption of the fetid hominids who actually get to run this country

---

2 "Dad, remember the time you locked me in the basement overnight?"

"Oh, gosh, honey, don't remind me about that."

"I told your father not to do that, but he was so mad!"

"Well, I did smoke dope and drive the car into the porch."

"And you were twelve. Twelve!"

"I guess I never did that again. On the other hand, I can't go into dark, wet places, and I'm terrified of spiders."

"Oh, honey! I'm so sorry!"

"I love you so much, Daddy!"

Happy tears.

becomes a confirmation, an objective correlative, for her own dark center. Everyone should be depressed "in a world like this."

So, for all these reasons, the depressed person is not wrong when she says her great *"j'accuse."* She is not wrong because she and most other depressed people are in fact realists. They are the *ultimate* realists. If it is the secret, lying world of mommy and daddy and the rancid behavior of the oligarchs that has made her sad, then her response must be honesty, the "ruthless critique of everything existing," as Marx put it. No one is more resentful of dishonesty than the depressed person. It's what makes her love Nietzsche. It's what makes her grateful to most of Western philosophy because, even if it is grim, at least certain philosophers—Nietzsche, Adorno, Sartre—care enough to bother to tell her the truth.

But this insistence on honesty is not without its own problems, as if the depressed person needed more problems. Her honesty is more often than not inconvenient for those who don't see the need to probe so deeply or so rigorously into the corpse of the world. Not all people, and certainly not the folk who believe they are prospering or may one day prosper under the current regime, are willing to hear the depressed person's realism. Everything the depressed person believes in her heart of hearts is an inconvenient truth to everybody else. So, she can believe what she likes, the crazy, but could she please keep quiet about it?

Premise four: Because the depressed person finds no possibility for life within the cloistered limits of the normal, she becomes radically open to other possibilities. She opens herself to the random. In this way, the depressed person becomes the portal of the beautiful. She becomes the creator of counter-worlds, other places where she might be able to live without being this miserable thing that she ineluctably is. Through her, a sort of happy-making playfulness comes to rule. She learns how to laugh. When she laughs, she really laughs. She is an incredibly great laugher. This is of some considerable consolation to her and her depressed friends.

Whether they know it or not, they have come under the aura of art.

Here's where it gets strange. A much larger number of normally cheerful people who have been brutalized in one way or another by states, business, religion, etc., also see the utopian appeal coming from the artful, handmade world of the depressed person. They think it looks like fun, a risky fun, but fun. Hey, they realize, it looks like life, like *freedom!*

The depressed person's therapeutic play becomes a social movement (Romantic poets, beatniks, folkies, hippies, punks, Goths, etc.). They begin the hard work of creating resistant communities, and, marvelous to say, the world actually begins to change as a consequence, even if just a little bit, even if just in a few wayward neighborhoods in Portland, Seattle, or Brooklyn. But for these comrades-made-miserable-by-chemical-destiny-or-by-the-meanness-of-the-world-and-then-made-happy-again-by-the-lively-culture-of-the-arts, the world has changed. What they all see in the art inventions of the depressed is actually the promise of happiness that they feel is terribly lacking for them in the world as it is. At a certain point, even chemically happy people revolt against the world's mendacious contention that they already have all the happiness they need or deserve, even though they may be eyeball deep in poverty and blood or deathly boredom when their masters make the claim. We, for instance, in these unhappily united states, are eyeball deep in blood, circa 2011, oh fuck whatever year it may be as you read this, and yet there is no shortage of well-dressed puppets tottering around on their rigid pins talking about US as the "last best hope" for something, the "indispensable nation." It's so maddening that it's enough to actually *change* your brain chemistry.

In short, happy people who have been taught to despair by the world are returned to happiness and hope by the desperate, playful inventions of depressed people.

Depressed people are always, or, okay, disproportionately, enemies of the state for these reasons. Unhappy people are always a threat to the current regime, but people who are unhappy for no good reason at all, who are metaphysically unhappy, are the most dangerous of all. All revolutions are alliances of the inventive depressed and the hapless despairing who find what is in the end a revolutionary hope in the creations of the chemically sad. The depressed are those human sacrifices that the species offers up as the evolutionary price to be paid for the occasional joy of feeling alive and free, and those rarer moments still when we feel that our chests are thrust forward into the world and into the future and our personal darkness merely purls in our wake. That is the triumph of depression.

Premise five: Without depression the world would not only suck but it would suck in exactly the same way century after century.

"The History of Sadness" first appeared in *Spolia*.

Drama

Kymberly Harris

Faith

…Oh. Well. Native Companion was—yeah, Kymberly went with me to that. It's not really her voice, it's somebody else's voice, if you can get my drift. But um, yeah, she was not pleased to have somebody else's voice put in there. But all that stuff happened, like she really did get put in that thing called the Zipper. Nothin', nothin' in there is made up.

—DFW, Although of Course You End Up Becoming Yourself

ACT I

SCENE 1:

(A club in Chicago. FAITH has just performed. She raises her arms—feeling the spotlight. Then she passes out. Her parents, SIMON and CLARK, rush the stage to try to revive her and then carry her out. As soon as they pick her up, SIMON, faints, dramatically, and CLARK has to figure out how to carry both of them out.)

SCENE 2:

(FAITH's family home in Normal, Illinois where she grew up. FAITH's mother SIMON is sitting at the kitchen table, eating popcorn frantically. FAITH enters with her father, CLARK, carrying her baggage. FAITH is strung out, black-eyed, shaking.)

SIMON: Faith?

FAITH: Mom?

SIMON: My Faith, you're fine.

CLARK: We got her out of there.

SIMON: Where's the rest of her stuff?

CLARK: We left the rest of her stuff.

SIMON: You left the rest of her stuff? How could you leave the rest of her stuff?

CLARK: The roommate was there.

SIMON: She was there?

CLARK: Clearly she had been doing drugs.

SIMON: You left her stuff?

CLARK: She was hysterical. We had to get out of there. She threatened me, with a dirty needle.

FAITH: Needle?

CLARK: Threatened to stab Faith, then herself. I went over and took the needle from her. Where's the hand sanitizer? *(Puts on Purell.)* She stole most of Faith's things to buy drugs. Tell her, Faith. She stole grandma's ring, tell her, Faith.

SIMON: Grandma's ring? That was an heirloom.

CLARK: She looks a little thin, doesn't she?

SIMON: It's good to be thin! Lookin' good babe.

CLARK: She has bills.

SIMON: How much?

CLARK: They wrote bad checks. I don't want to know what for. Banks are after her, her credit is shot, now.

SIMON: I'll take care of it!

CLARK: Thousands. Tell her, Faith.

FAITH: Thousands, mom, thousands. And the heirlooms. Everything. Gone. I'm gone.

CLARK: Jeeeeeeeez, criminy.

SIMON: I'll come up with it.

CLARK: Well, honey, how are you going to do that?

SIMON: *(Starts to eat popcorn frantically.)* I'll find a way. I'll-I'll-oohh.

CLARK: Do you see what you do to your mother?

SIMON: Ahh....

CLARK: Honey, why don't you go to bed, get some rest.

SIMON: We've a plan to enroll you in graduate school. At the University.

FAITH: I'm a singer.

SIMON: And a writer.

FAITH: A songwriter.

SIMON: You'll go in as a writing student. Is academia really so bad, you can be a scholar one day like dad and me.

FAITH: I don't want to teach, I—

SIMON: We've recruited Fitzpatrick George! You remember I sent you his short stories? Recipient of the *(Glowing in unison to say the words.)*

Kymberly Harris

SIMON/CLARK: MacArthur Genius Grant.

SIMON: He's coming into the department. We had him to dinner and then he made his decision to stay. I showed him your picture. The one that looks like me at your age.

CLARK: You're even prettier now.

FAITH: What the fuck does this have to do with anything?

SIMON: He liked it very much. *He's* just adorable.

(*CLARK turns to leave.*)

FAITH: Where are you going?

CLARK: To put your things away. What's left of them.

SIMON: Oh Clark, don't be so dumb.

FAITH: Mom, he's—

SIMON: We'll have Fitz to dinner tomorrow night. So the two of you can meet. He is a remarkable human being. A kindred spirit to me. Would you like that?

FAITH: Sure, Mom. Mom, I'm freezing.

SIMON: Let me open the door.

FAITH: My eyes are burning.

SIMON: You just have to get your mind off of it.

FAITH: My ears are ringing.

SIMON: Did you enjoy Fitz's short stories that I sent to you?

FAITH: (*Shivers.*) Do you have any wine?

SIMON: That sounds good to me, too. Red or white?

FAITH: Red. Blood red. Like family.

CLARK: That's it. I'm going up.

SIMON: Oh, I just can't wait for you to meet our Fitz.

SCENE 3

(*Living room, the next night, family home. FAITH is chugging red wine, listening to music. FITZ and SIMON enter, having been to the movies.*)

SIMON: (*Entering.*) How do you find the time to learn so much about extinct animals? It's remarkable.

(*FAITH turns off the music.*)

FITZ: Just a silly hobby. The name Tyrannosaurus Rex means, "King tyrant lizard."

SIMON: No kidding?

FITZ: The largest meat-eating animal ever to walk earth. The Stegosaurus is a plant-eater. Weak teeth, though. One of the first to extinguish itself. Ask yourself, if you were a dinosaur, which would you be? A king meat eater who rules her territory and lives the longest, or the humble plant eater that didn't have the heart to eat other animals, but as a result, becomes extinct first.

SIMON: Most people would say that I'm the Rex and Clark the humble pacifist, but I haven't been able to really talk to anyone but you in such a long time. So I ask you, what do you think?

(FITZ notices FAITH, who has been trying to hide by sinking into the couch.)

SIMON: Why, Faith, hello there, little girl. You disappeared.

FAITH: Just couldn't hang…. Weak teeth, I guess?

FITZ: *(Laughs out loud at her wit, then too enthusiastically.)* Hey there, Faith!

SIMON: Oh, you have a highly developed mouth, dear.

(SIMON goes over to fix Faith's hair.)

FAITH: Mom, what are you doing?

SIMON: Your hair looks so pretty out of your face.

FAITH: Stop. Please.

SIMON: Can't do anything right around here. Fitz, I guess I'll "perchance to dream." Thanks for the movie.

FITZ: *(His focus on FAITH now.)* Thanks for dinner.

SIMON: Tomorrow, then? 7 p.m.?

FITZ: *(Confused.)* I'll see if I can.

SIMON: You have to eat, don't you?

FITZ: *(Back to SIMON.)* Yes, I do.

FAITH: It's like they've adopted you. Careful, some people bring in stray dogs; my Mom brings in stray people.

(FITZ laughs again.)

SIMON: Don't call Fitz a dog.

FAITH: Not what I meant. Not that it matters. I'm going out, Mom.

SIMON: I think Fitz would like it if you kept him company, Faith.

(SIMON stays and lurks around.)

FAITH: *(Put on the spot.)* Mm-k? Uh, Fitz, would you like a beverage? Red wine?

FITZ: *(Shows Diet Coke.)* Got one.

FAITH: Right.

(FAITH gets more wine.)

FITZ: So, I couldn't help but notice you left the movie halfway through?

FAITH *(Laughs.)* I'm not much of a dinosaur fan.

FITZ: Yep, but it's not really about dinosaurs, see…

FAITH: You do realize your interpretation of the movie is much better than the movie itself?

FITZ: *(Blurts out.)* I haven't written anything since I moved here!

FAITH: Me either.

FITZ: Was that your own song playing when we walked in?

FAITH: Yeah, I—.

FITZ: It's much the same as coming from Chicago to here, I guess. Hard to write until you get your bearings. Right? You do write—

FAITH: Just songs.

FITZ: That's very cool.

FAITH: Thanks.

SIMON: (*Takes FAITH's wine glass and drinks from it.*) And now she'll study English at the University!

(*CLARK enters.*)

CLARK: What's going on down here? Am I invited to this little shindig?

SIMON: (*Handing back her wine glass.*) Sure, Clark, have a stiff one.

CLARK: I'll have a Coke.

(*FITZ offers CLARK a Diet Coke.*)

No thanks, none of that fake sugar for me. How was the movie?

FAITH: The two geniuses took me to see *Jurassic Park* at the dollar theater. You know, where they show movies nobody wanted to see the first time around?

CLARK: Faith has sophisticated taste, just like her mother.

SIMON: I enjoyed it.

CLARK: I thought I was going to meet you there?

SIMON: You wouldn't have liked it.

CLARK: Well, congratulations, Fitz, I can't get her to see anything but foreign films with me. In fact—

SIMON: I don't remember you trying, Clark.

CLARK: I gave up after awhile.

SIMON: Fitz, it's such a joy to have you here, a poet and a gentleman. Goodnight, all.

(*She sweeps out.*)

FAITH: Night, mom.

CLARK: Whelp, I guess I'll go up too.

FITZ: Goodnight, Clark.

(*CLARK goes up, too.*)

(*FAITH waits to make sure they're gone and removes a prescription bottle from her pants.*)

FAITH: Crap. Do you have a, a pocketknife? Or keys, maybe?

FITZ: Uh, yeah, keys.

(*FITZ hands her his keys.*)

FAITH: Great. Thanks so much. (*FAITH crushes the pills and makes lines. She takes out a straw and proceeds to do lines, whose effect she feels progressively throughout the scene.*)

FITZ: What is that, exactly?

FAITH: One of mom's prescriptions. She's got a whole drug store up there, cabinets full. It's a good thing, too, because I don't know where to get anything around here. You haven't met anyone who parties, have you?

FITZ: Uh—

FAITH: It's not cocaine, but it's a poor substitute.

FITZ: I'm in the program.

FAITH: Huh?

FITZ: I'm in AA.

FAITH: AA? That's for alcohol right?

FITZ: I can't really do anything.

FAITH: Suit yourself, but it's gonna get mighty boring here in the cornfields.

FITZ: It's not exactly a choice, drugs almost killed me.

FAITH: Sorry about that.

FITZ: Why'd you come back?

FAITH: I was kidnapped.

FITZ: I heard what happened at your show.

FAITH: Yes, that was kind of an unfortunate finale.

FITZ: I'd like to hear you sing one of your songs sometime.

FAITH: Okay. I'm working on some new—well. Wow. You must feel very proud of all your success as of late. The "genius" grant?

FITZ: All I can think about is what I have to do next. It's like my worst fear, to be popular for what I used to write. More public success brings more deadlines. Sometimes I think I should have never published.

FAITH: Well, I'm impressed. You should let yourself feel it.

FITZ: *(Feeling lifted up.)* How do you do that?

FAITH: *(Sings something original.)*

FITZ: *(He's surprised by how good she is. After a moment he takes to collect himself.)* If I could sing like that, I'd sing all the time.

FAITH: *(Speeding now.)* I read your short stories. You really articulated it. Isolation. Like being in a coma where everyone is talking around you and at you, and you can hear them, but they don't think you can, so the world is moving and moving about you, and you are paralyzed, and can't respond, even to say you can hear them, but if you could you'd say: stop speculating! You don't understand me better than I do myself! But since she's paralyzed, she can't even chime in about my own life.

FITZ: No one has made a coma analogy for that story before.

FAITH: Mmhm, mmhm.

FITZ: *(Pause.)* Maybe you could read the book I'm writing now?

FAITH: *(Light bulb moment doin' lines.)* Cockroach!

FITZ: What?

FAITH: Like the cockroach; you know, Kafka? Perception, it's all perception. Your expectations of yourself versus what you perceive are society's expectations of you? I know, very intellectual, and all that good genius grant stuff. But there are feelings, too. It's not just a writer's trick; I mean you have to think about the heart of the person who is being overlooked. She can't respond to her own life. How does she feel? It shouldn't be just a device, it's important what you're saying—you gotta get inside her.

FITZ: Well, the character *is* autistic.

FAITH: But she knew enough to know what she wasn't feeling, right? That she was too weak or limited to respond? She's aware of this limitation. And that she could have made better decisions for herself if that weren't the case. And instead she's at the mercy of the doctors, when she actually understands much more than they do about life, about humanity. She just cannot express it in a way they understand. In fact it's they, it is they!

FITZ: They?

FAITH: —who aren't aware of their limitations; even more than the autistic girl.

FITZ: That's a pretty fuckin' good read.

FAITH: It's brilliantly written but I wish I would have gotten more from the perspective of her, heart, you know? That's just my take on it.

FITZ: Thanks for reading it.

FAITH: No problem. *(FAITH snorts a line.)*

FITZ: Feel better?

FAITH: Not like coke, but—. She could get the best stuff she turned me on to it.

FITZ: Who?

FAITH: No one you know. She's in the Miami woman's detention center now. Day after I left. Coming down is a slow death, you want to die sometimes. But that twenty minutes after a line. You are really… you, well, you know, right? You feel you can do anything. No fears, no doubts, no awareness that I'm the cockroach not meeting anyone's expectations and afraid not to care…. *(FAITH laughs it off, then starts putting on lipstick from her purse, and dabs her cleavage with perfume.)*

FITZ: Isn't the Miami woman's detention center a prison?

FAITH: Let's get out of here, my new friend.

FITZ: W-where?

FAITH: The Hole.

FITZ: The——. It's 1:30.

FAITH: We can catch last call.

FITZ: Past my bedtime.

FAITH: Please don't make me dance alone.

FITZ: I really don't dance.

FAITH: Well, I'll dance. You can watch.

FITZ: Will you sing to me in the car?

FAITH: Will you autograph my… stomach?

SCENE 4

(FITZ's house. FITZ and FAITH enter after dancing.)

FITZ: So, welcome. Would you like some tea?

FAITH: Tea? No.

FITZ: I don't have anything to drink.

FAITH: That's okay, I can make it an hour or two.

FITZ: *(Stares.)*

FAITH: I'm joking!

Fitz: Oh. 'LMAO'.

FAITH: Do you mind if I smoke?

FITZ: Here? Well, jeez, I just quit. Could I have one? Uh no, I'd better not. Would you mind doing that outside? Oh no, then you'd have to actually go outside and then you wouldn't be right here glowing in my den. So go ahead.

FAITH: That was a long answer.

FITZ: You sure no tea?

FAITH: No, I'm good.

(FITZ prepares tea.)

FAITH: I can't believe I met you through my parents.

FITZ: Simon took out your picture, over dinner, and said, "Would you like to marry my daughter?"

FAITH: How generous.

FITZ: I took it as she liked me. Thought I might get the job at that point!

FAITH: I love being offered as a gift.

FITZ: I wrote to you.

FAITH: I wrote you back. Didn't I?

FITZ: Your letter was one long run-on sentence. What do you have against punctuation?

FAITH: Cocaine.

FITZ: Cocaine is what you have against punctuation?

FAITH: Cocaine was what I had against anything that would make me stop long enough to realize how much cocaine I was doing.

Kymberly Harris

FITZ: Damn interfering commas.

FAITH: And colons! I find colons to be very demanding.

FITZ: Are you?

FAITH: What?

FITZ: Demanding?

FAITH: No.

FITZ: I just got outta something....

FAITH: I bet I know what your favorite shape is.

FITZ: What's that?

FAITH: The triangle.

FITZ: You mean in terms of female anatomy? It would be a tossup between that and the circle, and your very heart shaped ass.

FAITH: I meant more in terms of floor plan.

FITZ: Floor plan?

FAITH: Yeah. You here, and one woman here, and another woman here, vying for your attention.

FITZ: I don't know if you've noticed but I'm not exactly young Marlon Brando.

FAITH: You're Fitzpatrick George.

FITZ: That I am. But flexing the cerebral muscle wasn't impressive until recently. I always thought of myself as a misfit with women. You, for example, are very pretty.

FAITH: Who are you used to dating?

FITZ: My hand. Is this a date?

FAITH: So I won't ask to see old prom pictures then?

FITZ: I have a family picture of my last girlfriend. Her family. Carrie, her husband, and her child.

FAITH: Oh, nice triangle there. Big one.

FITZ: I'd fake laugh, but I reserve that for my agent's office. Are you always this spiny?

FAITH: Spiny?

FITZ: Porcupiney.

FAITH: Prick, prick.

FITZ: Quick, quick. So.

FAITH: Carrie....

FITZ: Carrie. But it's over. (*Pause.*) You were stunning out there. On the dance floor. You're like some forest creature.

FAITH: So like an animal?

(*FAITH stops and drags her cigarette.*)

FITZ: No , I mean, instinctual.

Faith: Yeah, right.

FITZ: You wanna put that out?

FAITH: 'K.

(*FITZ hands FAITH his teacup. FITZ and FAITH kiss and stare into each other's eyes.*)

I should go.

FITZ: Tomorrow I, oh you probably wouldn't be interested. *Atlantic Monthly* commissioned me to do a story on the State Fair, in Springfield? I have to drive up and research the hog ties and other titilating contests.

FAITH: Tit contests?

FITZ: Titilating... anyway. Never mind—.

FAITH: Are there roller coasters?

FITZ: Yes. And the mayor will be there. And the Allman Brothers. And the mayor's wife. And her hair.

FAITH: What time?

FITZ: Oh, I think her hair is with her all the time. Early. Ten.

FAITH: Sure, I'll go.

FITZ: I could pick you up.

FAITH: Okay. (*Kisses him on the cheek.*) Bye.

FITZ: (*Alone, to himself.*) What am I doing?

(*He takes her cigarette from the ashtray and smokes. There's a knock at the door. He puts out the cigarette, waves the smoke away, hides the ashtray and answers.*)

FITZ: Hi!

FAITH: Can I get a ride home?

SCENE 5

(*Illinois State Fair. We hear the sounds of a crowded fair. FITZ and FAITH enter sweaty, buttoning and straightening their clothes. They just had sex in the car. FITZ is dazed, FAITH is energized.*)

FITZ: I have to say I never expected that. Did you expect that?

FAITH: Yeah.

FITZ: I think I lost my credentials.

FAITH: You have been with a woman before this, haven't you? Because you're acting awfully frazzled.

FITZ: (*Fearing he is getting distracted by something dangerous.*) Well, I can't find my credential name-tag and without it I can't go anywhere I need to go to get what I need to get for my story, the whole reason I'm here! For work, to work—! Oh shit, there's the mayor. I have to interview him later. I don't want him to see me like this. Get down, get down! (*FITZ shoves her head down and leads her to run and duck.*)

FAITH: What are you doing?

FITZ: Oh boy. There's a cotton candy vendor. Do you want to get some and sit and eat it for a few hours?

FAITH: I beg your pardon?

FITZ: It's already 2 and I meant to get started at 10. I have a deadline. *(Regarding schedule.)*

I've missed the hog tie, the best legs contest was at 11—

FAITH: *(Lifts up her skirt and kicks.)* I won. In the car, remember?

FITZ: P-please don't do that.

FAITH: What do you want me to do, extinguish myself? Like a grass eating dinosaur?

FITZ: Plant eating, I can't do grass anymore, just— I'm here for a purpose.

FAITH: Gee, I'm sorry fucking me interfered with your purpose?

FITZ: C-c-can we meet back here in a couple hours?

FAITH: No way.

FITZ: Could you just give me a couple hours? Or could you come with me and be *quietly* supportive.

FAITH: I dated this guy in Chicago. We were at a movie and he shushed me when I laughed, said my laugh was "too loud." So I dug the post of my earring into his balls until he screamed bloody murder, and then asked him to please keep it down.

FITZ: Look, I'm not going to leave you here, Okay? We can't even get past the gates until I find my credentials anyway. Oh, here they are. *(FITZ finds the credential card, attempts to pin it on FAITH's blouse.)*

FAITH: What are you doing?!

FITZ: I'm giving you credentials.

FAITH: What?

FITZ: Credentials.

FAITH: I don't want them.

FITZ: You need them to get in. *(Tries to pin them on her again.)*

FAITH: Would you stop!

FITZ: You need them!

FAITH: No, you need them.

FITZ: You get special privileges with these.

FAITH: I'll get special privileges on my own.

FITZ: No, you won't. They sent me all this literature on the rules. Like this gate. It's got a red tag on it. You can't even get in this way without these credentials.

(A CARNIE saunters over.)

CARNIE: Help yew?

FITZ: Uh, well, I don't know what to do, Faith, I have to go in. I'm supposed to be writing a story right now. This very minute, now.

FAITH: Do you mind if I escort this freakish young man? He's not from around here and as you can see, he's a bit nervous.

CARNIE: *(Snort laughs.)* He looks content as a pig in shit to me.

FITZ: Delightful.

CARNIE: What yew say?

FITZ: Please don't harm me.

CARNIE: Well, jest don't tell on me, luscious, or I'll get my hind end skinned.

FAITH: My lips are super glued.

(FAITH motions for FITZ to come on; he hesitantly follows.)

FITZ: That was impressive.

FAITH: I have my own credentials.

FITZ: And that doesn't bother you? You heard him, right. He called you "luscious." *(He takes some notes.)*

FAITH: And you disagree?

FITZ: Is that the objective here—overwhelming consensus?

FAITH: I'm going to find the Zipper!

(FITZ jumps back and protects his zipper with his hands.)

FAITH: It's a ride.

(Seeing Zipper ride, FAITH points to "it.")

Yes! There it is!

(CARNIE reappears. There's some semblance of a fast ride-sound and pantomime motion.)

FAITH: Excuse me. Do you think that you could give me a quick ride?

CARNIE: Whoo! Let the lady through. Hop on the big Zipper lady! Lady on the Zipper, lady ridin' the Zipper!

(FAITH climbs on. The whole time she is riding, the CARNIE is yelling remarks about her on the Zipper and controlling the ride. She is squealing with sexy delight and periodically yelling "Faster!" FITZ is getting progressively more nauseous observing this. The ride ends and FAITH hops off, bums a cigarette from the CARNIE, and goes to FITZ.)

FITZ: *(With serious concern.)* Are you all right?!

FAITH: That was awesome!

FITZ: Did you hear what he was saying to you? He was looking up your skirt every time you twirled up!

FAITH: So what?

FITZ: So what? Boy, you wouldn't hear that response from a woman in New York, she would slap them with a sexual harassment suit so fast, it would shut their Zipper down.

FAITH: Who's "she"?

FITZ: Just any female East Coaster.

FAITH: What would you have me do?

FITZ: Don't you care that he was violating you?

(Mimicking CARNIE.) "Look at her ride!"

FAITH: That's his problem.

FITZ: No. It's your problem. It was your skirt he was looking under.

FAITH: I was riding a ride. Having fun. If he's an asshole, why should I get upset?

FITZ: Well. Really, really different.

FAITH: Look, I thought you were off tying pigs to the Mayor or something.

FITZ: That ride was really dangerous.

FAITH: I'm fine.

FITZ: Can you just—?

FAITH: Can I just what? Be someone else?

FITZ: No.

FAITH: You're obviously thinking about your ex-girlfriend.

FITZ: Who—Carrie? No, I'm not.

FAITH: "She" would object to the carnies.

FITZ: Could you maybe just—

FAITH: What? Be quietly supportive while you do your research?

FITZ: Yes, please. Because here you are, this divine creature and so alive, and yet I've got this blank pad to fill and I haven't had nicotine for well, 17 days, and then the sex with no condom, I might add, and—!

FAITH: Alright, already.

FITZ: You really were beautiful up there. Like a beautiful colorful bird. You stun me.

(FAITH and FITZ kiss and hug.)

FITZ: So will you help me get this done? Please?

FAITH: I'm Simone de Beauvoir to your Jean Paul Sartre. I'm very familiar with *The Second Sex,* you know.

FITZ: I'll give you second sex.

FAITH: Focus on your work, young man.

SCENE 6

(FITZ's House.)

FITZ: *(Calling to FAITH.)* I've got to get some of these notes into form.

FAITH: *(Toilet flushes. She enters adjusting her skirt.)* Oh, enough work, some play.

FITZ: Faith, we've done it three times today, I'm suddenly feeling our age difference.

FAITH: Only 9 years.

FITZ: I've got to write for a few hours. Can I see you later?

FAITH: Now.

FITZ: I can't now.

FAITH: Did I tell you I learned to salsa just before I left Chicago?

(FAITH takes her shirt off down to her bra and starts to show him an impressive salsa that she's learned. She is trying to include FITZ, who is unenthusiastic.)

FITZ: Faith, I can't dance right now, I have important—

FAITH: Clearly, everything's more important to you than me. Everything.

FITZ: We've only really known each other for a few days. We should be friends. I want to be your friend.

FAITH: That wasn't the impression I got when you pulled over on the freeway on the way home so we could fuck.

FITZ: Why can't you understand this?

FAITH: Don't you want me?

FITZ: A blind man would want you.

(FAITH leans in to kiss FITZ. He is resisting anyway, but she doesn't make it easy.)

FITZ: Were you drinking in the bathroom?

FAITH: No.

FITZ: I smell it.

FAITH: Mouthwash. It's yours.

FITZ: It's just... I'm in recovery. I can't be around it all the time. Do you drink every day?

(FAITH starts to leave.)

Where are you going?

FAITH: *(Slamming the door.)* To Happy Hour. Of course.

SCENE 7

(FAITH's parent's house, two weeks after the fair. FAITH, FITZ, SIMON and CLARK sit around the table, eating dinner. FAITH is feeling up FITZ's leg under the table and they are making out. Parents are in discussion, they are disagreeing. Discussion is finally upstaged by making out.)

FITZ: What is this, "comin'"?

FAITH: Cumin.

FITZ: Cumin?

SIMON: Such taste buds! Yes, there is cumin in the lamb.

FITZ: Could you pass the corn?

SIMON: You don't like cumin?

FITZ: I may be allergic. But I love corn.

SIMON: *(Victimized.)* Oh, well. Shall I whip something else up?

FAITH: Will you pass the wine? Dad?

CLARK: What?

FAITH: The wine? Would you please pass it?

CLARK: *(Passes it, plugging his nose.)* Never could stand the smell of alcohol. So Fitz, how's your story for *Atlantic Monthly* coming along? Hope you don't mind I took a little peek at it. Nice of you to give it to Simon to proofread.

FITZ: Nice of her to do it.

FAITH: I took a "little peek" at it too.

FITZ: What did you think?

FAITH: It's the most fictional fiction I've ever fucked.

SIMON: Only you could fuck fiction, dear.

(CLARK coughs and clears his throat to mask what he just heard.)

FAITH: I mean it's not true.

FITZ: Do you have any Diet Coke?

FAITH: I mean the girl you were at the fair with was a psychotic exhibitionist stripper and who you were really with was me.

SIMON: You are a psychotic exhibitionist stripper, honey.

FAITH: Thanks, Mom.

CLARK: *(Solving a mystery.)* Very interesting how you employ the perspective of a "native companion" showing you around. The "native companion" blends with the local folk, so you remain the outsider.

FAITH: Yes, except the "native companion" was me and I don't blend with the local folk.

CLARK: You should be flattered, Faith! It's not every day that an award winning writer puts you in a story.

FAITH: I have never done cocaine. In public. Nor did I forget to wear my underwear under my skirt.

CLARK: Poetic license. It's not you. *(Proudly.)* But we know you were there.

SIMON: You really capture the way the locals talk. I couldn't believe how accurate you were.

FAITH: I don't talk like a hick!

SIMON: It's not about you, Faith.

FITZ: It's really not. I hope you made some edits, Simon?

SIMON: Very few. Mostly commentaries. I was really moved by your lens.

FAITH: Yeah, bi-focals.

FITZ: Clark?

CLARK: Oh, no, you didn't ask me to edit. You've got the best there in Simon.

SIMON: You don't have to say that, Clark.

CLARK: Well, I know, but, it's true. You're the best editor in the department.

SIMON: It's so refreshing to see some good literature. The tripe that's being passed off as essays now, some of it really isn't even worth reading.

FITZ: Well, they want the final draft by Thursday, so I really appreciate it. Could I have more corn?

FAITH: Yeah, you'll want to load up if you're going to mess with wild-ass me. Oh, I get it, wait a minute, it just came to me. Your ex-girlfriend, that explains it. She's the southerner. Her voice, my body, it's like a combo deal. Biggie fries and biggie shake. (*FAITH pours another glass of wine. There is a awkward silence.*)

CLARK: Did Faith tell you about her writing? She's had many songs optioned by different bands around the city.

SIMON: It's poetry, it really is.

FAITH: No, Mom, you teach poetry. I sing.

CLARK: Sing something for us!

SIMON: And she has a weekly music review she writes published in a Chicago paper. Do they know where to send you your checks for that now?

FAITH: It's a free paper.

SIMON: Sing something! Fitz, you are in for a treat.

FAITH: Mom. You're always critical of my songs.

SIMON: How could you say that?

CLARK: Mom is your biggest fan.

FAITH: Sorry, Mom.

CLARK: Sing the one I like....

(*Improv: Fitz, Simon and Clark all begin to talk at once about their "singing careers/ histories/family members who sang", until Faith interrupts with—*)

FAITH: (*Sings a pointed song. Then—*)

CLARK: That wasn't it.

FAITH: Do you have any Prozac?

SIMON: The Prozac is in the lazy Susan, honey.

FITZ: They should pay you. Someone must read the paper.

FAITH: It's a free paper.

CLARK: A free paper. Who ever heard of that?

FAITH: Uh, everyone.

CLARK: Oh, okay, Faith. You might want to pay attention to who you're in the room with.

FITZ: You could do better than that.

FAITH: (*Goes to get Prozac, pops them with wine, and loses it.*) So! Maybe I'll write something based on the State Fair, too.

(*Sings in hick voice.*)

Kymberly Harris

"I said pass the white powder and the thong please! Don't want you to see the sign on my genitals that says, 'Vacancy, open for renovation, according to my family!'"

(The rest stare at the elephant in the room.)

SCENE 8

(Same night, front porch, or porch swing. FITZ is addictively drinking Diet Coke, several empty cans strewn at his side. It is a black night with the stars gleaming in the sky. FAITH joins him sitting at the front of the house.)

FAITH: You're still here?

FITZ: Yeah, I'm still here.

(FAITH starts crying.)

Come on.

FAITH: It's not that.

FITZ: I just exaggerated things to make it funny—

FAITH: It's not that—

FITZ: Most people prefer not to be identified in a story, it's for the sake of privacy that—

FAITH: It's not that! I'm not the girl in the story. But I'm not the girl here either. I'm not the girl who was singing and writing in Chicago. I'm not the girl who was at the Fair. I'm not the girl who lives here with her parents. I'm just, not the girl! I don't know what's wrong with me? I'm here by default. I had to stay. We sold everything in my apartment for coke—it was all gone. We didn't have anything; I couldn't work anymore. I wouldn't have left—.

FITZ: But aren't you glad you did?

FAITH: I don't know.

FITZ: How can you not know?

FAITH: What's true for everybody else isn't necessarily true for me.

FITZ: Yeah. I wanted to talk to you about something, not a good time, maybe—

FAITH: Go ahead.

FITZ: My sponsor warns me every day. It's…it's not happening yet and maybe it's a good sign that I'm telling you now. Kind of nipping it in the bud. See, I never really allow myself to grieve the person I'm breaking up with before I start the new thing, so then I'm like you said, overstuffed with both the biggie fries and the biggie shake. You know technically that is too much food. One should have one or the other. But, no. Wendy's is smarter than that. They offer one at a discount if you get the other, and then what are you going to do, turn it down?

FAITH: I knew I shouldn't have told you about my past.

FITZ: I already figured most of that out, Faith. It's not that. I'm just saying that I do this. I loved you from the first moment I saw you, but—

FAITH: You just said you love me.

FITZ: I do.

FAITH: I love you, too.

FITZ: Did you understand what I just said? I'm telling you, it matters, I could change from a butterfly back into a cocoon right before your very eyes, any minute now, any second.

FAITH: I'll take my chances.

FITZ: Why would you do that? Haven't you had enough heartache?

FAITH: *(Smiling.)* I'm fine. Can I spend the night tonight? I don't think I can bear my parents' punishing silences. They think I drove the boy genius away.

FITZ: I don't think I'm over Carrie. We were together for two years and I'm just not ready for— I don't even think I can promise anything at all right now.

FAITH: Can we just go back to your place.

FITZ: I don't think it's a good idea tonight. I have to get home, do some work. Let's take a few days off, just to... I don't want to hurt you.

FAITH: *(Turning on the charm.)* You're not going to hurt me!

FITZ: You know what kills me? I know you must be in so much pain. I can feel it off of you. It's exquisite. Palpable. And yet, you smile and you smile and you smile.

(FITZ leaves.)

FAITH: *(Screams at the stars.)* I'm not the girl!

SIMON: *(Comes out smiling.)* Kids? I made Eskimo pies! Where is he?

FAITH: He's gone, mom.

SIMON: *(Sadly, goes back inside.)* Of course he is.

SCENE 9

(FITZ's house, later that night.)

(FAITH is knocking crazily at the bathroom door by now, as she has been trying to get in for several minutes. Before lights rise, we hear the incessant knocking and deliberating.)

FITZ: No! You have to leave. My whole support group says this is bad.

FAITH: They say I'm bad? How is that supposed to make me feel?

FITZ: Not you're bad. We are bad together. Please just go.

FAITH: Let me in, Fitz.

FITZ: Why?

FAITH: Why? Because I'm a human being knocking on your door!

FITZ: We're using each other like a drug. We're addicted to each other so it's not real. I've got to stop this pattern. So please go away.

FAITH: I'm not a pattern! And I'm not using you.

FITZ: You are, you just don't know you are. Besides I'm writing.

FAITH: In the bathroom?

(Silence.)

FITZ: Faith? Faith?

(Turns on light, lights up in full, opens the door. She plunges at him, hugging him.)

FAITH: Stop saying I'm a pattern.

FITZ: Let go.

FAITH: No.

FITZ: You've been drinking.

FAITH: You're into this. I can feel that you are.

FITZ: I can't be.

FAITH: We are.

FITZ: I don't want to be.

FAITH: That makes me want to die. Do you want me to die?

FITZ: Stop drinking.

FAITH: Fuck you! I'm lost. Lost. And all anyone wants to do is criticize me.

FITZ: I can't do this.

(FITZ escapes to the bathroom and locks the door.)

FAITH: *(Knocking.)* Let me in, please!

FITZ: I'm working.

FAITH: Please. I have to go!

FITZ: How are you going to do it?

FAITH: Slit my wrists.

FITZ: At your parent's house? One of them would find you, you know.

FAITH: Pills and alcohol.

FITZ: Same problem.

FAITH: Please unlock the door.

FITZ: I'm not the answer.

FAITH: But you could be a friend.

FITZ: As your friend I'm telling you to go. This isn't good for either of us.

FAITH: But, we love each other.

SCENE 10

(Therapist's office.)

(FAITH is drunk and on pills.)

FAITH: I think I might be losing it.

DR. LEONARD: Why?

FAITH: I can't touch anything in my life. It's all waving in front of me and offering itself and then I reach out to touch it and it's not really there.

DR. LEONARD: Mmm, hm.

FAITH: *(Blurting out sentences, not very logically.)* I share anti-depressants with my mother. I don't think they're working.

DR. LEONARD: Why?

FAITH: Life just doesn't seem worth living anymore, can't, please, anyone…

DR. LEONARD: They said at the front that you threatened to kill yourself.

FAITH: I didn't mean it as a threat, it's a solution. I'm not worth the space I'm takin' up.

DR. LEONARD: And how do you feel now?

FAITH: He said, "How do you want to die?" I said maybe pills, knife. Hanging's out. A little dramatic even for me. I don't believe in guns. I was trying to find a way we could both agree on. Cooperation is important in a relationship, as are mutual tastes. I read that somewhere. He said, "Well, I could drive you to Found Clinic and you could talk to a doctor there." I said, "What about graduate school?"

DR. LEONARD: Graduate school?

FAITH: It's just that he's so brilliant, you know? And it's not like what I think is complicated about me is scary to him, it's the drugs, but sober is not my bag. God, it's hot in here. *(Begins to have a panic attack and strip her clothing.)* Having said that though, the path to oblivion is not all it's cracked up to be. I mean the betrayal! Kerouac, Joplin. You drink to try to please them, to try to emulate something that they are, but they still can't be with you. Even though you're trying to cooperate with them. You're trying to have mutual tastes. Cocaine. Red wine. Sure I'm easy. Prozac, why not? But then the fucking stuff ups and stops working. You sure as hell don't read about that in *On the Road*.

DR. LEONARD: Are you saying you have a problem with addiction?

FAITH: Well, it's kind of like if you have a best friend, your only real friend. And she starts schtuping your husband. You know you're gonna leave his ass because he's been a bastard and besides, he doesn't want you anymore. But you only have one friend who will never leave no matter what you do. Even if she's not dependable anymore…. *(FAITH suddenly realized she had stripped down to her underwear and bra, and panics.)* Why am I always taking my clothes off?

(There is an uncomfortable silence.)

DR. LEONARD: You're hyperventilating. Put your head between your knees. *(FAITH does so. DR. LEONARD picks up FAITH's purse, takes out her wallet, reads driver's license.)*

DR. LEONARD: Faith, I'm going to have you admitted to the psychiatric ward here for some tests. *(Picks up phone. Dials.)* I have a Faith Gold here. It's a 911. I'll need you to contact her parents. Address is 1405 Kingsland Lane.

(BLACKOUT)

ACT II

SCENE 1

(Psych ward at Found Clinic, specializing in addiction. Empty room, one chair. NURSE is outside door. Inside, FAITH is in withdrawal, rocking herself.)

NURSE: Miss Faith, are you dressed?

FAITH: Name, name go away don't come back some other day. Name name go away. Name name go away....sticks and stones may break my bones but names will never hurt me. Shouldn't have played that game. Russian roulette with a child; stuff the competition in her mouth and see which way it comes out. Life or death? As you can see it's neither, both. The worst. You always come to take him away. Him being whoever I loved. Stuff the jealousy in her mouth; see which way it comes out. Name rhymes with shame rhymes with game rhymes with blame. Little girl no bigger than a thimble. And very nimble. Very nimble. Gets to a master writer. Why? Because Simon says. Mama. Shouldn't play Russian roulette with something no bigger than a thimble. My shrinking heart. Too easy to miss.

NURSE: Miss Faith, are you dressed?

FAITH: Yes, Miss Nurse.

NURSE: *(Enters.)* Would you like to meet with Dr. Leonard now?

FAITH: Nope. Thanks for askin'.

NURSE: Miss Faith, you know that's not good answer.

FAITH: Oh, you want the good answer? Why, then, yes, I am peeing myself with anticipation to see the doctor!

NURSE: We don't say "peeing ourselves."

FAITH: We don't?

NURSE: No, we don't. We say, "So grateful to have opportunity to see doctor."

FAITH: I see.

NURSE: She make us well!

FAITH: Oh, are you seeing the doctor, too?

NURSE: *(Quite offended.)* Not funny, Miss Faith.

(LIGHTS DIM on FAITH.)

SCENE 2

(Hospital, group therapy.)

(GROUP MEMBERS sit in a semi-circle:

    DR. LEONARD

    KIRK—*a philosopher*

    ANDREW—*a people pleaser/depressive*

SHEILA—*sex and cocaine addict*
MAYA—*a religious freak*
FAITH—*new to the group)*

DR. LEONARD: We have a new member coming today and as you know when someone new joins us, we start the session with a life or death topic. When you get out of here, what will stop you from being influenced against your best interests?

ANDREW: The Group?

DR. LEONARD: Please state your name before you speak today.

ANDREW: Andrew. The Group?

DR. LEONARD: Yes, of course, you'll keep in touch with certain members of Group after your treatment here. But, even so, there will be parties, peer pressure. Even pop culture often glamorizes addiction.

SHEILA: *(Raps.)* My name is Shei-*la*. And I'd really hate to be *ya. (Cracks up laughing.)* Because it's a well-known fact that eating pussy is far better on cocaine then off. For both parties, doc. How am I supposed to forget that?

DR. LEONARD: We'll keep working, Sheila. Any other revelations?

KIRK: Well, Doc, I'm Kirk. You and I have worked together for a long time. I have given this quite a lot of thought. You must regard each person, each situation, and each image individually. Take Gaga: a pop culture icon, true, but an artist. She's using her music to forward her concepts.

SHEILA: I'd fuck her.

KIRK: Take Born This Way. She's singing in her bra and underwear, in crazy makeup, with vaginas eating everybody, but it's a commentary, not to be taken literally. Wake up, people!

ANDREW: I long for her message. I wish it would reach out and eat me whole.

KIRK: She wanted to be a performance artist. It just so happens that the media latched on and she becomes a media sensation. But that is not her fault! And she continues to create concepts, to challenge us artistically—she's not just a fantasy girl-slash-sex kitten. No!

DR. LEONARD: I'm not sure I understand the relevance of this, Kirk.

KIRK: The relevance! The relevance is she stands out.

SHEILA: I would definitely fuck Kesha.

KIRK: Most of them can't sing, can't dance, don't challenging us to think, but are media sensations. Is that Okay, I ask you? It's not Okay. It's a cheap short cut. She looks sexy in the video. But it's just empty images. Same result. But the route there has no integrity. Same result though.

(DR. LEONARD sighs, gets up and turns off the TV.)

(Faith enters, late.)

DR. LEONARD: Oh, hi, Faith, take a chair. Welcome to your first Group! To help you create a focus for your recovery, we are discussing what might influence vs. prevent relapse when you are done with your stays here.

KIRK: As I was saying, why doesn't it matter how we get where we get? If two people are rich but one made their money legit, and one robbed a bank, how come they're the same? They're not.

SHEILA: He's a fucking wackadoo—

KIRK: No, actually I'm sober and not currently taking any meds like I'm sure the rest of you are. So you might want to pay attention to what I'm saying. Because they're going to give you meds in here, and so you'll be "their" kind of high, and ask yourselves, why is that okay, but the drugs you were taking that got you in here, are T-A-B-O-O?

DR. LEONARD: *(Having heard this concern from Kirk at the beginning of each new session.)* The problems we treat with medication are a result of medically diagnosed chemical imbalances. That is quite different than self-medicating.

ANDREW: *(Tearfully.)* Andrew. You want us to take our meds just so we'll act right, but that doesn't mean we're right inside. *(Suddenly self conscious.)* I didn't say it.

FAITH: So you're saying that drugs that are prescribed are socially acceptable, so they're okay?

KIRK: You have to say your name before you speak.

FAITH: What's your name?

KIRK: *(Like it's obvious.)* Uh, I'm Kirk.

FAITH: *(Right back at him.)* Okay. Well, I'm Faith.

KIRK: *(Laughs particularly loudly)*

FAITH: What?

KIRK: Addicts don't have faith in anyone or anything. Well, Faith, and everyone, the point is, they are going to claim they are going to treat you for a chemical imbalance, but there is no such thing as chemical imbalance. Everything is chemically unique and we accept it for what it is, but not people. The leather chair doesn't have to change chemically to be more like the felt chair. Cheddar doesn't change to be more like Swiss. But we're all supposed to be chemically the same? We have to be homogenized?

DR. LEONARD: Not homogenized, just not self-destructive.

ANDREW: *(Screams.)* I'm trying to listen to the doctor!

FAITH: How is taking a happy pill going to address my real feelings and thoughts. What happens to my real feelings and thoughts?

DR. LEONARD: Prozac cannot annihilate our psychology. It just feeds you serotonin so that it's easier for you to cope. If you take it as prescribed.

ANDREW: What about Lithium?

DR. LEONARD: Well, Lithium does change your personality slightly, but it is clear that the benefits outweigh the side effects in your case.

SHEILA: What about—

DR. LEONARD: We have discussed that at length! Did you take yours today or hide it under your tongue?

SHEILA: *(Stands and flaunts tongue.)* Finally, you're talking about something interesting: my tongue.

DR. LEONARD: Sit down, Sheila.

MAYA: Maya. The only real cure for addiction is the contemplation of God.

KIRK: That's so full of shit.

ANDREW: *(Still screaming.)* I can't hear the doctor's voice!!

FAITH: For Christ's sake.

MAYA: *(Accusingly.)* Faith! The Lord's name in vain? Keep it up, heathens!

DR. LEONARD: Is "Oh, you're so full of shit" an affirmative, pro-active statement? You can challenge me all you want but I will not allow any of you to insult your peers.

MAYA: Thank you, Doctor.

DR. LEONARD: From here on in the one who may speak is the one holding the Stone. Who would like to start?

(KIRK grabs it. Holds the stone with his life.)

Fine, Kirk's up. Why do you feel that Maya is being disingenuous?

KIRK: Because giving up all of her responsibility to God is so lame.

MAYA: *(Grabs the stone.)* God is in charge. It is all predestined.

KIRK: *(Grabs the stone.)* She's trying to glorify life to make herself feel better. It's so self-centered. Life is not a massive energy source sitting on the pot waiting to be manipulated to make Maya feel better.

DR. LEONARD: Why does it affect you if Maya perceives the world in a way that makes her feel better?

KIRK: Why not just take crack, heroin, meth, X, booze, pills? Same thing: escaping your reality.

DR. LEONARD: Wouldn't you say that relinquishing your control to a higher power as opposed to drugs and alcohol is a healthier choice?

KIRK: I say that religion's just another way to get high.

DR. LEONARD: That is a very interesting thought, Kirk.

KIRK: And recovery is just another dealer that wants to pay his bills.

FAITH: Do you agree with him?

DR. LEONARD: Kirk is holding the Stone.

FAITH: No! You make us read all this shit about putting our faith in a higher power, and we have to sit here and listen to him go on and on while we willing people are hanging on by our fingernails—

DR. LEONARD: It seems that Faith has a pressing need—

FAITH: Fuck you.

DR. LEONARD: Abusive. –to speak now. Kirk can you agree to pass the Stone?

(KIRK passes stone to FAITH. FAITH reluctantly has to accept.)

DR. LEONARD: Your turn, Faith. What's on your mind?

FAITH: Why do you let him go on like he's Kierkegaard or something? You like his dark ideas. What kind of an example is that for the rest of us? We're sitting here trying to believe we can survive without drugs if we believe in the twelve steps and a Higher Power when our very leader is practically handing out pamphlets to the contrary?

DR. LEONARD: I do not espouse to any one idea except that each of you has a right to express yours. If you aren't aware of your feelings, you can't deal with them.

MAYA: But Kirk somehow gets to spew his sacrilege—

DR. LEONARD: Kirk doesn't have any more right to speak than any one of the rest of you. Perhaps you feel threatened by Kirk's comments today. Perhaps you should ask yourselves why?

MAYA: We're threatened because he is going to burn in the bloody fires of hell and I don't want to be caught in the crossfire. Right, Faith?

DR. LEONARD: Whoever has the Stone may speak.

FAITH: Please don't side with me, Maya. I don't agree with you either.

MAYA: Atheist!

DR. LEONARD: You have the Stone.

FAITH: Yeah.

DR. LEONARD: So. Your turn.

FAITH: What is your personal belief, Doctor? I mean do you believe in a higher power?

DR. LEONARD: The success of 12-step recovery programs proves that if there is a spiritual force greater than yourself at work in your life, you will not feel the same debilitating pressures you're accustomed to, pressures that can lead to drug abuse, and even lead some to want to die. My personal beliefs aren't relevant to the Group's recovery.

SHEILA: Ha! Maya, your doctor's a Satan worshiper. Maybe you are in hell.

(MAYA starts crying. ANDREW empathizes and so starts crying.)

KIRK: Does scaring her really make you feel that much better, Sheila?

SHEILA: I'm just saying that if she let me into that tight little hole of hers, she'd loosen up a little bit.

DR. LEONARD: Sheila, strive for honesty, not hostility.

SHEILA: Huh? Fuck me. We're already in hell.

DR. LEONARD: It's group therapy in the psyche ward of the Found Clinic specializing in addiction.

KIRK: So in other words, "Hell."

DR. LEONARD: Interesting sentiment coming from the one voluntary patient we have.

KIRK: *(Stands.)* Betrayer! This session sucks shit! *(He paces furiously.)*

FAITH: I don't understand why you can't reveal more about your personal beliefs? You're sitting here with us. You're a human being.

DR. LEONARD: As your doctor, I'm in a position where I might influence someone's opinion.

FAITH: We need that. We need positive influences.

DR. LEONARD: Well, not everyone agrees with you.

FAITH: Do you agree with me?

DR. LEONARD: In part.

FAITH: Which part?

DR. LEONARD: That you need positive influence. But not by my subjective beliefs.

FAITH: That's what we're dealing with: subjective beliefs?

DR. LEONARD: What's your real question?

FAITH: My question is, do you believe this? That if we put our faith in an invisible God of our understanding that we'll get better? That's the answer?

DR. LEONARD: Do you believe it?

FAITH: No, do you believe it? You're the expert.

DR. LEONARD: It is irrelevant—

FAITH: You keep saying that, but the alternative is that you're sitting here lying to us. Patronizing us. What's good for us isn't necessarily good enough for you. And I'm asking you what would be good enough for you? That's the "program" I'm betting on. But let's face it, you're probably not even an addict.

KIRK: Oh, God! You are the first person who has asked her a real question in so long. In so fucking long. Baby! Yes! *(Jumps to his knees before FAITH.)*

> My mistresses' eyes are nothing like the sun;
>
> Coral is far more red than her lips' red;
>
> If snow be white, why then her breasts are dun;

If hairs be wires, black wires grow on her head.

I have seen roses damasked, red and white.

But no such roses see I in her cheeks,

And in some perfumes there is more delight

Than in the breath that from my mistress reeks.

I love to hear her speak, yet will I know

That music hath a far more pleasing sound;

I grant I never saw a goddess go;

My mistress when she walks treads on the ground.

And yet by heave I think my love as rare

As any she belied with false compare.

DR. LEONARD: So you identify with Faith, Kirk, excellent.

KIRK: Don't. Even. Look. At. Me.

MAYA: Doctor, I'm afraid that you did not understand what he just said. I must inform you, a "mistress" is a whore.

ANDREW: I'll give you five dollars if that's not what Shakespeare meant! Five dollars!

DR. LEONARD: Yes I understood him Maya, and a mistress in Shakespeare's day was simply a maiden, not a prostitute.

MAYA: Well, I see that Satan has gotten a hold of you, too.

DR. LEONARD: Good work. Many good questions were raised about how you will survive without drugs and alcohol. And our time has flown.

KIRK: Right over the cuckoo's nest.

DR. LEONARD: We have a lot to consider until tomorrow.

FAITH: Can I get a straight answer for once!

DR. LEONARD: Yes, Faith?

FAITH: Do you believe that if I put my faith in a higher power that I will stop needing drugs?

DR. LEONARD: Perhaps, but, I believe that your need isn't for drugs.

KIRK: What?

MAYA: Praise Jesus. Praise the Lord.

ANDREW: I want my five dollars back!

DR. LEONARD: *(Firmly.)* Your disease is that you try to be everything to everyone. And it is impossible. You are addicted to trying to gauge and control how people think about you. You've engaged in drugs and with drug addicts to avoid the pain of dealing with the fact that you can't please anybody, including yourself, all of the time. Many of us were trained to answer the needs of our parents before we could identify our own. Here we're learning to identify our own real needs and responsibilities. But that's not going to happen overnight. And that is why you're here. *(Pause.)* Time is officially up. Until tomorrow.

(DR. LEONARD briskly departs.)

FAITH: Don't do that! Don't drop a bomb on me and then leave. Don't walk out on me! You always leave, everybody always leaves.

(The Group sits in wonder.)

SCENE 3

(Hospital recreation area. FAITH and KIRK are playing ping-pong.)

KIRK: You did good today.

FAITH: I made an ass of myself.

KIRK: Yeah, everybody else in Group is so composed, what were you thinking?

FAITH: Well, I'm not like that. I don't break down.

KIRK: What's that supposed to mean?

FAITH: I'm not crazy.

KIRK: Oh, but the rest of us are.

FAITH: I'm not talking about you.

KIRK: Whatever you think of everyone else here, think of me, because we're all the same.

FAITH: Why are you getting upset with me?

KIRK: Maybe if you didn't put all your energy into trying to be better than the rest of us you'd have more left over for recovery.

FAITH: Recovery from what? I was going through a bad breakup and freaked out, it's common.

KIRK: You think the normal reaction to a breakup is wanting to off yourself?

FAITH: Oh, so now I'm abnormal.

KIRK: I think so.

FAITH: So who wants to be normal anyway? I'm *from* Normal, Illinois; I don't want to *be* normal.

KIRK: I'm so sick of you always setting yourself apart. You're the same as the rest of us. Have you even bothered to find out their stories?

FAITH: No, I'm too busy kicking your ass at ping-pong.

KIRK: Sheila. Raped as a child by her stepfather. Now a staunch lesbian, who has been self medicating with cocaine and sex to counter her severe depression, probably caused by repressing the rapes.

FAITH: Maya?

KIRK: She's an orthodox Jew.

FAITH: She's Jewish? *I'm* Jewish. Not Orthodox, but—

KIRK: Well, obviously.

FAITH: How do you know these things?

KIRK: I was interested, so I asked them.

FAITH: And, you?

KIRK: I tried to gas myself in my car, my girlfriend who was also my pot dealer, broke up with me. Thought I couldn't live without her.

FAITH: I know that feeling.

KIRK: Yeah, too bad you don't have anything in common with the rest of us.

(Game ends as Kirk scores the winning point.)

SCENE 4

(GROUP MEMBERS are playing with puppets that they made in Arts and Crafts. They use their puppets to encourage free dialogue and express their inner monologues.)

DR. LEONARD: Does everybody have his or her Puppet?

(They all hold them up.)

DR. LEONARD: Good. Now the topic is relationships, which is difficult for many of you. Know that you have your Puppet to shield you, and hopefully that will help you to interact more freely. The goal is to become more comfortable being intimate with the other Puppets. Let's begin.

KIRK: Mine's fucked. Give me the Stone.

MAYA: We're not even using that right now. We're doing Puppet Play.

(KIRK tears open his Puppet and sticks the Stone inside. He holds up his Puppet.)

KIRK: There! Now it won't blow away! My puppet was filled with air. It could have blown away with a mere gust of wind.

MAYA: You can't just put the Group's Stone inside your puppet.

ANDREW: That is very selfish, Kirk.

KIRK: Survival of the fittest, my friends.

MAYA: No! Adam and Eve!

SHEILA: *(Stands up and begins to strut her stuff.)* I'm Megan Fox.

FAITH: You're more than your body, you know.

SHEILA: Strip with me, baby.

MAYA: I had a dream last night about blood.

DR. LEONARD: What was the dream, Maya?

MAYA: Blood. You know, *the* blood.

SHEILA: Damn, I was this close to getting the clothes off Faith's puppet.

ANDREW: Bullshit, you liar!

FAITH: Stop it, you guys. You mean your period?

MAYA: When I first got my period I didn't even know what it was. I was eleven. I noticed a little blood on my panties for three days, and kept hiding them, and changing into new ones. The third night I woke up to a pool of blood on my bed and started screaming. My mother came upstairs, saw my period blood and smacked me across the face. After that, I hardly ever get my period. In fact, when I was pregnant, I didn't even know it. I just thought I was getting fat for six months.

FAITH: *(Skeptically.)* You were pregnant, Maya?

KIRK: Have you ever been pregnant, Faith?

FAITH: Have you ever gotten a girl pregnant Kirk?

ANDREW: I would love to be pregnant.

MAYA: *(Begins to pray.)* "Our father who art in Heaven…."

(There is a silence.)

ANDREW: If I weren't nothing, I would make a baby with you.

FAITH: You're not nothing.

KIRK: You don't care about Andrew. You just don't want to have to deal with that so you beef him up. Maybe he is nothing. Maybe he is something. But he has the right to feel the way he feels today without you giving him false hope and denying him that right.

FAITH: Oh, so would you have me say, "Yes Andrew, you're nothing"?

ANDREW: *(Tearing up.)* What?

FAITH: *(To ANDREW.)* No, I'm not saying that to you.

KIRK: It's not your place to say anything. Just accept it.

FAITH: Sorry, I care about people.

KIRK: Da Nile is a river in Egypt.

ANDREW: Thank you for sticking up for me, Faith, I love you! I love you! I am telling you I—!

SHEILA: Do this Faith. *(Puppet strip tease.)* Yeah, baby. Take it off. Yeah baby!

FAITH: Andrew, don't love me, okay? I'm a heart breaker.

ANDREW: No, you're just heartbroken.

(FAITH tears up.)

KIRK: You care-take everyone. How can you really love anyone if you're always second-guessing what they want and trying to give it to them. Just be.

FAITH: Why do you even care?

KIRK: Oh, for a woman who could understand herself.

FAITH: I understand myself, thank you.

KIRK: You just want goddess worship.

ANDREW: I understand yourself.

KIRK: Bleeding heart.

MAYA: *(Tormented.)* Ohhhhhh….

SHEILA: All right, you want to play rough, will that do it for ya? Take your clothes off you little slut. You little cock tease!

FAITH: A woman isn't a cock tease just because she won't take her clothes off, Sheila.

SHEILA: How would you know what a woman is? You wanna find out?

KIRK: Everything isn't about you, Faith.

ANDREW: Yes, it is!

KIRK: Rent a clue, Andrew.

ANDREW: Dr. Leonard. I am professing my love to Faith, and everyone treats it like a joke. I am trying to express my intimacy, and no one is taking me seriously!

FAITH: You love me.

ANDREW: Yes!

FAITH: Alright. Let's go out on a date.

ANDREW: W-w-w-where do you want to go?

FAITH: To the movies and then out for Italian food, where we feed each other at the table. I will suck up your linguine and you mine, and then I'll get up and sing a song to you, and then we'll go home and make hot love and wake up and have coffee and strawberries in bed and read the paper, then go for a run, and come home and take a shower together and make love again.

ANDREW: W-What movie do you want to see?

FAITH: Something romantic. *Juno.*

ANDREW: I-I've seen that.

FAITH: Well, what about the rest?

ANDREW: Italian is way too filling. On second thought, I-I better stay home.

SHEILA: Why would you want to go out with him? Don't you see he doesn't know what to do with a real woman? I'll take you out.

ANDREW: I'll take her out.

KIRK: Cut this unreal shit!

FAITH: You think anything that doesn't come out of your mouth is unreal.

KIRK: Exactly, because I'm the only one here who insists on emotional truth.

MAYA: Andrew, will you pray with me?

FAITH: Is that why you don't you find me attractive?

KIRK: See, like that. Does everybody need to find you attractive?

DR. LEONARD: There is something to be looked at here, Faith. All of the puppets have asked for your company except for Kirk's. Why are you focused on him?

FAITH: I want to know what he thinks is wrong with me. He obviously thinks something is wrong with me.

DR. LEONARD: It is interesting that you are only attracted to those who resist you, though.

FAITH: I'm not attracted to him!

SHEILA: Maybe something's wrong with him.

KIRK: *(To SHEILA.)* Maybe something's wrong with you.

SHEILA: Ain't nothing wrong with me baby, I could take her to the moon and back with three little fingers if she'd let me. I don't need a dick for that.

ANDREW: Will you show me how to do that?

SHEILA: Yeah, but you might want to get over your agoraphobia first.

ANDREW: My what? My *what!* (*ANDREW makes troubled muffled sounds.*)

MAYA: Stop it all of you. None of you have any idea what love is! My mother was virgin until she was married.

SHEILA: Aren't you a little old to be a "virgin"?

MAYA: How do you know I am a virgin, Sheila, stupid.

SHEILA: What did you do, fuck an imaginary angel? You're a virgin, believe me. I can smell 'em a mile away.

MAYA: Well, this time—*MS.*—you are wrong.

FAITH: You've had sex, Maya?

MAYA: I got screwed at fifteen.

KIRK: Did you say screw? I think I'm titillated.

ANDREW: Me too.

SHEILA: Me, too, girl.

MAYA: Mother was a virgin until she was married but I sinned—

SHEILA: Mary Magdalene was a hooker.

MAYA: You don't know the first thing about her plight. Jesus paid for her sins.

(*MAYA crosses herself.*)

FAITH: What happened to you, Maya?

MAYA: I don't remember much. I was drinking beer for the first time. I was dating a boy, sort of, and we were at this party. I was drinking a lot, and we went outside and I don't remember anything of it, except that we came back in and everybody was looking at me.

FAITH: What did you do?

MAYA: I sort of knew to act like I hadn't done what must have just happened.

FAITH: Had you been sexual together at all before this?

MAYA: We had always done everything "but." The next day the boy brought me a T-shirt to school with my blood on it. A souvenir. He said I was saying things during it like, "Oh, it hurts so good." Why did I talk like a whore? I was a virgin.

ANDREW: Your first sexual experience was rape?

SHEILA: Holy shit!

MAYA: What? No it wasn't. I—we were going together. Mary sacrificed her body and so did I.

FAITH: It's Okay, Maya. I lost my virginity when I was fifteen, too.

Kymberly Harris

ANDREW: I wish I could lose my virginity.

SHEILA: Oh my God! See you're a bunch of impotents. That's why I only date celebrities. They're the only ones with enough ego to handle IT, if you know what I'm sayin.

MAYA: *(Inspired by a fury of religious judgment, gets in each of their faces.)* You're all sinners. *(To SHEILA.)* You're a disgusting heathen and you're going straight to hell. *(To ANDREW.)* You're too weak. *(To KIRK.)* You're too proud. *(To FAITH.)* You're vain. God doesn't want us to be this way. Take Him into your hearts or you are going to hell!

FAITH & KIRK: *(To MAYA.)* Maya, you're Jewish!!

SCENE 5

(FAITH's hospital room. FAITH is alone, writing. She had the pills she's been harboring in a line in front of her. She is taking them as she writes.)

FAITH: Intimacy, in to me see, in to me see, in to me—

(She runs out of paper. Starts writing on her arm, runs out of space on her arm, starts writing on her chest.)

See—

(Stabs herself in chest.)

Ow!

(She uses blood to continue writing, feeling the pain. She enjoys that she is no longer numb.)

Faith without works is dead.

SCENE 6

(Found Clinic, DR. LEONARD's office. CLARK and SIMON sit in the office with Dr. LEONARD.)

SIMON: She—she tried to cut her heart out?

CLARK: She cut her chest. I don't think she tried to cut her heart out.

SIMON: Why else would she be stabbing at her chest, Clark?

CLARK: She was out of her mind on drugs, Simon. One of the kids gave her their Valium, and then she took the Ritalin and the Prozac they gave her, which she shouldn't even be on. They found it when they pumped her stomach. And right before visiting day. I was going to show her she was mentioned in the magazine article Fitz wrote and she goes and does this.

SIMON: Why doesn't she feel our love?

CLARK: She got influenced by a bad seed in Chicago, and now she's bringing it home to Normal.

SIMON: You're such an idiot! *(She starts beating on him. He maintains the stance of a man who can take it and endures.)*

CLARK: Get it out.

SIMON: Don't tell me what to do.

CLARK: Get it out.

SIMON: Where are my pills?

CLARK: Gee, I wonder where Faith gets it from.

SIMON: You bastard.

CLARK: Faith doesn't need all of those pills. That's what's making her crazy.

SIMON: They give her pills to mend what is broken.

CLARK: Oh, bull. What's broken? She's a good kid from a good family. She's spoiled. "What's broken."

SIMON: Clark, we have not had sex in 12 years.

CLARK: What's that got to do with the price of rice?

SIMON: We're broken.

CLARK: We just haven't felt that way in a while, Simon, with your illness and now Faith's problems. Things have been rough.

SIMON: You can't keep doing this to me.

CLARK: What am I doing? I'm comforting you.

SIMON: I want to have sex! I want to get laid! I want to get fucked every which way possible. *(She is freaking out. Clark slaps her face.)*

SIMON: You hit me!

CLARK: You're hysterical.

SIMON: Then get me my fucking pills.

CLARK: What in the heck is going on in this place?

SIMON: Clark, just let the doctor explain

CLARK: God dog it, missy. I send my daughter here to get well, better, to get better for life, and we get a call that, what?

SIMON: It was our daughter, right? Faith Gold? There was no mistake? It wasn't someone else's daughter?

DR. LEONARD: No, Mrs. Gold, it—it—

CLARK: What the hell is going on!

SIMON: *(Sarcastic.)* Oh, my, Clark, you cursed. You're losing control.

DR. LEONARD: Please sit. Can I get you some tea? Aspirin?

CLARK: I think an explanation is what we need.

DR. LEONARD: There's a saying that goes, "She who rides a tiger is afraid to dismount."

CLARK: What? What?!

DR. LEONARD: Faith tried to hurt herself, maybe even to take her own life, it's true. But it is important to look at how she did it. She-she tried to write out her thoughts and feelings on her own body. To literally embody her own thoughts and feelings. In a way, this is progress.

CLARK: Jeez Criminy!

(SIMON weeps.)

DR. LEONARD: You see, while very empathetic to other people's feelings, she couldn't feel her own heart, because she didn't feel she had a right to. She shared this with me in session. But what you need to understand is, that although the action is regrettable, her motivation was based on new self-awareness, which in itself is a step towards recovery.

CLARK: *(Spitting with anger.)* Are you a patient here? You are trying to tell me that there is something good about my daughter stabbing at herself repeatedly?

(SIMON starts praying in Yiddish.)

DR. LEONARD: I assure you. It will never happen again.

CLARK: You better believe it won't. Because we are getting her out of here.

DR. LEONARD: I implore you not to do that.

SIMON: Are you serious?

DR. LEONARD: If you take her away now you will once again be telling her that her truth, her real expression, is something to be moved on from rather than something worth exploring. That your feelings and thoughts about her, about anything for that matter, are more valid than her own.

CLARK: That is horse manure!

SIMON: Bullshit, Clark. For god's sake at a time like this, just say bullshit. You cursed before, you're already tainted.

CLARK: This is not about cursing, Simon.

DR. LEONARD: What is it about?

CLARK: It's about Faith!

SIMON: Faith. Faith! *(SIMON breaks down.)*

DR. LEONARD: Faith felt her feelings for the first time and they were so painful that it made her want to die. But she didn't die. And she did experience and live through her genuine feelings—

CLARK: My daughter has always been an emotional person.

DR. LEONARD: Yes, a reactionary. Reacting to other people's big emotions. Engaging with people with big emotions. Bringing out people's emotions. But last night she was alone with her emotions for the first time. Not yours, not Simon's, not a boyfriend's, hers.

SIMON: Well, if it caused this suicide attempt how can this be good?

DR. LEONARD: What's the alternative?

CLARK: Living.

DR. LEONARD: But not for herself? Never accepting and trusting her own passions and desires and instincts.

CLARK: Her instinct was to die.

DR. LEONARD: It's a real instinct. Not to be dismissed.

CLARK: It's a crazy impulse.

DR. LEONARD: According to whom? You? That's your label? Great minds have contemplated suicide.

(SIMON screams in agony, crying louder, because to her, it's all about her.)

CLARK: Is that what you teach here? That suicidal impulse is the sign of a great mind?

DR. LEONARD: Of course not. But we don't discourage our patients from their thoughts or how will we understand how to truly help them? If they pretend they're feeling other then they are, why even be here to get healed? Denial is what society demands of us, it's not what recovery demands of us. Recovery demands the opposite. And the reward is mental health.

CLARK: *(Snidely.)* "Recovery," huh? How did she get the drugs?

DR. LEONARD: You're absolutely right. That won't happen again.

CLARK: We should sue you.

DR. LEONARD: Well, in fact, we're protected, Mr. Gold. In fact, we have the right to kick Faith out for harboring drugs. But I don't want to do that.

SIMON: Why not?

DR. LEONARD: Because believe it or not, I see this as a breakthrough for Faith.

CLARK: Am I having a nightmare?

SIMON: Yes, Clark, you're having a nightmare! Booga booga booga!

DR. LEONARD: We have work to do. To heal Faith.

SIMON: I need to see her. I need to see my baby.

DR. LEONARD: Not yet. She's too fragile to see family now.

SIMON: I beg your pardon. I am her mother.

DR. LEONARD: I can tell her you were here. I'll tell her.

SIMON: You are not her mother. I am.

DR. LEONARD: And she is here, now.

SCENE 7

(Hospital room/hallucination. FAITH is on a hospital bed. She is groggy, in pain, experiencing an hallucination.)

SIMON: You were cutting other people's pain out of your body.

FAITH: Somebody's got to get rid of it, mommy. And I never could. Tell me it's not my responsibility anymore.

SIMON: It's not your responsibility anymore.

FAITH: Tell me it never was.

SIMON: It never was.

FAITH: Tell me I'm not a failure because of it.

CLARK: You're not.

FAITH: Tell me I am free.

SIMON & CLARK: You are free to live for you now.

FAITH: And I won't be punished for taking care of myself and growing?

SIMON & CLARK: You won't be punished for taking care of yourself and growing.

FAITH: And even if it means being alone sometimes, I have to do it anyway.

FITZ & KIRK: Even if we don't love you anymore because of it, you have to do it anyway.

FAITH: Let it be.

SCENE 8

(Found Clinic lunchroom. FAITH bursts in with her tray and sits next to KIRK, who is already eating.)

KIRK: Your bandages are off.

FAITH: Yeah.

KIRK: Lookin' good.

FAITH: Thanks. *(Pause.)* I wonder if Fitz will show up for Visitor's Day? Three days before my release. He's going to ask me a bunch of questions. I don't think that I have any answers.

KIRK: What is this, Jell-O or pudding?

FAITH: What am I going to tell him? "I'm sorry I was drunk every time we got together? I couldn't face intimacy sober?"

KIRK: This isn't even any one color. Is this puce?

FAITH: "You're the most talented man I've ever known and I couldn't really see or hear you or let you see or hear me? My fear of rejection took precedence over your feelings or thoughts, forgive me?"

KIRK: Now I know what color puce is. It's not yellow, it's not green—

FAITH: You have so much unsolicited advice all the time and here when I am asking for—

KIRK: Ask your Dr. Leonard.

FAITH: I'm asking you.

KIRK: You want to have your cake and eat it too.

FAITH: Have you ever even eaten cake, Kirk? Or are you an expert simply by looking in the bakery window?

KIRK: Oh, I've eaten my share of cake baby, and it just made me hungrier.

FAITH: Well, maybe you should upgrade the quality of what you're putting in your mouth.

KIRK: *(Right at her.)* This isn't about whether or not I want to put you in my mouth. *(Pause.)* Chemicals. Everybody needs chemicals. You just can't get enough of them. I'd like to be pure just for a while.

FAITH: Okay, "Maya."

KIRK: No pure, clean pure. To live for two seconds without the need to stuff myself with something to make me feel better. Could be good for a person. Could let a person learn what they're truly ready for.

FAITH: Not everything is a drug. I want real love in my life.

KIRK: As much as you don't want to be alone? Do you want to give unconditional love as much as you want to receive it? Do you have any idea how to do that? Have you seen a relationship that you can emulate? There are muscles that a person has to develop.

FAITH: Well…

KIRK: You, for example, Okay, are really good at engaging, and really good at telling people to fuck off. But you have to ask yourself if you have the strength to develop the muscles in between. To hang in with someone, even if they disappoint you, even after they don't meet your expectations, that is love.

FAITH: You won't disappoint me.

KIRK: *(Yells.)* I'm not talking about me! I'm talking about you! Be accountable for yourself, for once!

FAITH: And this coming from a man who won't leave rehab?

KIRK: I know I have to work out more to have a relationship. You need to decide if you do.

FAITH: This is ridiculous. You can't be this self-aware, and in the psyche ward.

KIRK: Self-awareness has nothing to do with hanging in with someone. And hanging in with someone is all that life's about.

FAITH: Oh, really.

KIRK: Really, "He who rides a tiger is afraid to dismount."

FAITH: Excuse me?

KIRK: It's a proverb.

FAITH: From who?

KIRK: From the proverb people. Faith, building a bridge back to life, everybody has to do their part. To bring the materials they need to make the bridge. It's not about the individual people, it's about the bridge, and can you really trust Joe to bring the cement, and Faith to bring the drill?

FAITH: Who the hell is Joe?

KIRK: Love, baby. Can't be rushed. The bridge has to be solid enough to get from one side to the other, every day. And if it isn't, you better be man enough to know that. One of us has to.

(There is a pause. FAITH understands him.)

FAITH: Jell-O.

Kymberly Harris

KIRK: What?

FAITH: It's lime Jell-O.

SCENE 9

(KIRK's room.)

(FAITH sneaks in and shakes KIRK awake. ANDREW, his roomy, sleeps then fake-sleeps throughout this dialogue.)

FAITH: Kirk, I've come to tell you, you're driving me a little crazy.

KIRK: Faith, you're in a nut house. You have to be crazy to get meals and clean sheets. Go to bed.

FAITH: I brought you a Ding-Dong.

KIRK: You mean you?

FAITH: *(Hands him the pastry.)* It's a bribe. I need to talk.

KIRK: Now?

FAITH: Now. Wait. Give your Ding-Dong to Andrew and see if he'll go into the bathroom. I don't want him to hear.

KIRK: Andrew has too many sedatives in him to wake up until morning. What's up, pussycat? I'm not going to Da Nile in Egypt with you if that's why you're here.

FAITH: If you think I understand so little about love, why did you say that sonnet to me that time? I had been a total bitch to you in Group and you got down on your knees—

KIRK: I like it when you're a bitch. It's real.

FAITH: Oh, this just gets better and better.

KIRK: It's okay to be you, Faith. No one is better or worse than anybody, nobody's better or worse than you. Now, go to sleep.

FAITH: If you know so much, what are you doing in here?

KIRK: Where else am I going to go?

FAITH: Home.

KIRK: Home is inside.

FAITH: Where you came from.

KIRK: Where I came from isn't my home. Home is where you can feel like you. This is the only place they're speaking in a language I can understand.

FAITH: If you want to talk psychology, become a therapist.

KIRK: I'd rather just stay crazy; less responsibility.

FAITH: But it stigmatizes you.

KIRK: As what?

FAITH: As a crazy person who keeps getting released and checking himself back in.

KIRK: You're a crazy person and you're as beautiful as could be.

(They jump each other with the passion that has been building up, and then KIRK suddenly pushes her away, screaming.)

I'm not fit to touch! *I'm not fit to touch!*

(ANDREW shoots up. FAITH jumps out of bed. KIRK is revealed and shaken. He holds himself. ANDREW goes back to sleep, traumatized.)

FAITH: I'm not the girl.

(Shaken, FAITH curls up at the bottom of the bed like a kitten. Slowly, KIRK reaches out and almost touches her.)

SCENE 10

(Found clinic public room, Visitor's Day, three days before FAITH's release. THE GROUP sits around waiting for visitors. FAITH sleeps. DR. LEONARD comes in and waves different patients out to see their visitors, until FAITH is left alone sleeping. Lights change on the action to reflect that FAITH is having a dream.)

FITZ: Hey.

KIRK: Hey.

FITZ: Um, do you know Faith Gold? The nurse said I'd find her in here.

KIRK: What if I do?

FITZ: Uh. Well, do you?

KIRK: Why in God's fuck would I tell you who I know and who I don't know?

FITZ: I'll just wait.

KIRK: I wouldn't if I were you.

(FAITH walks into her own dream.)

FITZ: Hey!

FAITH: Hi!

(They embrace tenderly and for a while. KIRK sits stoically watching, and clears his throat several times.)

FAITH: Uh, Fitz, Kirk; Kirk, Fitz.

FITZ: How ya doin man?

KIRK: My muscles have atrophied and you're definitely puce but besides that—

(There is an uncomfortable silence.)

FAITH: Um, Kirk?

KIRK: Yeah?

FAITH: Could we have some privacy?

KIRK: This isn't your room.

FAITH: We can't bring visitors to our rooms.

KIRK: Never stopped you before.

FAITH: Kirk!

KIRK: *(To FITZ, trying to stand up and deal with this perceived threat.)* I'll be in the next room buddy. *(He departs never taking his eyes off of FITZ.)*

FITZ: Okay, man. Nice to meet ya. What the—?

FAITH: Sorry about that.

FITZ: No, it's cool.

FAITH: He's another patient here. He's going through a hard time—

FITZ: That's cool. How are you?

FAITH: Great.

FITZ: Ready to come home?

FAITH: I guess.

FITZ: You're almost out, right?

FAITH: Three more days.

FITZ: You all right?

FAITH: What do you want me to say, Fitz?

FITZ: Nothing. No. You look good. I mean do you feel good? You look good.

FAITH: How do I feel? I feel like I don't look good.

FITZ: Oh, you do—wow—terrific. Lost weight, huh?

FAITH: Insanity diet.

FITZ: So, I heard—

FAITH: Yeah. I tried to off myself. But I can't take credit for it. I was out of my mind on drugs.

FITZ: How could it happen when you were in here?

FAITH: Where there's a will—

FITZ: What happened, if you don't mind? I wanted you to be somewhere safe; getting you here was all I knew to do.

FAITH: Everyone has been making decisions for me; I had to make one for myself.

FITZ: Couldn't you've just written a song?

FAITH: It was my heart. I couldn't see what good it was doing me, you know? I guess I wanted to get rid of it.

FITZ: And now?

FAITH: Now I think I just need to get to know it better.

FITZ: Faith, I came to tell you something, I've realized...I have to get this out, or I won't. I rehearsed.

FAITH: You rehearsed?

FITZ: I'm goin'.

FAITH: Okay.

FITZ: Here goes. You— You're like a great novel. You have to read you, think about you, and then re-read you to understand all that's there and what it's trying to say. And nothing seemed further from what I wanted then re-reading you. But it's taken me over since you've been gone. When you tried to kill yourself, I felt so, I felt like it was happening to me. I love you. I want to be with you. And this isn't something that's going to go away. I've felt this way for weeks and.... I understand that they're probably telling you to steer clear of relationships right now. And they're right, you should. I don't want to overwhelm you with this. But if I don't tell you how I feel I'm going to go the whole rest of my life wondering.... *(FITZ does a little jig.)* I'm learning how to dance, Faith, I'm learning how to dance. I'll leave you with that. I'll be waiting for you. I love you. But, Faith, one thing? With all we've been through, we hold people, especially people that can truly see us, at arms length. Can I ask you for something?

FAITH: Yes?

FITZ: Help me love you.

(He leaves.)

(KIRK bursts in.)

KIRK: What did that son of a bitch do?

FAITH: What?!

KIRK: Tell me!

FAITH: He didn't do anything.

KIRK: You're crying. He's such an asshole. He practically ushers you in here—

FAITH: Nobody can do that—

KIRK: He was glad you came. He was glad to get rid of you. What'd he say, he's sorry?

FAITH: —it was me, too.

KIRK: I suppose he wants you back now, right? A little late for that.

FAITH: Hey! Let me ask you something. You've been in and out of here for three years, and seem to like it. If I get out of here, are you coming with me? I didn't think so. So don't fight for me. Don't fight for me if you're not a possibility for my life. I'm going to be attracted to enough things I can't have outside these walls. Don't make yourself one of them.

KIRK: You have me.

FAITH: This is not having you. This is being in rehab with you.

KIRK: I hope edging me out makes your departure easier for you.

FAITH: You want to come with me? Come on. Come with me.

KIRK: Not yet.

FAITH: Then leave me alone.

(DR. LEONARD enters.)

(KIRK exits.)

(FAITH is still.)

DR. LEONARD: Faith, wake up.

FAITH: What? Where's—?

DR. LEONARD: Your parents are outside. I wanted to talk to you first.

FAITH: Did Fitz come?

DR. LEONARD: Faith we got some bad news. I thought I should tell you. Fitz committed suicide last night. He hanged himself.

FAITH: No. He's learning how to dance!

DR. LEONARD: What?

FAITH: I was dreaming—.

DR. LEONARD: He didn't make it. Some don't. I took the liberty to call his doctors, and he was very depressed. He couldn't break out of it. He wanted to very badly, but no medication could work for him, and he really wanted to die for a long time. Even before he moved to take the job here, he thought that would help, but it didn't. He was very sick.

FAITH: I should have been there—

DR. LEONARD: People can't save each other, we can only save ourselves, and be there for the living.

FAITH: I thought he wanted to come see me.

DR. LEONARD: I'm sure he wanted to do a lot of things. You are lucky you can do what you choose to do. Not everyone can. Some people are crippled and guided by their condition, and don't have a choice.

FAITH: Oh, Fitz—

DR. LEONARD: Do you want to see your parents?

FAITH: Yeah.

(DR. LEONARD opens the door or SIMON and CLARK. They come running in and the three embrace.)

SCENE 10

(On a club stage. FAITH sits on a stool alone and stares out, preparing to sing.)

(LIGHTS OUT)

END

www.ingramcontent.com/pod-product-compliance
Lightning Source LLC
Chambersburg PA
CBHW070221030726
47505CB00006B/1770